BACKUP PLAN

SILVER RIDGE SERIES: BOOK ONE

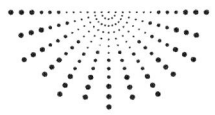

EMILY GOODWIN

Backup Plan
Silver Ridge Series: Book One
©2020 Emily Goodwin
www.emilygoodwinbooks.com
www.facebook.com/emilygoodwin

Cover Photography: Wander Aguiar
Editing by Contagious Edits
Proofing by My Brother's Editor

All rights reserved. This book or any portion thereof may not be reproduced or used in any manner whatsoever without the written permission of the publisher except for the use of brief quotations in a book review.

This is a work of fiction. Names, characters, businesses, places, events, and incidents are either the products of the author's imagination or used in a fictitious manner. Any resemblance to actual persons, living or dead, or actual events or places is purely coincidental.

To Figment and Captain Jack: thanks for bringing so much joy to my girls.
(Yes, I dedicated a book to my guinea pigs.)

CHAPTER ONE

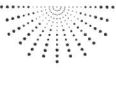

CHLOE

FRESHMAN YEAR...

Swallowing the lump in my throat, I blink back tears and slowly turn away from the register after swiping my lunch card. I grip the edges of the tray so hard my fingers hurt. The cafeteria is a sea of mostly happy teenagers, excitedly talking—and bragging—about their summer vacations, comparing tan lines, and complaining about being back at Silver Ridge High.

Taking a slow step forward, I concentrate both on not slipping and falling in these heels while at the same time, looking around the crowded lunchroom for a place to sit. Knowing pretty much everyone is both the blessing and the curse of this small town, and right now I'm wishing I could curse every single of one them in this room.

Okay, not every single one. Just Derek Rogers and everyone within a ten-foot radius of him. I clench my jaw, preparing to walk past his table. Busy talking and laughing with his football buddies, he pays me no attention, but Lauren Wallace does. She makes it a point to give me a pressed smile and slip her arm through Derek's right as I walk by.

The lump rises in my throat and I know I'm going to lose my battle with my tears. I stare straight ahead and keep walking, praying it's not obvious that I'm frantically looking around for a place to sit. We have what's called a "mixed lunch" here at Silver Ridge High, were students of all grade levels eat together. The entire school is put into one big group and then randomly divided. My best friend, Farisha, is in the lunch hour after this one, along with our friends Courtney and Arron.

Which reminds me of the *second* curse of a small town: there are fewer people to try and fit in with. Farisha is the peanut butter to my jelly, and not being together sucks more than I thought.

Especially since Lauren is now sticking her tongue down Derek's throat. I speed forward, almost slip since I'm not used to wearing heels, and sit at the table in the back with a group of kids everyone calls "the stoners." Whether they actually smoke pot all the time or not, I have no idea, but they look at me like the outsider that I am.

Still, I'd rather be here than anywhere near Derek and Lauren fucking Wallace. I'm not jealous, or even all that upset Derek dumped me over an instant message that I didn't read until *after* he stood me up for a date. No, it's not that I wasted a whole summer with that asshole because—hah—he wasted it with me too, and I never put out, which was part of the reason he dumped me.

But it's what he said.

We're different. You're weird and not like the other girls.

Farisha held my hand as I read the message over three times, trying to figure out if I should take it all as a hidden compliment or accept his words at face value. Because I know I'm different. I know I'm not like most of the girls at Silver Ridge High…or in the rest of the world for that matter. I try not to let it bother me, but what if it's true?

"Hey," a deep male voice comes from across the table, and I

jerk up, blinking back tears. Sam Harris sets his lunch tray down and takes the seat opposite me. "You okay, Chloe?"

My heart flutters in my chest, and I'm well aware half the female population of the lunchroom is looking at me right now. And I hope that includes Lauren fucking Wallace. "I'm fine," I say with a fake smile, picking up my fork and stabbing it into my salad.

"Really?" Sam cocks an eyebrow and reaches for a greasy piece of pizza. "You don't look fine."

"It's just first-day jitters," I lie, though I know Sam can see right through me, which is why he came to sit with me in the first place, I'm sure of it. I'm thankful, of course, because now I'm not alone and I have someone familiar with me, but I hate the feeling of needing to be rescued. My day just got significantly better, that's for sure, and being with Sam always puts a smile on my face.

My parents were friends with Sam's parents back in the day, and Sam's mom was over-the-moon happy that her childhood best friend moved back into town. And Mrs. Harris was there for us after Mom died, bringing us a casserole every week for nearly a year.

Sam is two years older than me but only a grade above me, thanks to cutoff dates and him being one of the oldest in his class and me being the youngest in mine. We became instant friends when we first met, and have somehow stayed close despite him being Mr. Popular and me being dubbed Creepy Chloe because of my interest in the paranormal and slight borderline obsession with all things *Harry Potter*. Though Sam's baby sister is just as into magic and fantasy as I am, and having that camaraderie with the youngest Harris has always been respected by Sam, as well as his other brothers.

But I worry that's all he sees me as…another little sister. The thought alone devastates me because for as long as I can remember, I've been in love with Sam Harris.

"So," Farisha starts, closing her locker at the end of the day. "What do you think? Does it feel good to be a high schooler now or what?"

I shove my English book into my locker, messing up my neat stack of school supplies already.

"It's not that bad," I say with a half-smile. And really, the rest of the day wasn't, thanks to Sam sitting with me at lunch. It brightened my whole mood, reminding me that I don't have to conform like everyone else in order to have friends. Closing my locker, I swing my backpack up on one shoulder. "You really think you can get your lunch switched?"

Farisha nods. "All I have to do is tell Mom I was feeling a little shaky and she'll freak out and insist I need to eat a whole thirty minutes earlier."

"It's nice to have your mom be the school nurse," I say, though we joked that Mrs. Kapoor only got a job as the school nurse so she could keep an eye on Farisha's diabetes. After one incident last year where her blood sugar dropped so low she fainted, Farisha's mom has been way overbearing.

"Or I could have you moved to mine," she tests, trying not to smile.

"How would that make sense?" I play dumb to her hidden question. "You're trying to eat earlier because of low blood sugar."

"I can make it work. You wouldn't care, would you?" We start walking down the hall.

"No," I say with a straight face, unable to look her in the eyes. "As long as we're together."

"Really? You're sure you don't want to give up being able to look at—"

"Sam!" I interrupt, seeing him turn down the hall. I elbow Farisha in a not-so-obvious move meant to shut her up. She knows about my massive crush on Sam Harris, though could you blame me?

He's tall, somehow always tan, and muscular. The blue shirt he's wearing matches his dark blue eyes, reminding me of the lake at night. They're eyes you can drown in, and when I look at Sam, I'll gladly let him pull me under. Pair them with his sharp jaw, full lips, and perpetually messy yet sexy dark hair, and it's no secret why every girl in Silver Ridge has eyes for Sam.

"Chloe," he says back, smiling. "How'd your first day go?"

"Cood," I say and then close my eyes, willing my face not to flush.

"Cool and good?" Sam questions, smirk on his lips.

"Yeah." I flick my eyes to him and then back to the floor. "I was going to say cool and then realized that's not an answer to how my day was."

Sam chuckles. "Are you headed home? I can drive you if you want."

My mouth goes dry, and I look at Farisha. We were going to walk home together and I'm not blowing her off.

"Mom wants to drive me home today," she says without missing a beat. "I've got to go hang out in the nurse's office for a bit now. I'll talk to you later," she tells me, and I do my best to nonverbally thank her. "Bye, Sam."

"See ya," he tells her, and as soon as she's a few paces away, I get nervous. I've always been myself around Sam, but now that we're in school together, I'm aware of everything. Of the way everyone looks at him. How well-liked he is by the students and the teachers. He's an all-around good guy, even if he does go through girlfriends faster than I can binge read the *Harry Potter* series on a rainy weekend.

"I have to pick up Jacob and Mason," he tells me as we walk out into the parking lot. It's mid-August and still super hot outside. "So we have like twenty minutes to kill before going to the middle school. We can go by the lake."

"Sure," I say, ready to agree with just about anything Sam suggests. His birthday was only two weeks ago, and I know he rushed out and got his license as soon as possible. I'm not positive he's supposed to be driving me, or even his siblings for that matter, but I'm sure as hell not going to question it.

I relax as soon as I'm in his Jeep. The top is off but when the door shuts, it's like I'm shutting out school and I can be myself again. I tip my head up, feeling the wind in my hair as Sam speeds out of the school parking lot, heading to the lake Silver Ridge was built around. Neither of us talk as we get out, climbing down a rocky hill to the shore. We only have about seven minutes until we need to go and pick up Sam's brothers, but I'll take whatever I can get.

"So what was really going on today?" Sam asks as I take my shoes off and dip my feet in the water. There's no way I'm making it back up past those rocks in these heels without breaking an ankle.

"Nothing."

"Really?" He picks up a rock and throws it into the lake. "That didn't look like nothing."

"Fine," I huff. "You know I was dating Derek over the summer, right?"

"Was? Did that asshole do something to you?"

I press my lips together. "If he did, I'd handle it."

"I have no doubt you would," Sam laughs.

I step deeper into the water, gathering the hem of my black dress up to my thighs. "He said I was too weird to be with," I admit, shaking my head. "And I let his words get to me. Maybe I am too weird. Maybe I will be alone forever because I'd rather stay home and write fan fiction than go see Derek's brother's band play in Missy Spencer's garage. It smells like soup in there. Always."

Sam laughs and runs his hand through his hair. "It does. Tomato soup. I've been in there before watching said band. You didn't miss anything."

"Well, good." I bend over to pick up a rock, not thinking that with my dress gathered up, I just flashed Sam my butt. At least I have cute undies on today.

"And Chloe," Sam starts when I straighten up, looking at the smooth rock in my hands. "You're not going to be alone forever. You are weird, but that's what I like about you."

My heart swells in my chest. "I hope you're right about that."

"Hey. I'll make you a deal. If you're still alone when you turn thirty—and if I am too—let's run away to Vegas and get married."

"Sure," I agree with a giggle, knowing there's no way Sam will still be single by the time he turns twenty, let alone thirty.

"I mean it!"

"Well, then we better start planning *our* wedding," I tease. "I'm undatable."

"Oh please," he waves his hand in the air. "Any guy would be lucky to have you."

My heart flutters again and hope bubbles up inside of me. Maybe I do have a chance with Sam. Maybe he looks at me the way I look at him and we—

"Shit," he says suddenly.

"What?"

"I was supposed to meet Tiffany after school. Fuck, she's going to be pissed." He shrugs. "I'll just make it up to her later." He wiggles his eyebrows at me and laughs. My heart sinks, and I let the rock fall out of my hands, splashing into the water and washing away the little hope I had.

Sam's just being nice. Saying things to make me feel better. But he'll never see me the way I want him to. Who I am kidding? I'm Creepy Chloe, the weird girl who wears too much black, brings tarot cards to school, and wrote a fifty-five-page *Harry Potter*-meets-*Charmed* fanfic for her eighth-grade creative writing assignment.

And Sam is, well, Sam. Smart. Good-looking. Athletic. *Normal.*

As much as I want to believe fate will intervene and Sam and I could end up together, I know the only way it would happen is if everything falls apart and he has to resort to me—his backup plan.

CHAPTER TWO

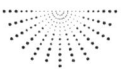

CHLOE

PRESENT DAY...

Spiraling.

It's what's happening to me…I think. And the fact that I'm not sure only proves just how fast I'm spiraling. Falling down at a dizzying rate. The world spins so fast I can't make out anything around me. I'm a big fat fucking fake and it's only a matter of time before they expose me, and what better way than to do it on live TV, broadcasted nationally to several million viewers.

Fuck.

What was the question? Sweat drips between my breasts, thankfully out of sight from the live audience's prying eyes. I'm regretting turning down that pre-show glass of wine, going instead for some gross concoction of kale, green tea, and some nasty shit that was probably scraped out of a dirty fish tank with a fancy name slapped on it.

I swallow hard and force a smile, flicking my eyes from the show host to the audience.

"Fight like a girl," I say, not recognizing my own voice leaving my lips. It's not an answer to the question I was asked, I know, yet the audience erupts in cheers nonetheless when they hear the catchy tagline to my series. I take their enthusiasm in stride, stealing a few seconds to close my eyes and try and find my center—which I've never been able to fucking do, even after overpaying for private yoga session for the last five years.

"You've started a feminist movement," Helen, the show host goes on, fanning the flames of my rabid fans. "Was that always your intention?"

My smile turns genuine, and I push myself back into the game. *I've got this.*

"Honestly," I say slowly, leaning forward. It's one little word, but three killer syllables. Because honesty and Hollywood aren't things you say simultaneously. "I had these voices in my head that demanded I tell their stories. And it just transpired from there."

The crowd breaks out into cheers again, and my heart swells in my chest, sucking it all in. The fame. The love from perfect strangers. Knowing my words have touched so many people. It's surreal, even after all this time. I may have twenty novels under my belt, had my name appear on the New York Times bestseller list multiple times, have an insanely supportive fanbase, and a super popular paranormal romance series that got made into a TV series—and season one won two fucking Emmy awards—but I still feel like the same outcast I did the day I moved to LA.

A loner.

The weirdo.

Forever alone.

Too much for anyone to handle.

Surround me a thousand adoring fans, and all it does is remind me how alone I actually am. I'm a walking and talking cliché, I know. And I hate myself for it.

I made it.

Did the impossible.

And for that, yeah, I feel like the bad-fucking-ass my

fanbase thinks I am. The nerd, the underdog, the girl everyone made fun of made it not only in the scary world of publishing but now is flourishing in Hollywood. I've dated actors. Gone out with producers. Partied with reality TV stars. Signed books all over the world and had my novels translated into more languages than I knew existed. I went from writing fan fiction to my own original stories, and those novels hit it big time with the paranormal and sci-fi loving crowd. My characters became a voice in the much overdue feminist movement, giving hope to those who'd otherwise been hopeless, as well as just providing an entertaining-as-fuck series for pretty much everyone to enjoy.

"Tell me more about Kellie," Helen says, and the audience eagerly agrees. "How did you come up with such an interesting character?"

My lips pull into a smile, genuine this time, because I can talk about my characters all day long. They're all me in some sense, just a little less neurotic, even the ones who fight demons on the regular. I've put myself into each and every one of my characters in some way or the other, and I stand behind creating realistic and relatable characters one hundred percent, which I know caused waves at last year's Comic Con.

I have a degree in sociology. I grew up wanting to be a social worker and didn't study English for years like some of my peers, who look down on me for said lack of degree But I'll look out at the audience and tell them with confidence that you either have what it takes to write or you don't, and wasting years studying "the craft" won't make up for your lack of talent.

I've pissed off my fair share of wealthy parents by saying just that, but I stand by it. Anyone can get a fancy degree if you can wrangle up the money. Creativity can't be taught. You can learn how to unlock what you already have, but if you don't have it then you don't have it.

Squeezing my eyes closed, I refocus my energy on the live interview, telling myself I'll get a burger—a real one, not that vegan patty shit—if I can pull this off. Deep down, I know I can. I've done tons of interviews just like this one, and I love talking about my characters. A rush goes through me, and I reach for the glass of water on the coffee table in front of me. I take a careful drink, always afraid I'm going to dribble water down my chin or drink it the wrong way and spend the next three minutes coughing.

Never in my life did I think taking a drink of water could be this stressful, but welcome to show business. I'm able to drink without choking, drooling, or spilling water on the table when I set the glass back down, ready and excited to launch into a full conversation about Kellie, the leading lady in my paranormal series.

We take a few questions from the audience, and we're getting close to a scheduled commercial break, signaling that I'm nearing the end of my interview, thank goodness. It's always been a little difficult for me to keep my eyes on the host or the audience and not get distracted with what's going on backstage, with the things I can see, but you have no clue about when you're watching a show.

"Before we go," Helen says, seamlessly lifting her own glass of water to her lips and taking a drink like a pro. "I think we all are dying to hear about this." She smiles, flashing perfectly straight, white teeth. "The romance," she says, and the crowd cheers again. My stomach tightens and I smile, suppressing the fact that she got me. "Who inspired Marcus?"

I can talk about feminism, kick-ass-take-no-shit female leads all day. But ask me about love? Hah. This is where I'm exposed, where it's obvious I'm a big fat fucking fraud. I've been in relationships before, all ending the same way: epic failure. I know nothing when it comes to matters of the heart.

And the truth could put a damper on my career as a romance novelist. I write about true love. Soul mates. First kisses and transcendental lovemaking. Of being brave enough to follow your heart. To fight tooth and nail for that person you know you're meant to be with.

But the truth of the matter is I'm still hopelessly clinging to a ghost of my past. It's pathetic, I know. But the heart wants what the heart wants, no matter how stupid it is.

CHAPTER THREE

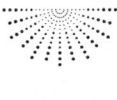

CHLOE

"I'm not going to lie," Karina starts, sitting back in her leather chair. Her jet-black hair falls in perfect waves around her pretty face. "That was rough."

"I didn't think it was that bad," I counter, internally wincing. We just got done watching my interview from this morning. I might have cringed more than once while watching. I looked aloof, and you could tell my heart just wasn't in it. Because it wasn't.

"I've seen worse," my publicist agrees, brushing dog fur from her ivory-colored suit jacket. "Never from you, though. What's going on?" Her brown eyes pierce mine, waiting for a response—an honest response. She'll keep her gaze trained on me until I crack, and I love and hate her for it. She's petite and girly but is ruthless when it comes to her clients. We started working together when *Nightfall* got optioned for film and has gotten me an impressive amount of sponsorships and exposure since then.

"I don't know," I say with a sigh. "I feel…off."

"Does this have to do with the shitstorm that happened on Twitter a few weeks ago? We resolved that. Do not bring it back up."

"No, I hadn't really thought about that until now, so thanks." Said shitshow was the result of too many mimosas that led me to respond to some asshole on Twitter saying how disappointed she was in me for including LGBTQ characters in my books. She was trying to get her conservative 'mom friends" to share a petition to get my show taken off the air because it was a "bad influence" for kids. Not to mention I'm going straight to hell for writing about vampires and witches.

My show just got renewed for a new season, and I know the season after that is in the bag already too. I wasn't worried about that but was just fed up with assholes like her. As if it's not hard enough for the LGBTQ community already... My fans rallied with me, and the comments went from trying to nicely educate this woman to threats and digging up personal information about her and her family, which got publicly posted. While my own comments were a little over the edge, I didn't cross any line, yet I was seen as the ringleader for the rapid responses that followed.

I've always had a good reputation in both publishing and producing, and the fact that I'm *not* a drama-llama has worked in my favor. It didn't help that only two days after said Twitter shitstorm, I went on a date with the son of a movie producer who got a little handsy, repeatedly tried to slide his fingers under my dress while at the table of a crowded restaurant, and then called me a prude when I told him to knock it off. I threw my drink in his face and walked out, and yes—*that* part got caught on camera by the paparazzi, but not him touching me without consent. It was a big his-word-against-mine mess, and with the threat to get lawyers involved, he issued a public apology but then days later Tweeted a list of all my ex-boyfriends, saying I was obviously the issue and there must be "something wrong with me." It's so fun to have all your failed relationships scrutinized publicly on social media, and as much as I hated it, as much as I tried not to let it get to me...it did.

Because there I was again, lonely and doubting myself.

Maybe there really is something wrong with me. Maybe I really am too weird, too dark, too lost in my own head for someone to handle.

"You've been going nonstop," Karina goes on. "Normally, I'll keep pushing you because I know you can handle it. But maybe it's time to take a break. Get out of the spotlight for a while and catch your breath. You haven't gotten very far with the next book in this series, have you?"

I shake my head. "Not really," I say, trying not to cringe. I have half of the first chapter written and keep fizzling out the second I sit down to write. I've been super busy the last month too, with book signings, interviews, and collaborating with the show runners for next season. "I haven't had much time."

"Exactly, and I just had a conference call with your agent and editor this morning. If you can get the first draft done a month ahead of schedule, we'll be able to line up a three-week-long tour in Europe. For you *and* Charles. He's in if you're in, and we can schedule it perfectly with his break between filming."

My face lights up. Charles Baldwin is the mega movie star who plays Marcus, the vampire lead in my book-turned-TV series. He's one of Hollywood's biggest heartthrobs, has a reputation of being a suave playboy, just crossed thirty-million Instagram followers, and was named the Sexiest Man Alive last year.

He's also my on-again, off-again boyfriend, but the whole thing was set up by Karina, who's his publicist too. Our relationship sparked interest in the two of us—and *Nightfall*—perfectly timed when the show was announced to the world. We "break up" often, needing to uphold Charles's playboy reputation and keep his female fans pining over him. Being seen with him made me recognizable, something I wasn't quite used to before. As an author, my name was my claim to fame, not my face. But now I'm photographed, pictures slapped all over TMZ and social media, tagged as "Charles's ⌐ only way to identify me is by who I used to "belong to."

It's strange, faking a relationship with someone. And faking, I mean literally faking every single romantic part of said relationship. Because Charles is gay, and it breaks my heart that he's been advised to keep his sexuality hushed out of fear it will hurt his career. I've encouraged him to come out, but he's not ready, and I respect that. He's one of my very best friends now, and our tight-knit bond of platonic friendship is what sells our fake relationship so well.

Touring Europe with Charles will be so fucking fun. I can probably convince Farisha to sneak away for a week too. She's a sucker for anything European.

"Can we make it so we have at least two days at Disneyland Paris?" I ask, hiking my brows up.

Karina rolls her eyes. "Charles asked for the same thing."

"Yes!" I pump my fist in the air. "I knew I could count on him."

Karina laughs. "Fine. You can get a few days in Paris to yourselves. But only if you get this book done ahead of time."

"I'll get it," I say as if it's no big deal at all. Because, you know, there's no pressure in not only writing the highly-anticipated eighth book in a popular series but getting it done a month before I originally planned on finishing. "I'll take a staycation somewhere quiet, lock myself in a room and write nonstop."

"Where are you going to go?" Karina asks. "Bali again?"

I think about it for a few seconds but shake my head. I've been struggling a bit with getting this book started, and I know what I need to do: go back to the place that inspired this book, back to the real town my fictional one is based on. I'll walk through the woods and will write by the lake. If any place is going to inspire me, it's where it all started. "No, not Bali." I look up at Karina. "I'm going back to Silver Ridge."

CHAPTER FOUR

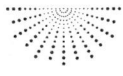

SAM

"You're overthinking it." I cast my line into the water and let my eyes fall shut, face bathed in the warmth from the sun. The boat gently rocks back and forth, and it would easily lull me to sleep if I were to sit down. Finishing a string of twelve-hour shifts does that to me.

"That means shit coming from someone like you," Jacob deadpans. "You don't think. At all. You'll fuck anything in a skirt."

"I have standards," I toss back, trying to act offended.

Mason lets out a snort of laughter and slowly reels in his line.

"You're worse." Jacob sets his fishing pole down and turns to mess with the boat's radio, which isn't picking up any signal this far out on the lake. Country music crackles through, and the fucker leaves it.

"If getting some on the regular is worse, I'll take it." Mason reaches for his beer. "And Sam's right. You're overthinking it. Go out with her. It's just one date that'll lead to one night, well, if you can be the least bit competent for a few hours. And lord knows you need to get laid. I've been home for all of five hours and am already sick for your crab-ass attitude."

"I don't do one-night stands," Jacob immediately counters, eyeing both me and Mason. "Unlike you two."

Mason looks at me, rolling his eyes. "I'm not entirely sure he even does people anymore at this point," he whisper-talks. "Maybe there's a reason he went into veterinary medicine. All those late-night calls to horse farms…"

"Fuck you, man." Jacob throws a handful of bait at the back of Mason's head and I laugh, always enjoying passively egging my younger brothers on like this. But the truth is we're all so fucking glad to be together again because it doesn't happen very often. Jacob stayed in Silver Ridge and is the small town's only vet, and Mason and I left the first chances we got. But this place will always be home for all of us, and we've all been looking forward to this weekend more than any of us want to admit.

Rory, our baby sister, is coming home this weekend as well, along with her husband and their newborn son, Adam. I haven't seen my nephew since the week he was born, and I need to make sure Rory's husband is still treating her well. I take my role as older brother seriously, as I always have, and will cut throats and throw punches without a second thought when it comes to my sister.

"If you don't want to go out with Annie, then don't," I say with a yawn. My line bobs down and I wait a beat, secretly hoping I *didn't* catch anything. Fishing isn't my favorite thing in the world, but we grew up doing this. I like being out on the lake with my brothers more than I actually like trying to catch a fish, and we put back most of what we catch anyway.

Dad started taking me out here on a rickety-ass boat when I was the only Harris kid yet to be born. Mom hated it, and I still remember being three years old and Mom putting blow-up water wings on my arms along with a multi-colored life vest. I couldn't put my arms down—just like that kid from *A Christmas Story*—but in the opposite season.

Dad's not out here with us today, though; he's anxiously

waiting for Adam to arrive at the house. There's no doubt both Mom and Dad will point out how they only have one grandchild, and it's the youngest of the bunch who settled down, got married, and popped out a kid first.

Mason and I already took bets on how long it'll take Mom to remind me that I'm the oldest, the one she expected to get married first, yet here I am, single once again.

Though I'm not complaining.

There's another tug on my line and I jerk it back, waiting half a second to see if I caught anything. The line doesn't move again, so I slowly reel it up, somewhat thankful the bait is gone. Resting my pole against the side of the boat, I heft into one of the seats, warmed by the sun, and grab a beer from the built-in cooler.

The boat is only two years old, and was a much-needed upgrade from the old hunk of junk Dad insisted still "ran just fine," despite us getting stranded in Lake Michigan for five hours during a storm until the Coast Guard could come out and tow us in. I bought this new boat for Dad on his birthday two years ago, and while it's a bit over the top for a birthday gift, I figured it was the least I could do after my parents footed the bill for me to go to medical school and become a doctor. I had it paid off in only a year, and we've already got our money's worth out of this thing.

We're on Silver Lake today, much smaller than Lake Michigan, and the breeze coming in over the water is hot and sticky.

"Or go out with her," Mason counters. "Wine and dine her, fuck her good, and then ghost her."

"You're despicable," Jacob quips, leaning over the boat railing and looking down into the water. He won't say the real reason he's on the fence about going out with this girl is because he's still bitter over his last relationship ending with his girlfriend cheating on him after two-and-a-half years together. Only Mason and I know he'd gone out looking at engagement rings the week before things blew up in his face.

"Tell her from the start you don't want anything serious," I suggest. "That's what I do, and it's worked out so far."

"Yeah, it's worked out well." Mason rolls his eyes. "How many times have you and Stacey broken up and gotten back together?"

"Four," I say with a shrug. We started dating a few years ago, and we get along just fine. But *fine* is all I can describe us as.

The sex is fine.

Her company is fine.

Everything is so *fine* there's no substance to it. She agrees with almost everything I say, and I don't actually know what she really likes or doesn't like, even after three years off and on. If I want to get Mexican food, she does too. If I want to watch hours of murder documentaries, she does too. It sounds ideal, I know, and I fumble every time I try to explain why having someone just blindly go along with me is off-putting.

It would be one thing if she enjoyed the murder documentaries, or got excited to watch football with me, but she doesn't. She'll just sit there, looking bored as she stares at the screen of her phone. Physically, she's there with me, but she mentally checks out the second we get together. No, she doesn't actually enjoy any of that, and instead it feels like she's doing it to appease me so she can get something out of it in the end...which she usually does.

I spent the weekend watching sports with you, take me shopping now?

"It must be good pussy to keep going back," Mason notes.

I shrug. "It's okay."

"Just okay?" Mason's brows rise incredulously. It's the first time I've so much as hinted that things between Stacey and me aren't hot and heavy. I've had a reputation to uphold, but honestly, I'm just tired right now. "Time to move on."

"I plan on it," I say, not going into detail that we were

together just two months ago. I had a particularly rough shift at the trauma center and burn victims are some of the hardest to treat and to see.

It's worse when said victims are children…burned by the result of evil, vile parents who inflicted the burns as a form of punishment.

A brother and sister were airlifted to us, and we lost the three-year-old girl. I put the five-year-old boy in a medically induced coma, and we didn't know the extent of the brain damage until he was stable enough to wake up.

I was exhausted but couldn't sleep, and Stacey was still up when I called her at one AM. She came over, and sex has always been my go-to solution of all of my problems, no matter how temporary it is.

"Shit," Jacob mutters, looking at his phone.

"What?" Mason and I ask in unison.

"Mrs. Nelson's horse has colic again. I'm sure it has *nothing* to do with the low-hay, high-grain diet she's feeding him," he grumbles. "Mind if we head in early?"

It's not quite four in the afternoon again, and while we had planned on being out here until we had to go home for dinner, I'll gladly check in early and get a nap in before Mom calls the whole family down for Friday night dinner. "I'm good with it."

"Me too." Mason wipes sweat off his forehead. "It's hot as balls out here today."

"I'd say jump in the lake to cool off," Jacob starts, looking at the water. "But it feels like fucking bathwater this late in the summer."

We put our fishing supplies away and Jacob starts up the boat. The lake is small, and we're close to our childhood home, where everyone but Jacob is staying for the weekend. He's the only one out of the four of us who still lives in Silver Ridge. Mason moves all over as an FBI agent and is currently residing in Detroit, working at the Michigan FBI headquarters, and I did my residency in Indianapolis and ended up at a hospital with a trauma center in Chicago. Rory is four or so hours way in a small town in Indiana, not too far from me, actually. We're all within driving distance, at least for the time being.

About half an hour later, we're pulling off the road onto the gravel driveway that takes us to the farmhouse we grew up in. It's been updated over the years but has retained the overall look and feel that brings me an instant sense of comfort. I hated living in a small town in my youth, but now that I've been out and living in big cities for years, I've developed a certain appreciation for the slower pace of Silver Ridge.

"Rory's here already," Mason states the obvious when we see her car parked in front of the garage. I smile, looking forward to seeing my sister, but more so my nephew. We park the boat down near the barn and get out, grabbing our shit and heading inside. There's a note taped on the door leading into the mudroom from the garage, saying Adam is napping so be quiet.

"Hey!" Rory says quietly when we get inside. She's sitting in the kitchen with her husband, Dean, and gets up, coming over for a hug. "You smell like lake water and worms."

"Nice to see you too, sis." I pat her on the back and turn to Dean. "How was the drive up?"

"We didn't hit a second of traffic, but Adam cried for the first half of it," Dean says, slowly shaking his head.

"He wore himself out." Rory goes back into the kitchen and takes something out of the oven. "I just laid him down in the pack-and-play upstairs. We've been having a hard time getting him down for naps. He just wants to be held, and we've kind of caved to it." She looks at Dean, smiling guiltily.

"If he wants to be held, then I'm going to hold him," Dean says back. "I can't say no to that face."

"It's good to see you both," Jacob tells them. "I've got to run and take care of a horse. I'll be back by dinner…hopefully."

"You're always rushing out as soon as I get here," Rory heckles. "I'm starting to take it personally."

"And I'm starting to wonder if there's a little" —Mason jerks his hand up and down in a crude gesture— "going on with the horse."

"Fuck you," Jacob said pointedly. "Tell Mom not to wait for me to start dinner. Just save me food."

"I'll let her know," Rory tells him.

"Thanks. Nice to see you again, Dean," Jacob says and hurries out the door.

Rory pulls out a box full of takeout bags, and I recognize the smell instantly. Silver Café is one of the few places in Silver Ridge that's open past ten PM. It's right along Silver Lake, with a large outside patio dining area that offers amazing views of the lake at night. And they have the best damn Detroit-style Coney dogs and fries.

"I've been craving these," Rory muses as she unrolls the takeout bag.

"Craving?" Mom comes around the corner, holding a sleeping baby.

"Mom," Rory quips. "We're trying to get him to lie down in his crib for naps."

"Oh hush," Mom tells her, smiling down at Adam. "How often does Nana get to hold him?"

Rory opens her mouth to protest, but Dean rests his hand on her shoulder, stopping her. He knows it won't do any good.

"And you're craving food?" Mom asks hopefully, eyes wide. "Are you pregnant?"

"No," Rory says back right away. "Adam isn't even four months old yet. It's not even possible."

"Well, it *is* possible," Dean whisper-talks to Rory. She blushes and elbows him. "I'm not pregnant, it's been a while since I've had these."

"They are good," I agree, grabbing a hot dog and sitting at the island counter. Mason takes two and goes to the table, checking his phone for any calls from work. He can never tell us all the details of what he's working on until the cases are closed.

"Is Dad picking up Nana Benson on the way home from work?" Rory asks.

"Yes, and she's so looking forward to seeing her great-grandson," Mom tells her.

"I don't know how she's still alive and kicking," Mason says casually. "Don't get me wrong, I'm glad she is, but that woman just won't stop. I hope I inherited her genes."

"Remember that mouse I had when I was a kid?" Rory asks. "Goldie."

"That thing wouldn't die," I laugh. "Are you making a Nana Benson-Goldie comparison?"

"Yes," Rory chuckles. "Goldie was like eight before she finally passed. Nana is just like that. She's in her late eighties, went through hip and knee replacements, and is still as spunky as ever."

"You had a mouse live for eight years?" Dean asks dubiously.

"Maybe seven and a half. I took really good care of her."

I look at Mason, knowing he was responsible for the murder of the OG Goldie when he went into Rory's room to get something, forgot to close the door, and our family cat ate her. Mom and I spent six hours driving around trying to find a mouse that looked like Goldie, putting her in the cage before Rory noticed.

And when Goldie Number Two died on Christmas Eve, Mom wasn't going to let it ruin Rory's holiday. Rory was seven at the time and spent an entire day making a Christmas village out of cardboard boxes for her damn mouse. That time Dad drove all the way to a pet shop in Indiana to get a replacement.

Mason gives me the slightest shake of the head, saying he wants to let Rory keep believing it was her impeccable care and love that kept the mouse alive for an impossibly long time. She has to know, I'm sure, because that's not a normal lifespan. At all.

"You're just staying the weekend?" Rory asks.

"Yeah," I tell her, even though I don't have to be back to work until Wednesday. Trauma has a high burnout rate and our clinic has set everyone up on an impressive rotation schedule, giving us a much-needed break every few months. Stacey and I had plans to go to New Orleans for a quick four-day getaway, staying in a historic bed and breakfast. I considered going on my own, but canceled at the last minute. My current plan is to visit with family for the weekend and then go home and spend the rest of my time off watching TV, playing video games, and eating junk food.

I'm okay with that.

"Oh, you'll never guess what I heard," Rory says, taking a bite of her hotdog. We all look at her, waiting for her to finish chewing to go on.

"Yes?" Mason asks impatiently.

"Chloe Fisher is in town!"

My heart skips a beat and my stomach tightens at the mention of her name. It's been years since I've seen her, and I've worked hard over those years not to think about her, which is hard to fucking do since her name and face are all over the place. If it's not an advertisement or article about one of her books, TV series, or upcoming talk show interviews, then it's pictures of her with the various celebrities she's dated.

I'm happy for her, really, I am. Chloe got exactly what she wanted, and I know it wasn't easy for her. She worked hard to push forward with her dreams of writing despite being bullied. She stood her ground and refused to bend, saying she'd rather be herself and alone than fake and popular. I always respected the hell out of her for it. It's not easy to have that sort of confidence, especially when we were teenagers.

Chloe got everything she deserves, and I *am* happy for her...

yet I have to remind not to be bitter or resentful. Not towards her, but towards myself.

Because as far as I'm concerned, Chloe will always be the one that got away, even though she was never mine. It would be one thing if she slipped through my fingers, but it's much, much worse as I practically shoved her away.

I had my chance with Chloe and I fucking blew it. There's no way she'll ever forgive me for it.

CHAPTER FIVE

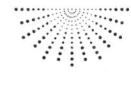

CHLOE

Eyes closed, I lie back on the dock. The hot sun beats down on me, and I've been sweating since the minute I came out here. There are quite a few people out on the lake today, and the distant sound of boats and jet skis interrupts the quiet of the forest surrounding the lake. Silver Lake is large and kind of horseshoe-shaped. It's divided into two parts, with the part Dad's house is on being the "quiet side" of the lake reserved for fishing or any other sort of activity that doesn't produce a wake. Its counterpart is where the fun happens, and the annual boat races are still held every July, just like they were years ago.

I didn't grow up right along the lake like this. We lived in a small house right in the middle of Silver Ridge. Mom always wanted to live on lakefront property, but even in this small town, it was too expensive. It was her dream to buy one of the historic homes and fix it up, but she died before that could ever happen.

When this house popped up for sale, I jumped on it, but then almost backed out at the last minute because the thought of fulfilling Mom's dream without her hurt too much. I'd only been living in LA for a few months at that time, and *Nightfall* had just gotten optioned for film, so I was overwhelmed on all ends. I went to bed with every intention of getting up and calling the bank to tell them I'm out, and that night I dreamed about Mom. She told me we all needed this house, and she'd be mad if I let this house go and someone else bought it and turned it into a cheesy bed and breakfast. Plus, she didn't like seeing Dad alone in the house she died in, and said this house would be good for him. Dad likes a project, even though I was planning on hiring contractors to handle the much-needed renovations.

Three months after moving in, Dad went on his first date since Mom died. And to this day he's still dating Wendy, the next-door neighbor who lost her husband in a car accident three years after Mom died.

A fishing boat goes by, with county music playing too loud for my liking. Any volume is too loud for country music in my opinion, though. Male voices drift over the music and the water, and I'm tempted to sit up and glare at them. Instead, I cover my face with my dark red hair, using it to block out the sun.

I doze off, startling awake when the dock shakes under someone's feet. I sit up, blinking in the bright light, and see Dad coming down toward me.

"Hey, kiddo."

"Hi, Dad. It's five already?"

"Five-thirty, actually. I got held up at work." Dad's a supervisor at an electrical company, and after years of working holidays, weekends, and midnights, has a nice Monday-through-Friday, nine-to-five job.

"Everything good?" I ask, lazily stretching and grabbing my cover-up. I pull it over my head, and the sheer material sticks to the sweat on my back.

"It is now. I thought you were joining us for dinner."

"Go without me," I say. Coming home was so spur of the moment, I didn't realize that today was Dad and Wendy's anniversary. They've had reservations tonight at a nice place half an hour away for weeks, and a mini-vacation planned a few days later. Dad feels bad they're leaving basically as soon as I got here, but the quiet will help me concentrate on my book.

"I already ate."

"Really?" Dad questions. "What did you have?"

"Half a jar of blue olives and almost a full bottle of Merlot."

"And here I was, worried that living in LA would turn you into a health-conscious hippy who only eats kale and seaweed."

"Hah. Though I am all about kombucha right now." I get up feeling exhausted from the heat. "And seriously, Dad, go out with Wendy tonight. I'm going to get my laptop and come back out here tonight and try to write. Karina's already texted me three times asking how much I've gotten written."

Dad chuckles. "She does know you just landed this morning, right?"

"Late this morning." I use the bottom of my swimsuit cover-up to blot up the sweat on my face. "And Rebecca is going to start hounding me soon too."

"She's your editor? Agent?"

"Personal assistant. Lupe is my editor and Vanessa is my agent."

Dad smiles, looking at me in the way only a proud parent can. "You have people. Too many to keep track of."

I wave my hand in the air. "It sounds fancier than it actually is."

"And you're still modest to boot. We're all so proud of you, you know. Your picture is still up in City Hall."

"That's a horrible picture," I laugh, knowing exactly which one he's talking about. *Small Town Girl Gets Big Time Publishing Deal* is the headline of the newspaper article, with a hastily snapped photo of me holding up my book, smiling like a lunatic. Only Farisha knows I was drunk at the time of the interview and photo. She came over with two bottles of wine, with the intention of choosing one to crack open and drink to celebrate the news.

Of course we drank both, and the reporter from the Silver Ridge Times showed up an hour before I expected him to, though it's not like an hour would have done me much good after consuming an entire bottle of Shiraz.

"Your most recent headshots are nice," Dad says. "You look like your mother in a few of them."

We both smile, hearts aching, and start to walk down the dock. "Maybe I'll sneak in and tape one of my better photos over that horrible one."

"The article is in black and white and your photos are in color. No one will notice."

"See? It's a solid plan."

"How's Charles?" Dad asks. He and Farisha are the only ones outside our little PR bubble who know the truth and Charles was the one to break down and tell Dad a few Christmases ago after Dad misread Charles's weird behavior as him being nervous to ask my father's permission to marry me.

"Busy, but good. They're wrapping up filming the end of the season and then he's going right into production for that new action movie you're excited to see, and yes, he already said he'll make sure you get to go to the premiere." I shake my head. "Walk your father down the red carpet once and he gets addicted. I've created a monster."

Dad laughs and rests his hand on my shoulder. "I'm so proud of you, Chloe. And I know your mother would be too."

My eyes prick with tears and my throat tightens. I give a small nod, knowing if I opened my mouth to say something back, my voice would come out all squeaky. Balloon, Dad's dog, yips excitedly by the gate when we come into view. The dog came with his name, given to him by a three-year-old boy. I'm not sure why the dog was surrendered to the animal shelter, but at five years old, he was used to his name and Dad didn't have the heart to change it. Shortening it to Ball or Loon didn't really work, so Balloon it is.

"Hey, buddy," Dad says, picking up the little dog. I pet him, knowing he won't calm down until he's got his greeting in. Yawning, I go right into the kitchen and grab the bottle of Merlot from the counter.

"Please tell me Uber Eats or DoorDash has finally come to Silver Ridge."

"What is that?"

I raise an eyebrow, letting Dad know I'm not amused. "So that's a no."

"Correct, kiddo. But Silver Pizza delivers. I don't think they'll put spinach or broccoli on the pizza for you, though," he teases. Overly stereotyping me as a *valley girl* is a running joke between us.

"I just do tofu now. On a cauliflower crust."

"I almost want to be there when you order just to see their faces," Dad laughs.

"A normal pizza sounds really good right now, actually."

The front door opens, and Balloon goes running through the kitchen, nails clicking against the wooden floor. A few seconds later Wendy comes bustling into the kitchen, carrying a tray full of baked goods.

"Chloe!" she coos, setting the tray down on the counter. She pulls me into a tight hug. "It's so good to see you." She pats my back and lets me go, looking me up and down. "And look at you! I swear you look younger than the last time I saw you. LA has been good to you!"

"It's the Botox," I admit with a laugh.

"Take me with you next time!"

"I'll schedule us a double appointment when you guys come out next."

"Oh please," Dad huffs. "Neither of you need that. Especially you, Chloe. You're only thirty-two."

I bring my fingers to my forehead. "I had lines, Dad," I say dramatically.

Dad holds his hands up. "Oh no, not lines! Anything but the lines."

Wendy laughs and rolls her eyes. "What am I going to do with this one?"

"He's your problem now, not mine," I say, laughing as well. "You guys better get going if you want to make it to your reservation in time."

"You're not joining us?" Wendy brushes her blonde hair back off her neck.

"No, I'm not going to crash your date. And I have work to do."

"Ohhhh, and maybe later you'll tell me spoilers! You're not going to kill Marcus, are you? That cliffhanger was cruel, lady!"

I laugh. "Oh, I know. I drank my coffee out of that *tears of my reader's* mug every morning while writing that book."

"Fitting," Wendy chuckles. "But really, Marcus is going to be okay, right?"

"I don't know. The demon hunters do have him cornered."

"Enough shop-talk," Dad says and picks up Balloon. He puts the little dog in my arms and opens the junk drawer in the kitchen, pulling out a card and a small box wrapped in pretty purple paper. It's not a ring, I know that for sure. Both Dad and Wendy said they weren't sure if they ever wanted to get married again, but here they are celebrating yet another anniversary. And I know for a fact Wendy spends most of her time here at this house with Dad. They've talked before about having her move in officially and then rent out her house for extra income, enabling them both to retire earlier than they planned.

I don't know what it's like to be with someone you love more than anything, who loves you right back. And I certainly don't know what it's like to have that person taken away from you. I really like Wendy, and Mom totally approves of her, as she told me in another dream. She's the opposite of my mother, who was creative and free-spirited. Wendy's a paralegal at Silver Ridge's only law office. She's worked the same job her whole adult life, has short, blonde hair, loves routines, and owns more cleaning products than the cleaning company who cleans my house every week.

But she's fun and caring and makes Dad happy, which is all that matters. We get along well, and she's one of my biggest fans, raving about my books to anyone who'll listen.

"For me?" Wendy asks, blue eyes widening when she sees the card and present in my father's hands.

"You have to wait until after dinner. And after you give me my gift," Dad says with a wink.

Wendy rolls her eyes again and loops her arm through Dad's. "I'll see you in the morning, then, dear. And know I'm here to brainstorm ideas if you need someone."

"Taking one for the team, I see." Dad steps forward, tugging Wendy with him. "Enjoy your tofu and chia seed pizza."

"Bye, Dad."

I follow them to the front, locking the door behind them once they leave. "Want to share a pizza with me?" I ask Balloon, setting him on the ground. Going back into the kitchen, I pour the remaining Merlot into a glass and look up Silver Ridge Pizza's number.

"Yes," I say to myself when I see an option to order online so I won't have to call and talk to anyone. It'll be about half an hour for the pizza to get here. Taking the glass of Merlot with me, I go onto the screened-in porch, where I left my laptop and notebook. I know what I want to happen in this next book, and no, I'm not killing my vampire Marcus. Charles would kill *me* if I killed him off in the books, though I'm sure the showrunners would keep him in. The show follows the book pretty well, with some original storylines set up for some side characters, giving them more screen time than I'd written in for them.

Breaking my self-imposed rule of avoiding social media this

trip so I can focus on my book, I go to Instagram and reply to a few comments and messages. I do my best to interact with fans because it honestly still blows my fucking mind I have fans.

Then I fall down the *Free Britney* rabbit hole until the doorbell rings. My stomach grumbles at the thought of pizza, and I don't even bother with a plate. I take the entire box back to the screened-in porch, shoving a piece in my mouth.

"This is so good," I tell Balloon, picking off a pepperoni and tossing it to him. He gets gassy if he gets too much people food, but he sleeps with Dad and Wendy, not me.

There's a ceiling fan out here on the porch, and when the weather is a little cooler and you crank that thing on high, it's really pleasant out here. But with a warm, sticky breeze coming in from the lake, it's hot no matter how hard that little fan spins. I suffer through the heat so I can eat two more pieces of pizza, slowly sipping the rest of the Merlot. I look out at the water as I eat, doing my best not to think of anything, which really just reminds me how talkative my damn brain is.

Like for real, just shut up every once in a while. Live in the moment and feel the zen or whatever the fuck you're supposed to do, okay? Rolling my eyes at myself, I put the pizza crust back in the box. I ordered crust with garlic sauce brushed on it, thinking it would be like a breadstick and I'd be able to eat it. It's strange, I know, that I love breadsticks but don't like pizza crust.

Stopping myself from eating yet another slice of pizza and then being gassy the rest of the night just like Balloon, I close the box and get up, feeling instant relief when I step into the air-conditioned living room. The sun is still shining through the large windows, but it has that evening glow, the kind that promises a reprieve from the harshness of the hot sun while still holding onto the heat of the day.

My heart swells in my chest as I look around the living room. It's so different yet the same, with updated photos on the gallery wall. Most are of me, a few are of Balloon, and the rest are Dad and Wendy. Wendy's husband passed before they had children, and she confessed not that long ago she still regrets never allowing herself to move on and have a baby before she became too old to. But it all worked out, she says, because she met my father when she needed him most.

There's a large stone fireplace centered in the far wall in the living room, perfect for winter nights when the lake is nearly frozen over and frost and snow cling to the surrounding trees. I came here two Christmases ago, arriving the day before Christmas Eve and then not being able to leave until the end of December thanks to a snowstorm. Since I moved, I've only returned to Silver Ridge a handful of times, and it's all quick trips.

Two days for Thanksgiving. Three for Christmas. One for Dad's birthday. Dad picks me up from the airport and drives to the house. We're busy and time flies and I don't leave the house. It's safe, keeping me in a little bubble. Come home with a reason, stay distracted, and then leave.

I haven't been back like this in, hell, six years. Not having a busy schedule or an organized agenda makes me anxious. Because when I don't know exactly what to do every minute of every day, my mind starts to wander.

And being back here…looking around the house and hearing the happy chatter and distant rumble of boats out on the lake…it makes me worry my heart will wander as well.

CHAPTER SIX

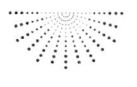

SAM

Chloe Fisher is in town.
Rory's words echo through my head for the millionth time. Chloe. In town. This town. The one I'm in right now. It's no surprise, not any more than it is for me to come back. Chloe's from Silver Ridge and her father still lives here.

So why the fuck is it getting under my skin so much? And why can't I get her off my mind? I've made it a point *not* to think about Chloe. I haven't let the vision of her dark auburn hair flash through my mind. I haven't missed the feel of her fingers sweeping against mine, wanting to grab my hand but too shy to link our fingers together.

I haven't let myself think about the pale orange and red freckles that dot Chloe's cheeks when she's in the sun too long, how her hair curls around her face at the base of her neck when it's hot outside, or how good she looked in a bikini the summer of her senior year. She visited her grandparents the first half of the summer and came back a cup size bigger, but I wasn't distracted with her breasts or her hourglass figure. Nope. Not at all.

Just like how she hasn't haunted me over the years, despite me refusing to believe in ghosts. Chloe is always there, in the back of my mind. Taunting. Teasing. Reminding me how much I fucked up.

"Sam?" Mom asks, in a tone that lets me know she's called my name before. We're all seated in the formal dining room, the large table and chairs rarely used unless we're all here together. We were never allowed in here as kids, with Mom saying she wanted at least one nice, clean room in the house when people came over. The dining room is one of the first rooms you see when you walk in the house, opposite a small sitting room. The day Mom ordered ivory-colored couches and a pale pink area rug was the day Jacob, Mason, and I were banned from going in it.

"Yeah?" I ask, realizing my fork is hovering in the air, a bite of grilled chicken halfway between the plate and my mouth. I can feel everyone exchange glances, aware I wasn't paying the slightest bit of attention to whatever was being said.

"Are you all right, honey?" Mom goes on.

"Why wouldn't I be?" I shove the chicken into my mouth, buying some time before I have to speak again.

"Mason said he put potato flakes in his bloody cut," Rory says slowly, brows pinched together. "Like the ones from the box."

"Why?" I ask, still chewing my chicken.

"I looked it up online and it said it would stop the bleeding." Mason holds out his arm, showing off a nasty-looking scar on the inside of his left arm. I know enough from working in trauma to recognize a knife wound when I see one.

"Please tell me you're joking." I set my fork down and reach for my glass of water.

"It worked." Mason runs a finger over the dark line on his arm.

"And it didn't get infected?" I ask incredulously.

"I didn't say that." Mason raises his eyebrows and we laugh.

"You know you could have—"

"Called, yes, I know," Mason huffs.

"Even I can get you antibiotics," Jacob goes on. "My patients are animals, so you'd fit right in."

"Hilarious," Mason spits, and Rory looks at me, silently laughing. It's a bit of a running joke between the four of us. Rory is a nurse, I'm an anesthesiologist, and Jacob is a vet. Mason is the only one of us who didn't go into medicine, and we love to give him hell over it.

"Got any good OR stories?" I ask Rory, winking. With us being the only two in *human* medicine, and both working primarily in operating room settings, it's easy for us to dominate the conversation with our most recent war story, dealing with difficult patients or going into the very real topic of losing patients, which is something you're never quite ready for, no matter how much they prep you for it in school.

When I was working general surgery, we had more success stories than not, but now that I'm in trauma, our "success stories" might mean someone pulling through but with life-changing injuries that require months if not years of therapy to get back to just a slice of normalcy.

"Oh, I do!" Rory cuts into her chicken, laughing at the thought of whatever she's about to tell us. "It was our first scheduled surgery of the day, so we had the guy come in at five AM. He showed up half an hour late and smelled like alcohol so strong I felt drunk just standing next to him. He had dried vomit on his chin and shirt, and when we asked if he'd been drinking, he flat-out denied it. Then his wife showed up demanding we go through with the surgery because they already put a deposit down or something that didn't even make sense. She was screaming, like literally screaming at the poor intake nurse."

"Gotta love when family members get involved like that," I say with a laugh.

"They're the best." Rory rolls her eyes. "So Dr. Jones came out and tried to talk some sense into them, explaining why he won't operate on someone who was clearly drinking right before surgery due to safety concerns, and the woman lost it even more. She threw a decorative vase from the end table in the waiting room at Dr. Jones, and we had to get security to escort her out. The drunk patient—who really needs his gallbladder removed—stumbled along behind her and then threw up all over the hallway right outside the OR waiting room."

"Lovely," Mom says with a grimace. "God bless you two for going into your line of work. You know I don't even like the sight of blood."

"You'd hate my job then," Mason quips. He's can't say much about his current case, but we know he's dealing with some sort of child sex trafficking ring. It takes a lot to unnerve me, but things dealing with violence against children gets to me, just like the two children we treated whose own parents were responsible for what happened.

"What about you?" Rory asks me. "You don't get too many crazy people anymore, do you?"

I shake my head. "A good majority of the people brought into the trauma center aren't even conscious. Family members can be irate, but it's usually because they're in shock and don't want to accept what happened to their loved one. Their misplaced anger is understood. We had an older man a few weeks ago lose it when we said he had to respect the wishes of his wife's advanced directive, which had DNR orders."

"That's tragic," Mom says, shaking her head.

"And you wonder why I chose to work with animals," Jacob grumbles.

"You've had some interesting owners to deal with, haven't you?" Dean asks. "Rory told me about someone getting pissed you couldn't reverse-neuter their dog."

Dad laughs. "That crazy lady still leaves one-star reviews all over Facebook." We all laugh and continue laughing over stories of difficult or just plain stupid people we've dealt with over the years, but my mind shifts back to Chloe.

I should have asked Rory what else she heard, but it's too

late now to bring her back up into the conversation without it being obvious. Is Chloe in town with anyone? She was reportedly dating Charles Baldwin, a famous actor who stars as the main character in Chloe's book-to-TV-show series.

And *why* is she here? To get away from the flashing cameras and prying eyes in LA? To bring home a guy to meet her father? But more importantly…why the fuck does that last question make me feel uncomfortable?

I don't care. Not anymore. Chloe isn't mine. She never was. I'm happy with how things are going in my life, and now that Stacey and I are officially over, I was looking forward to casual sex with a different woman every night. No strings, no obligation, no chance of getting involved and ultimately hurt.

And the best part is then *I* won't hurt anyone. I've been upfront with anyone I take home, making sure they have no expectations. I won't leave them broken and alone, too naive to admit I was running from myself and my own insecurities at the time.

But that was the past, and I doubt Chloe has even paid me even the smallest thought. She's probably changed now, and running into her again would be a disappointment. I miss the old Chloe, and there's no way years of living in LA, walking red carpets, and signing seven-figure book deals wouldn't change a person.

"Are you guys going out on the lake again tomorrow?" Rory asks.

"In the morning," Jacob tells her. "It's supposed to storm later in the afternoon, though, so we'll have to wait and see. You want to come?"

"I do!"

"Are you bringing Adam?" Mason asks with his mouth full, and Mom glares at him.

"No," Rory rushes out and looks at Dean. "We'd love a few baby-free hours together."

"So you can work on baby number two?" Mason teases.

"Let's hope not in the boat," Dad says with a grimace.

"If you're so eager to have another baby in the family, *you* have a kid," Rory says pointedly, and right on cue, Adam starts crying. Rory makes a move to get up, but Dean stops her, saying he'll get the baby.

"I wouldn't be surprised if there were half a dozen mini-Masons running around already," I say.

"Same can be said for you, you whore," Mason retorts, and Jacob laughs.

"Are we going to Silver Lake or all the way to Lake Michigan?" Rory asks, ignoring our bickering.

"Silver," Jacob answers. "By the time we go to Lake Michigan, it'll be storming, and I really don't want to get stuck out there—again."

"The boat is new," Dad grumps, offended when we insult the old clunker of a boat we had before.

"The lake is hot as fuck," Mason warns Rory, and Nana Benson swats him on the back of the head.

"Language," she hisses. "There's a baby present."

"It's not like he can—" Mason starts and then turns his head down. "Sorry, Nana."

"It is hot out there," I agree and take another bite of food.

"Good," Rory says. "It'll be fall before we know it and missing the heat of summer. And then we'll be buried under snow. Though it's not as bad in Eastwood as it is here. Funny how just a few hours down makes a big difference in the snow."

"If a transfer to Miami comes up this winter, I might just take it," Mason tells us.

"No, you won't," Mom says right back. "That's too far."

"Did you forget I spent two years in Arizona?"

"No, I didn't at all. I only saw you three times in that time."

"I was undercover," he reminds us. "And it paid off. We got the bad guys."

"What time are we going out?" Rory asks, taking the baby from Dean so she can nurse him.

"Seven?" Jacob suggests and everyone shudders.

"Why would I voluntarily get up at seven?" Mason looks at me, knowing I get up early for work a lot too. "Nine."

"Fine," Jacob huffs. "Nine it is."

"I THINK THE STORM IS ROLLING IN FASTER THAN WE EXPECTED." I twist in my seat, beer in hand. We're in the busy part of the lake today, and it's packed with people doing just the same as us. Saturdays are always busy, but with school starting next week, I think everyone is trying to get out and enjoy one last hurrah before going back to the grind.

I used to live for summer, and it seemed the older I got, the faster summers went by. Then I got into med school and summers were a thing of the past.

"It is," Dad says, looking at the weather radar. "We have time for one more time around and then we should head back. It'll take a while to cross the lake."

Since it was so busy today, we had to park and dock on the other side of the lake, the "quiet part" reserved for fishing and kayaking. It's a no-wake zone, so it takes a long-ass time to idle through the water until we get to this part of the lake.

"Who's up?" Dad asks, and Mason and Rory play *Rock, Paper, Scissors* to see who gets to go on the tube once more. Rory wins, and I'm pretty sure Mason let her. We're all big softies when it comes to our little sister, even though she drove us crazy when we were kids.

The gray clouds look like they're starting to clear up when Rory climbs back onto the boat, but the radar tells a different story, and I'd rather not get caught in a thunderstorm on the water. The boat ramp will most definitely be all backed up by then, with people clambering to get loaded up and out of the storm.

I pop the top on my third beer—I'm not driving or anything

—and sit next to Rory in the back of the boat. I don't drink very often, both because of being on-call throughout the week, and because I've gotten pretty damn dedicated to working out this past year. It's been a good distraction and the perfect way to blow off steam when I have a rough day at work.

"I don't even like beer but that looks good," she huffs.

"Can't you have a little?" I ask.

"I can, and I had like half a glass of wine the other night that pretty much made me drunk," she laughs. "I'm going to nurse Adam as soon as we're home, so no booze for me. My boobs hurt."

"But they look good." Dean playfully elbows her, and she giggles.

Taking a long drink of beer, I lean back and enjoy the breeze on my face as the boat gets going. It's hotter than hell out here, and with the storm approaching, it's getting humid. The sun is still beating down on us for now, and once we hit the fishing area of the lake, the heat will get to us all, I'm sure.

"You going to see your girlfriend later?" Mason asks Jacob.

"I don't have a girlfriend, dumbass." Jacob finishing his drink and tosses the empty bottle into the little recycling bin we have on board.

"Ah, right. Mr. Ed is your boyfriend."

"Hilarious," Jacob deadpans, knowing his lack of reaction will only piss Mason off even more.

"Are you dating anyone?" Rory asks, trying to come off as casual. "I have some single friends if not."

"No," Jacob tells her. "You are not setting me up with anyone, and don't all your friends live in Indiana by you now?"

"Yeah, but maybe you'll fall so madly in love you'll want to move!"

Jacob cocks an eyebrow. "And leave my own practice? She could come here instead."

"Maybe, but you'll never know if you don't get out there and try."

Jacob looks at me and sighs. "They're both still single too, you know."

"Yeah," Rory agrees. "But I'm going with the brother I have the best odds to match someone to. Mason is, well, Mason, and Sam is getting old yet refuses to believe it."

"I'm the same age as your husband," I remind her.

Rory looks at Dean, making a face as she slowly nods. "I know, and trust, me, I remind him all the time how lucky he is to snag a younger woman."

"So much younger," Dean says dryly as he puts his arm around Rory. "And I'm going to risk siding with your brothers for once," he goes on, looking at Rory. "Quinn used to try to set me up all the time and it was annoying," he says, speaking about his own sister. "Really annoying."

"Fine," Rory huffs. Yawning, she rests her head against Dean's shoulder. I slowly drink my beer, watching the lake whiz by, and the hot air slaps us in the face when we slow to make our way through the other part of the lake.

Rory pokes me, getting my attention. She points to a coastal-style house along the lake. It has a private dock, and a woman is lying out on it, long legs stretched out on her lounge chair. Her dark red hair is gathered up in a messy bun on the top of her head, and she has a book open over her face, shielding her eyes from the sun.

"I think that's Chloe!" Rory whispers, though there's no way the woman on the dock can hear us…I think. Almost choking on the mouthful of beer I just took, I cough, sputtering to turn and inconspicuously stare at the woman on the dock.

It is her. It has to be. And—fuck—even from here, I can tell time has done Chloe well.

"What makes you think that?" Dean asks, thankfully since I'm still not able to find my voice.

"Her dad lives in that house," Rory says, continuing to whisper. "She bought it for him a few years ago."

Right as we're passing by, Chloe sits up, blinking in the

bright sunlight. My heart skips a beat in my chest, and I don't know what I want more: for her to look our way or completely ignore us. She reaches down and picks up her sunglasses from the dock and puts them on. She's smiling, I can tell from here, and stands, bringing her phone to her ear.

Fuck, she looks good, and I feel like I did the summer I turned eighteen and Chloe went boating with us. I was so attracted to her it was hard to be around her. She was sixteen. I was eighteen. I knew I couldn't pull her around to the side of the boat and kiss her like I wanted to, and as a horny teenager, the sight of her in a yellow bikini was enough to get me hard. I avoided her the best I could, and she cried the next day, thinking I didn't want to be her friend anymore.

If only she knew.

Chloe brings one hand to her face, shielding the sun from her vision, and looks out at the lake. Rory makes a move to stand and wave to her, but Chloe turns at the last second. Relief washes over me, quickly followed by disappointment.

What the fuck?

I tell myself it's a good thing. That I really do want her to completely ignore us because there's no fucking point in a forced and awkward hello.

But even I'm not buying that lie.

CHAPTER SEVEN

CHLOE

"That wasn't very nice." I throw my pen down on my open notebook and flop back onto the lounge chair. I'm hot, sweaty, and want a drink, but I was determined to stay out here on the dock until I came up with a detailed outline for the next two chapters of my book. I got one chapter written in the early morning hours, after waking up at four AM with my characters talking in my head so loudly I couldn't *not* get up and write. I went back to sleep around six-thirty, woke up around ten, and have been out here, making myself suffer as punishment.

Because my characters are going in a totally different direction than I originally anticipated, throwing even me for a loop, which is why I'm speaking harshly to them right now. Trading my notebook for a paperback copy of the very first book in the series, I randomly crack it open and start reading, going over the details and plot I love so very much.

Three chapters later, I lie back, put the book over my face for shade, and get some sun before it starts to storm. Only about ten minutes later, my phone dings with a text, and I smile when I see Charles's name. Like me, he doesn't like to talk on the phone, yet we send each other voice messages via text message all the time.

No matter what someone says, it's different. Yeah, we're talking, but not in real time. And if I leave an awkward message, I can delete and try again. Which I do…all the time, even though I feel just as comfortable around Charles as I do around Farisha. But if anyone can second-guess any single little thing they say or do…it's me.

A boat passes by, and I divert my eyes from the lake to my phone, bringing it closer to my ear so I can hear.

"We just wrapped up another day of shooting," Charles says. "And I was thinking, because I know you're working on the next book, you should really write in a scene where Marcus has to sword fight someone."

I let out a snort of laughter and hold down the little record icon on my text message. "Marcus is a vampire. Why in the world would he fight with a sword? He's kind of made it a point to show off his fangs throughout this whole thing, if you haven't noticed." I send my voice message and gather up my stuff, needing a break from the sun. I get to the end of the dock when Charles sends another message.

"Maybe he and Kellie come across demons that can only be killed by consecrated silver?"

"Okay, I kind of like that idea," I send back as I let myself through the gate. Balloon, inside because of the heat, jumps up and down at the glass door as soon as he sees me. "Give me a day to work it into my outline. But why swords?"

I hang my towel, which is more damp with sweat than lake water, on the fence and go into the house, letting out a sigh of relief when the cool air hits me. Dad is over at Wendy's today, repainting the upstairs bedrooms. They're unofficially getting things one step closer to opening the house up to renters, and I'm enjoying the quiet of the house.

My phone vibrates in my hand, and I press play on Charles's message. "We had some spare time on set, and I messed around with Kellie's sword. If she has one, makes sense Marcus would be well-versed in how to use it."

"It does," I send back. "I'm going to think on this, but fuck you for messing with the flow of the story," I add with a laugh, though my story isn't flowing very well at all, and I hate how I'm stuck. I know what needs to happen, and I can see the ending unfolding in my head. It's just getting there that's tripping me up, and every time I start writing, my mind wanders, but where it's trying to go…I don't have a fucking clue.

"Hungry?" I ask Balloon, dropping my sunglasses, notebook, and book on the kitchen counter. "I'm starving." I go to the fridge, pulling up a text message to Marcy, the owner of the posh stable my horse, Spartan, is boarded at. He's the only pet I have, and I miss him dearly already. He's an off-the-track thoroughbred, rescued six years ago from an abusive life on the racetrack. He slipped in the pasture on a rare rainy day recently, and we've been taking the last few weeks off from riding, making my escape from Los Angeles a bit easier than it normally would be. He's well taken care of, and when I'm busy touring the world, a few girls who come to the barn for riding lessons brush him and feed him way too many treats.

Marcy texts me back only a minute later, while I'm still standing in front of the fridge looking at the vast array of food but not able to decide what to make. Spartan is doing just fine, and she adds a picture of him being loved on by three little girls. I feel a tug on my heart, missing my big beast. He's a character in my series, though unlike the fictional Spartan, my real-life horse doesn't have magical powers.

Settling on a block of cheese and a carton of strawberries, I plop down in front of the TV, watching a show about people with nasty wounds on their feet while I eat. Half an hour later I shower and move into the little-used office in the lake house, trying to force myself to write.

And only twenty minutes after that, I'm ready to throw my computer or cry. Or maybe do both at the same time. Closing my laptop before I chuck it out the window, or better yet, take it to the lake, set it on fire, and throw it in, I strip out of my blue dress, trading it instead for black leggings and a *Nightfall* merchandise t-shirt. I rake my damp hair into a messy bun and go into the kitchen, getting a water bottle and some snacks from the pantry. I shove them into my mini Gucci backpack along with my phone and a bottle of bug spray.

"Hey, kiddo," Dad calls from Wendy's front porch when I walk out of the house. "Going for a walk?"

"Yeah, I need to clear my head before I attempt to write another chapter."

"Having a bit of writer's block?"

"Kind of," I say, not sure how to explain it. I know what I want to write, but I have to get through several chapters first until I get to the big action sequence I've been dying to write since the conception of this series. So it's not really "writer's block" but more like "motivation block" crippled by a healthy dose of pressure to make this book better than the last, not disappoint fans, and leave them wanting more. And I'm hating every single freaking word I type in my document, which is a bit of an issue. There's nothing like deleting every other word to move a story freaking forward. "I'm hoping if I hang out at *the coven* I'll feel inspired again."

Dad chuckles, knowing exactly what I mean. When we were in sixth grade, Farisha and I found a little circle of rocks in the woods, and of course we thought the place was magical. A lot of weird things happened at *the coven*, leading us to one hundred percent believe it to be haunted. It inspired me to write my *Nightfall* series, and going back there has to give me the kick in the pants I so desperately need.

"A storm is headed this way," Wendy says.

"I don't plan on being out long, and if I do get caught in the rain, I'd actually like that, but it's only a five-minute hike to that covered picnic area. It's still there, right?"

"It is," Wendy tells me, picking up a glass of iced tea. She's sitting on the porch swing next to Dad. "They've added new tables and a few fire pits. It's a popular site now. It's probably busy today," she adds, knowing my general dislike for people, which is funny since I moved to the overpopulated city of LA, but it's easy to blend in there, well, it used to be.

Not like I'm some crazy popular celebrity or anything, but my fake relationship with Charles definitely got me unwanted—and honestly unexpected—attention. My name is known, and I naively thought it would stay that way. My publisher was happy to see the uptick in already-booming sales when TMZ starting reporting on the *blossoming romance* between the author behind the soon-to-be-streaming TV series and the star of said show. My social media followers doubled, which forced me to actually post stuff more than once a month.

Though, contrary to what the masses think, I'm not that interesting of a person. I spend most of my time outside in my little yard, lounging by my pool with my laptop in tow, or at the stable with Spartan. Luckily people seem to love horse content, but I think most of my followers are crossover fans of Charles and are hoping for more candid photos and videos of him.

"We're having lunch with Wendy's sister," Dad tells me. "We'll be back by six-thirty for dinner. You're eating with us, right?"

"Yeah," I tell him. "I'll be back before then, and will hopefully have a couple thousand words written by dinner. What are you making me?"

Dad laughs. "It's supposed to cool down after the afternoon storm, so I'll grill chicken."

"Sounds good. Want me to make a salad? I'll gather some wild mushrooms and dandelion greens from the forest," I say with a straight face.

Dad winks. "Make sure to get the good shrooms."

"Dad!" I say, faking my shock. "Are you suggesting I bring you illegal drugs?"

"Don't be so uptight."

We all laugh. and I wave goodbye to Dad and Wendy, setting off down the driveway. It's about a ten-minute walk down the street to get to the nature preserve, which surrounds the lake. There are hiking trails with gorgeous views, and it's so hot and humid today there aren't many people on them. Silver Ridge is a small town, but people travel from all over to walk these trails and use our lake. The stigma of glaring at outsiders is strong here, and it's easy to spot someone visiting from out of town.

The sky darkens and the air thickens with the electricity of the oncoming storm. I pull the hair tie out of my hair and flip my head upside down, raking my damp hair back into a tight bun, needing it off my neck. I take in a deep breath, feeling almost as if I'm breathing underwater.

At this point, I'll welcome the rain, though I am almost to the coven. A group of hikers passes me by in a hurry to the parking lot, suggesting I do the same before the storm rolls in. I smile, nod, and pretend to take their advice, but then veer off the path, using an old, gnarled oak tree as a guide. *The coven* is about a quarter-mile away from the trail, far enough to make us feel like we were in the middle of nowhere when we were kids, but not so far a search party needs to get called for us, though people do get lost out here quite easily.

In the summer, the canopy of trees makes it almost impossible to use thermal scanning to find anyone from the air, and the last time I was here visiting Dad, two thirteen-year-old kids wandered off and got lost. They were found six hours later, and the entire town was tense, thinking the worse. They were playing some sort of geo-tracking game and lost cell service in the woods, which I suppose could throw you for a loop if you're not used to the shitty cell service Silver Ridge already has.

I get a little turned around halfway to *the coven* and have to stop and gather my composure so I don't freak out. I used to pride myself on being able to find my way around the woods, and even ran into a black bear a time or two, and the encounter didn't end in bloodshed. I'm the outdoorsy one in my group of friends back in LA, but damn, it's been a while since I've been out here, and I won't do myself any favors pretending I know my way around.

It's changed a lot over the years.

Stopping to get my phone from my backpack, I hold my breath as I wait for the map to load. I have one bar of service, just enough for me to figure out I went a few yards in the wrong direction. I get back on the right track and come to the little circle of rocks in just a few minutes. Two are covered in moss, and beer cans, an empty bottle of whiskey, and food wrappers litter my sacred space. I'm not sure what pisses me off more: that someone else found this place or they were an asshole and left their trash.

Picking up a stick from the ground, I use it to push all the trash into one spot, intending to come back here tomorrow with a bag so I can clean up the area. I brush bird poop and dirt off a rock and sit down, closing my eyes and taking in the silence of the forest. I stay perfectly still for a few minutes, remembering sitting in this exact spot, excitedly scribbling down story ideas in a leather-bound notebook. Kellie spoke to me here, and I used to run around with a dull dagger hanging from my waist, pretending to have powers and fight demons.

Lauren Wallace teased me relentlessly for it, and when I was fifteen, she and her cronies crossed paths with me out here in the woods. Farisha and I were both wearing medieval costumes and were cooking soup in the coven over a tiny fire we built and lit all on our own. It took us nearly two hours to get the fire started and were quite proud of it. It had rained that morning, and I ventured away from the safety of *the coven* in search of dry sticks for the fire.

And that was where I ran into Lauren and company. It was back before every teen had a camera phone, thankfully, but

Lauren made sure to tell everyone just how much of a freak I was. Farisha was out of sight, thankfully, and I never uttered one word about her being a "freak" too. There was no need to drag her into it.

Reaching into my backpack again, I get out my notebook, hoping for inspiration to strike as strongly as it did all those years ago. It takes a while, but it does, and I outline the next three chapters, seamlessly putting in a sword fighting scene for Charles's sake—that totally fits with the story. Usually, I don't like to write longhand what I then have to go back and type, but the fight scene is so clear in my head I start writing it out—and then can't stop.

Rain starts to drip down on me, but I ignore it, not stopping until the drizzle becomes a steady fall. I close my notebook, blinking as I look up, and seal it safely away in my backpack. I stand, realizing just how long I've been sitting there on the rock. My left foot is asleep and my butt hurts from sitting in one position for so long. My head hurts from having my hair up in a tight bun, so I pull my hair tie out, giving my scalp a break. It's the only downfall to having such thick hair.

I hold out my hand, loving the feel of the rain on my skin. I slowly start walking back toward the trail. Thunder rumbles overhead, and I pause, mentally debating if I should just walk in the rain or if I should go to the picnic shelter and wait out the storm. When lightning flashes, I decide to take the safe route and go to the shelter. It's not a far hike, and I'll be there in just a few minutes if I pick up the pace.

Stepping over a fallen log, something crashes behind me. I freeze, straining to hear past the loud sound of rain falling in the leaves. A branch snaps. It's probably a deer. Or a bunny, even. They can be rather loud for how small they are. There's also a chance a bear has wandered down, tempted by the food left out at the campground and picnic areas. The fearlessness I felt facing bears from my youth has left me, and lying on the ground, slowly bleeding to death seems likely.

Swallowing hard, I slowly turn around, looking behind me. The rain starts to come down harder, and the wind picks up, rustling the forest and making it hard for me to hear if certain death is lurking closer and closer. A few seconds pass and nothing attacks me. Along with bears, my adult mind goes to serial killers or psychopaths living in the woods, kidnapping hikers and slowly peeling off their flesh in strips which they dry and eat like beef jerky.

Sometimes having an active imagination is problematic.

Forcing myself to stay calm, I increase my speed, not stopping until I make it back to the path. It's pouring now, and thunder crashes above me, reverberating through the forest. The dirt path under my feet is slippery now, and I almost fall a few times as I hurry to the picnic shelter.

I look like a drowned rat and don't feel like dealing with people right now, so I'm pleasantly surprised to see the covered area empty. Well, this side of it at least. There's a large stone fireplace in the center, open on both sides for people to warm themselves by in the colder months. Something moves on the other side of the fireplace, and all I see is a flash of black.

Now there *is* a real chance it's a bear. It might not be taking shelter from the storm like I am, but it's definitely eating any scraps of food left behind by picnickers. I slow right as lightning sizzles in the sky and another clap of thunder shakes the very ground beneath my feet.

Whatever is behind the fireplace moves forward. It's not a bear, but something much, much worse. Eyes, dark blue like the stormy sky, lock with mine, and the cold rainwater suddenly drenches my heart, making a shiver run down my spine.

"Chloe."

CHAPTER EIGHT

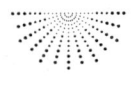

SAM

The world stops, and the air is sucked out of my chest. Wind and rain rage around us, and thunder booms when her full lips part, drowning out whatever she said. I blink, afraid if I look away she'll disappear somehow, that maybe I'm just imaging all this.

She's drenched from the rain, dark red hair hanging around her face, somehow highlighting her intense green eyes. Dressed in hiking boots, black leggings, and a white t-shirt with the words *Nightfall* along the collar, my eyes go right to her breasts on their own accord and—*fuck*—I can see the faint outline of her nipples through the wet fabric.

I've wondered what Chloe looks like naked multiple times over the years. I've caught glimpses of her here and there, most happening innocently enough. But seeing her—all of her—has been the subject of my dreams more times than once.

The years have been good to her, and even standing here, barely out of the pouring rain, with wet hair, no makeup, and mud splattered on her feet and ankles, Chloe takes my fucking breath away. She's even more gorgeous here than she is in photos—photos where her hair and makeup have been professionally done and she has her arm linked through some guy's.

The wind gusts, blowing rain into the covered shelter. The flames in the large fireplace, which were almost out, hiss in protest. More thunder rumbles overhead and lightning flashes across the darkening sky. I blink and the logical part of my brain kicks into gear.

It's storming, and my phone buzzed with a weather alert not long ago, warning about a tornado in the next town over. Chloe is still at the threshold of the shelter, at risk for getting hit by lightning or debris. I think the shelter might hold up in the event a tornado actually went through here, but we'd need to move to the center, hoping the great stone fireplace will hold and the structure won't lose its integrity if trees topple over.

Chloe shivers again, pulling her arms in toward herself. If I had a jacket, I'd take it off and give it to her. But I'm out here in athletic shorts and a tank top, having slipped away from the house for a jog through the woods to clear my head. I made it to the shelter before it started raining, and I decided to play it safe and wait out the storm in the picnic shelter. There were a few families here, rushing to gather their belongings and get out before the storm hit.

They were roasting hotdogs over the fire and didn't bother to put out the flames as they ran out. I'd been sitting here poking at the fire when I saw someone come out of the woods. There are a few more logs left to toss into the fire, and right now Chloe might be thankful for that. The heat of the day got washed away with the rain, and the constant wind is making even me a little cold, and I'm not soaking wet from the cold rain.

Chloe reaches up, moving several strands of wet hair that are stuck to her forehead, and continues to stare at me, unmoving. For a second, I think maybe she doesn't recognize me anymore. It's been years, and the memory of the last time I laid eyes on Chloe is burned in my memory.

Did that memory fade for her?

"Chloe," I say again, and those two syllables come out breathy, awakening something inside of me. Something I need to promptly fall right back to sleep. She slowly steps forward and regret weighs heavily on my chest.

"Sam," she finally replies, inching in. "It's…it's been a while."

"It has." I don't realize I'm walking closer until misty rain blows in, dampening my face. Goosebumps break out on Chloe's arms, and her pert nipples become even more obvious beneath the thin fabric of her shirt. "You look good."

"I'm wet," she says, and then immediately thinks exactly what I'm thinking. "From the rain," she adds quickly. "Not because, well, you know—but not—it's raining and…*fuck.*"

My lips curve into a smile, mind of course struggling to get out of the gutter, but happily surprised to see she's just as adorably awkward as ever. Leaves rip off the nearby trees, crashing to the ground in wet heaps.

"We should move to the center," I tell her, finding comfort in being rational. Think about our physical safety, not about how it would feel to have her *physically* closer to me. Chloe nods but stands rooted to the spot, emerald eyes piercing into mine, and I hate that I can't interpret the look on her pretty face.

We have so much history between us, history I left behind and couldn't go back to because I burned that bridge. Has enough time passed?

"I didn't think the storm would be this intense," she says quietly, moving next to the hearth. She takes her backpack off and sets it on a picnic table. "Or else I would have brought a raincoat."

"You knew it was going to storm and you still went out into the woods?" I ask, shocked again by how much of a *Chloe thing* that is to do.

She nods and turns, holding out her hands to the dwindling flames. "Yeah. I intentionally got caught in it. I figured it would be good inspiration."

I'm smiling again, forcing myself to take my eyes off of her and pick up two logs to carefully work them into the fire.

"Why are you here?" she asks, question coming out a little pointed.

"I went for a run and came here to wait out the rain. There was a family roasting hotdogs, hence the flames."

She nods, staring into the fireplace, watching the smaller of the two logs slowly catch on fire. "I mean in Silver Ridge." Snapping her head to the side to look at me. I see her there—the Chloe that I knew from our childhood—but it's then I realize how much of a stranger she's become.

And how much I fucking hate it.

I run my hand through my hair, brushing it back. I was hot and sweaty before stopping, and even with the temperature dropping a good ten degrees from the storm, standing here next to Chloe, and the fire, is making me hot again.

"Oh, we're, uh, all here," I say, confused as to why I'm suddenly so unnerved. "Mason and Rory too. Jacob never left."

"He's the town vet. My dad takes his dog to him. I didn't realize Rory moved, but I suppose it makes sense since she got married."

Chloe and Rory are still Facebook friends, and Chloe sent Rory a card with a very large amount of money inside the week before her wedding. Rory was so excited Chloe not only remembered who she was but took the time to write her a personalized note inside the card.

"Mason moved?"

"Yeah. He's an FBI agent now," I tell her. "So he's all over the place."

"That's fitting for him." She smiles. "What about you?"

"I'm a doctor. I've been at a trauma center in Chicago for a few years now."

"Wow," she says in a way that makes me think she actually had no idea what I've been up to. Not low-key stalking me like I do her…though really, I don't have to put much effort into it.

Anytime I log online or turn the TV on, I see advertisements and commercials for her books or the show her book is based on. And Charles Baldwin, the star of her show who supposedly dated her, is all over social media. "What kind of doctoring do you do? Is that even a word? Doctoring?" She laughs, and the smile on her face paired with the slight crinkling of her eyes is the most gorgeous thing fucking ever.

Dammit.

"I think so, and I'm an anesthesiologist."

"Oh wow," she repeats. "That's intense. And you said a trauma center, right?"

"Yeah," I say with a nod.

Her brows furrow and a sobering moment passes between us. "I've written about doctors before," she offers with a half shrug. "It's not the same, I know, but from my own research I know working trauma can be, well, traumatizing."

"I have my days," I admit.

"But we need people like you. God forbid I ever end up there…" She trails off, looking at the storm. I almost forgot about it. Being this close to Chloe after all this time is a fucking hurricane of emotion, paling in comparison to what could very well be an actual tornado.

"Cold?" I ask, though it's obvious she is. Nodding, she leans closer to the fire.

"This helps. Too bad those people didn't leave any hotdogs. I'm starving." Smiling, she looks at the picnic area. "I haven't had cookout food in a long time, and I miss it, though I don't really know why. Lukewarm potato salad, hotdogs and burgers that you know had flies walking all over them, everyone reaching their hands into the same bag of chips…it's rather unappetizing yet so good at the same time."

"Don't forget the taco tip that is always in direct sunlight."

She laughs and rakes her wet hair back again. "It makes the cheese nice and melty, though I know that had to be terrible for the sour cream."

"I'm surprised more people don't get food poisoning from cookouts, now that I think about it."

"We've built up an immunity, I'm sure."

We both laugh and then a moment of silence ticks by as we watch the storm and the fire. We're barely out of reach of the rain, and with the wind gusting harder now than before, we might not be out of reach for much longer. Chloe gets up, going to her backpack, and unzips it.

"Did your stuff get wet?" I ask.

"It's not too bad." She checks her notebook, nodding approvingly at whatever she just read, and pulls out a hair tie from a little zipper pouch on the back. Flipping her head upside down, she gathers her wet hair into a messy bun, securing it at the back of her head. "Much better," she muses to herself and goes back to the fire, standing with one foot on the hearth to try and dry her shoes a bit.

"You're a doctor, Jacob is a vet, Mason's in the FBI, and Rory is a nurse, right?" Chloe asks, untying the laces of her boots.

"Right."

"How are your parents?"

"Good. Mom still does alterations here and there, mostly for wedding dresses, and my dad is still working, saying he's going to retire every year but can't take the plunge. But they're good. How's your dad?"

"Same. Working but happy. He has a girlfriend."

"Is that, uh, good?" Chloe would want her father to be happy, but it could be hard seeing him with someone after her mom died, though it's been many years.

"Yeah. I really like Wendy. She lost her husband, so they connected over being widows, which sounds so morbid, but I guess it's nice to have someone who understands, ya know? They're both really happy."

"I do, and it makes sense. It's good he's happy." Another few seconds of silence pass between us and the wind starts to die down. It's disappointing, knowing the intense storm will be over as quickly as it came. Chloe will have no reason to stand here talking to me. "What about you? How are you doing?" Of course I know *what* she's doing, but I don't know *how* she's doing, and I mean it, I really do. I can't imagine the turn her life took, and I hate that I wasn't there to experience it with her.

"I'm...good," she says, hesitating slightly.

"That doesn't sound too convincing." She's never been a good liar, mostly because she doesn't like to lie.

"I've been really busy, that's all."

"Is that why you came back here?" I ask, hoping I sound casual. She hasn't come back to Silver Ridge in years, according to my sister, that is. "To take a break from everything?"

"Pretty much. My publicist is pushing for me to finish my next book a whole month sooner than planned so she can line up some promo for the book and the show. I'm officially behind now that I have a new timeline, so I thought it would be inspiring to come back to the place that started it all."

"You based your *Nightfall* series off of Silver Ridge?" What else—or who else—made it into the book? I was never able to bring myself to read them, though Rory and at least half the people I know love the series.

"I did," she answers with a smile. "You haven't read them then, I'm guessing?"

"I've, uh, intended to but haven't found the time."

She laughs. "They're not really your cup of tea, and I'm fine with that. Not everyone likes paranormal romance, though the books have a ton of action in them—sorry. If you get me started talking about Kellie and Marcus, I won't shut up."

"You're passionate, and that's not a bad thing."

"It's the one time my obsessive personality comes in handy." She casts her eyes down, and I hear echoes of the taunting in my mind...of Chloe being teased for being "weird" though I never saw a damn thing weird or wrong about her. Shame creeps over me like an itchy wool sweater, choking me and making me desperately want to claw my own skin off.

We were young.

I was lost.

And Chloe always knew exactly who she was.

Taking a seat on a bench of a picnic table, I'm just a few feet from Chloe right now. She picks a stick from the little pile of firewood and pokes at the flames, trying to get the second log to ignite. It takes a few minutes—and a lot of smoke wafting in both our faces—but she gets it.

"That feels better," she says quietly, twisting and pulling the hem of her top away from her body, doing her best to get it to dry. She inhales deeply, and I can't help but watch her breasts rise and fall as she breathes. Chloe has always been beautiful with her dark red hair and striking green eyes. She's thin but fit, and I remember a video Rory shared on social media—that I watched against my better judgment—of Chloe and Charles demonstrating their workout routine, which they did together.

I watch her for a moment, and all the words I should have said way back then bubble up in my throat, wanting to spill out at a dizzying rate. I swallow them down, eyes wandering over Chloe's body.

"The storm's dying down," she notes, voice soft, after a few more minutes pass. She gives the fire a final poke and gets up, reaching for her backpack.

"It's still raining."

"My clothes didn't dry at all." She motions to her body and, dammit, I'm staring at her breasts again. "It doesn't really matter. And I like walking in the rain, though it is a little cold and I have a long walk back to the lake house."

"I'm parked in that lot." I point to the parking lot right behind the shelter. It'll take only a minute or two for us to walk to the car. "I can drive you to your dad's house."

"I don't want to get your seats all wet."

"They're leather, so it would be fine, and if you're really worried about it, I do have a blanket you can put on the seat."

"Why do you have a blanket in your car?"

"Sometimes I take a nap in my car in between surgeries. It sounds weird, I know, but it's easier to relax in my car in the parking garage than the break rooms."

"It doesn't sound weird. I'd probably prefer to sleep in my car too than somewhere with other people." She bites her lip, no idea how fucking sexy that looks on her, and turns her attention to the fire. "Should we put it out before we go?"

"Probably," I reply and look around for something to use to extinguish the fire. We don't have any water, so instead, I dash out near the edge of the woods, retrieving a small broken tree branch with a thick cluster of wet leaves. I put it on the fire, strangling out the flames.

"Smart," Chloe says, eyeing me. She looks uncomfortable now, like the thought of getting in the car with me is unnerving. I wish I knew what she was thinking, or that we were still close enough I could just come out and ask her.

The clouds are just spitting out a drizzle of rain now. Thunder and lightning still rage on around us. The storm isn't over just yet, but we caught a break in the rain.

"Which side of the lake is the house?" I ask, pretending like Rory didn't point out her house like a stalker this morning.

"The quiet side. Dad's been there for a few years already. We bought and restored that house I liked as a kid. The one my mom liked too."

"I remember that house," I say softly, noticing the sadness that instantly comes to Chloe's pretty eyes at the mention of her mother. "Have you been out on the lake yet?"

She shakes her head. "No, just down to the dock. My dad and his girlfriend are leaving tomorrow for a romantic getaway, so I probably won't get out there this trip."

"They're leaving when you just got here?" We start walking down the stone path to the parking lot.

"They had the trip planned, and me coming here wasn't preplanned or anything. Though it works out, because as much as I love my father, he's a talker, and I don't get much work done when he's around."

"Yeah, I could see that. Having a lake house to yourself while writing a book is exactly what a movie about a writer would do."

She chuckles. "It is a little cliché, but it will be really nice and quiet. They're taking the dog too, so I'll literally have no one but myself to take care of. Though when I'm deep in the writing cave—not a literal cave, but a mental one, I guess?" She shakes her head. "It's just something us writers say. But when I'm in the writing cave, I can go like all day without eating and only drinking coffee and wine. And then it might be a few days before I shower, and I don't know why I'm admitting this to you, though I also admitted it on TV last year so…"

"That's also what I think of when I think of writers," I joke and playfully nudge her. The second my skin touches hers, a shock runs through me. I look out at the woods, having to talk down my cock—and my heart.

"Write drunk, edit sober," she says with a wink. "It's a Hemmingway quote and isn't that terrible advice."

"I can't imagine having a drink while working."

She laughs, and I love the way that little dimple on her right cheek is still there when she smiles. "Yeah, I don't think that would go too well."

We get to my car, which is the only one left in the parking lot. I open the passenger side door for Chloe and reach into the back, grabbing the fleece blanket. I really don't care if she sits in the car all wet from the rain, but I know Chloe doesn't like to inconvenience anyone in the smallest way.

"Thanks again for driving me to my dad's," she says, and I get a flash of driving her home after school. There were so many times when I wanted to pull over and kiss her.

But there were even more times when it just didn't happen.

Her phone goes crazy with text messages as soon as we're back on the road and within cell service range. I'm curious who the messages are from, mostly because I don't see how Chloe could be single. Jealously sizzles through my veins at the thought of her having a boyfriend, and I need to knock it the fuck off.

She's busy replying to the messages on the short drive from the park to her dad's house. The rain is starting to fall harder when I park in the driveway. My heart jumps into my throat when I turn and look at her. I put my BMW in park and shove that fucker back down where it belongs.

"It was really good to see you," I say slowly, resisting the urge to reach out and brush back that loose lock of hair that's starting to curl around her forehead. "You look…good. Really good."

"Even wet?" she asks and then closes her eyes, realizing she's said something awkward yet again. "You know what I mean."

I laugh, mind—again—going to her being a different kind of wet. "I do, and yeah, even after you've been caught in the rain."

She blushes and unbuckles her seatbelt. "You look good too, though you always have. It's not fair." Her lips pull into a smile. "I'm glad I got caught in the rain when I did."

"Me too." The car is in park yet we're still sitting here, hearts racing. "Do you want to go out and catch up?"

"I'm having dinner with my dad and Wendy tonight or, um…yeah." She leans toward me, just a bit, and the curl falls into her eyes. I can't help it this time. I reach out and tuck it behind her ear. I sweep my fingers down along her jaw, and Chloe shivers again. Part of me wants to kiss her right here and now, just to see what would happen.

If it would feel as good as I've imagined.

Her phone dings with another text, startling her. She tenses, and I jerk my hand back. "How…how long are you in town?" she asks.

"Until Tuesday," I say, though I'd only planned on the weekend. If she's here, I want to be here, trying to make up for all the lost time. "Come over sometime if you can take some time away from your book."

Her lips curve into a smile again, and the rain starts to come down harder. My heart is hammering in my chest, and I'm feeling entirely too vulnerable right now. She gets another text message, and when I shift my eyes down to the phone in her hand, I see someone named Charles is texting her. It has to be her ex. Are they back together? Maybe they—fuck—I need to give it up.

"Rory would really love if you came over. She'll be here for a few more days and she has her baby with her, of course. You were always like a sister to her…to all of us."

"Oh." The smile disappears from Chloe's face. "Yeah…a sister." She lets out a sigh. "Thanks again, Sam. Tell everyone I said hi."

Without another word, she gets out and walks away.

CHAPTER NINE

CHLOE

Like a sister.
I close the door to Sam's BMW with a little more force than necessary, fingers slipping from the handle due to the rain. Focusing my attention on the front door of the house, I walk up the driveway, each step squishing beneath my feet.

I'm so stupid. Naive. I guess I'll never change.

Sam is still in the driveway when I get onto the porch, and I make it a point not to turn around and look at him. Really, I shouldn't be mad. Not at him. He did nothing wrong, and offering to take me home so I don't have to walk in the rain was nice of him, and I'm quite thankful because thunder is rumbling overhead again. The storm is getting its second wind —literally. It would have taken me a while to walk back from the picnic shelter. I'm already cold, and there's no promise a tree wouldn't have fallen on me. If the impact alone didn't kill me, I could very easily become hypothermic and die a slow, painful death.

Okay, probably not since it's still seventy-five degrees out, but the dirt is cold, and I'd at least be chewed to near death from bugs. Sighing, I swing my backpack over my shoulder and get the house key, though I don't need it. Dad left the house unlocked, like so many others do in this small town. Yeah, Silver Ridge has a low crime rate, but walking into an empty house that's been left unlocked freaks me out a bit.

Balloon comes running, barking his little head off. At least I'd know if a stranger was hiding inside the house…unless they've secretly worked on slowly building trust and this little yorkie-mix sees them as a friend. Dammit, I overthink things way too much, but that's what makes me a good writer, I hope at least.

"Hey, buddy," I tell Balloon, peeling my wet clothes off in the foyer. I ball them up and bring them into the laundry room. I turn my boots upside down on a towel and make a mental note to put them out in the sun when the storm finally passes so they can dry.

I go right upstairs and get into the shower, grumbling to myself the whole time about how pathetic and stupid I am. It's easier to focus on being angry, to mentally kick myself over and over than it is to admit just how much it hurt—how much it still fucking hurt—to hear Sam refer to me as a sister again.

You were always like a sister to her…to all of us.

And she was to me, but Sam was never like a brother to me. So much for all the inspiration I found sitting out in the woods. If Kellie—my main character—were here, she'd slap me and tell me to get out of my funk. To get over it and not waste time on a guy. Though she'd also fight to the death for Marcus, her one true love.

"Fuck," I sigh and sink to the shower floor, putting my head in my hands. I stay there for a few minutes, doing the breathing techniques I learned during my yoga lessons, and actually feel a little better when I stand back up, quickly shampooing and conditioning my hair so I can get out of the shower.

I started writing my *Nightfall* series as an escape. Kellie is everything I wish I could be, and her romance is what I dream of. It's not perfect, she and Marcus fight and bicker, but their love is truer than anything, and it's one of the things people love so much about the series. Love *can* conquer all, even though you might have to kill a few demons here or there to get to that point.

Toweling off my hair, I dress in sleeper shorts and a baggy t-shirt. Balloon is waiting outside the door for me, and I go downstairs to get us both a quick snack. I have two and a half hours until Dad and Wendy will come back for dinner. I can get a lot written in two hours, leaving the extra thirty minutes to get myself looking halfway presentable.

But as soon as I open my laptop, I toss my head back in frustration. Charles matches the description of Marcus perfectly, and fans of the series had already envisioned him playing the sexy vampire before the books even got optioned for screen. Tall, muscular, with dark hair and dark blue eyes, Charles *is* perfect to play him, but I always envisioned someone else, and that someone just reaffirmed my worst fear from when we were kids.

The man I've been in love with sees me as his sister, and that's not sexy in the least. I need to give it up, to get over it, and accept—finally fucking accept—that Sam will never look at me the way I look at him.

Looking at my notebook, I start to type what I wrote longhand, but find myself secretly wanting Kellie to get possessed by an evil spirit so she can slap Sam—aka Marcus—around a bit. I laugh at my own stupidity and set the notebook down, going onto social media instead. I'm cheered up almost instantly when I see some fan-made teasers for the series and feel inspired all over again.

Turning on my playlist I put together just for this book, I get back into it, pounding out over a thousand words in just half an hour. I'm back in the groove, patching the part where I left off to where I wrote that sword fighting scene Charles will be happy about.

And speaking of him, I never listened to his voice messages from before. It's the downfall of sending each other voice messages instead of regular texts. Unless I have my headphones on, I can't listen to them in mixed company.

I press play on his first message, listening to him ramble about some gossip he heard on set. Most of our messages are this way, talking about nothing in particular. The fifth message asks if I'm still alive, since I haven't replied or even listened to his messages yet.

"Yes, I'm alive," I say and send the message. "I went into the woods to try to get inspired and you'll never guess who I ran into."

Three little dots show up in the conversation, followed by a text.

Charles: At the gym, can't listen. You're alive though, right?!

Me: Chloe is alive for now. This is her kidnapper. I expect a million dollars and some nudes sent right away or I'm going to off her.

Charles quickly sends a photo of a very obese naked man holding a bunch of dollar bills.

Me: You sent that WAY too fast, sicko.

Charles: hahahaha you know I have an arsenal of photos like that just for you.

Me: I don't doubt it.

I put the phone down and go back to my book, writing a few more sentences before Charles texts me again.

Charles: Just listened. Who did you run into?

I hesitate for a moment, feeling almost overly dramatic bringing it up. There's no point. I might see Sam once or twice before I go back to LA, and then it'll be business as usual. He'll forget about me and I'll get busy and remember I don't have time for a love life, even if the guy I do love decides to hook up with his sister—gross, Chloe. "Too far," I huff, though that is how Sam thinks of me. I stare at the screen of my phone for a few seconds before texting Charles, hesitant to say it because I know he's going to want details.

Me: Sam
Charles: The guy who humiliated you in college?
Me: Yep. That's the one.
Charles: Annndddddd?
Me: And what? We said hi, he drove me home because it was raining or else I would have had to walk through the woods and that's it.

A few seconds pass by and Charles sends a voice message. "Remind me what happened again."

I sigh thinking about it, refusing to let something that happened all those years ago embarrass me still...but it does. "They basically pulled a Vivienne from *Legally Blonde* on me and told me that a party was a costume party when it wasn't. I showed up dressed like a pirate—and not the sexy kind—and everyone laughed and took pictures, and one of the photos ended up on the front page of the university newspaper. The sorority got in trouble for it and lost their credibility, so the rest of my senior year, the girls had it out for me, blaming me for their charter or chapter or whatever getting shut down."

"Fuck," Charles says back. "That's fucking shitty—hang on, my trainer is coming back."

Me: Go workout and stay in tip-top vampire shape. I'm going to try to finish another chapter before dinner with my dad. And yes, I gave you a sword fighting scene that's really fucking cool, if I do say so myself.

Charles sends back a heart emoji, and I try to focus on writing again, but my mind goes back to that day in college. Sam wasn't the one who lied to me, who purposely tried to embarrass me, but he was on-and-off dating Heather Hunt, the head bitch in charge at the sorority. I was under the impression they were *off*, and Sam had asked me to go to the party with him.

I thought it was a date...a real date. Our *first* date.

Heather was jealous of my close relationship with Sam, as well as raging that my short story won in a contest and hers didn't even get an honorable mention. She was majoring in English and thought it was bullshit a sociology major was even allowed to enter the contest, let alone win.

The fake costume party was an elaborate setup, and she got a lot of people in on it. If Sam was with Heather the night before like she claimed, then he had to have known, and that's what hurt the most. He'd moved on to med school by then and wasn't at Michigan State anymore, and arrived that weekend just to party with us. The contest was supposed to be judged on historical accuracy, so I went all out with my pirate costume and even got fake teeth to wear since mine were white and perfectly straight, thanks to wearing braces in middle school.

Unlike Elle Woods, I didn't stay at the party, acting like it didn't bother me. If I'd shown up like a sexy bunny, maybe I would have. But I ran out in tears, blinded from all the cameras flashing. The last thing I remember was looking right at Sam, who was already drunk. He just stood there, the shock obvious on his face, while Heather threw her arm around him, cackling as she took photos.

That was the last time we saw each other. He called me nonstop, and emailed me three days after that, but Farisha deleted the email saying I didn't need to hear any bullshit apology. He didn't do anything, which she said was just as bad as being in on it. He didn't defend me. Didn't run out after me. And from what I heard, he kept dating Heather after that.

It was the ultimate betrayal and would have hurt even if I hadn't been secretly in love with Sam since childhood. Once a playboy, always a playboy, and I doubt he's changed.

So as far as I'm concerned, Sam Harris can go fuck himself.

"No phones at the table."

I flick my eyes from my phone to Dad, smiling. "Sorry. I've

been waiting for an email from my editor all day, and she just emailed me back."

"What did she say?" Wendy asks.

"She likes the chapter and outline I sent." I trade my phone for a glass of sangria, which Wendy made herself and is really good. Wendy asks me about the writing process, which she's asked about a dozen times before, but I have to give her props. She wants to be involved and wants me to know she cares, but also doesn't want me to think she's hoping to replace my mom. If I was younger, that could have been a concern, but it's not now. Especially since ghost-Mom told me to push them together. She loves Dad even beyond the grave and wants him to be happy.

"This is good," I tell Wendy, scooping up another bite of homemade macaroni and cheese. "I could eat my weight in cheese, you know."

"I do," Wendy says with a smile. "There are lots of leftovers for you while we're gone. It should last you a few days."

"I'm capable of cooking, but thank you. It'll save me time and save me from ordering pizza every day."

"You're sure you don't want to tag along?" Dad asks, worried my feelings are hurt that I got here only for them to leave. It's my fault, really, for not calling and making sure a visit worked for everyone.

"Yes. Having the house to myself will be peaceful. I'm hoping to have this book almost done by the time you're back."

"You can write that much in a week?" Wendy asks.

I nod. "I usually take like a month to write a book, well, the first draft. And that's while maintaining somewhat of a personal life and going to the gym daily. With no distractions or other obligations, I think I can double my daily word count."

"Just remember to shower," Dad adds with a wink.

"You might want to text me on your way back and remind me. Or else you'll come home to a week of me not showering."

"Go out and enjoy yourself too," Dad urges. "You can't man the boat well on your own, but the jet ski is a one-man vehicle."

"Or woman," Wendy adds under her breath, and Dad gives her a you-know-what-I-meant look.

"The keys to both are in the mudroom cabinet," Dad goes on. "Enjoy the silence while you can, but have some fun too."

"Writing is fun," I insist, though there are many nights where I'd rather park my ass on the couch and not move for hours while I binge watch some show I'm not all that invested in. It's easier than writing, after all. But I really do love what I do for a living.

"I might take the jet ski out for a bit," I say. "It sounds fun and is a good way to work on my tan without laying in the unbearable heat. It's so humid."

"You don't have much humidity out west," Wendy notes. "Lucky."

"Oh, trust me, I know how lucky I am." It was one of the main reasons I moved to California in the first place. I was sick and tired of being cold in the winter and then melting from the humidity in the summers. LA is nice and all, with ideal weather, but it never felt like home.

For some reason, I always had it in the back of my mind that I'd come back here. It was home for so long, and even though I'd prefer to be on the west coast in the winter, I can't deny how pretty everything looks when it's covered in frost and snow, looking like Elsa came through and dusted everything in reflective glassy ice.

And maybe, just maybe, another part of me thought Silver Ridge would be my home again because I loved something—okay, some*one*—in it.

CHAPTER TEN

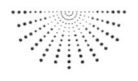

SAM

"You need a pet." Rory spreads a hand-drawn map on the reclaimed wood dining room table. We're at Jacob's house, and baby Adam is home with my parents. We were supposed to have a fun "sibling night out," but Rory insisted on playing a game instead.

"I'm not home enough for a pet," I counter, picking up my empty pie plate so the extensive map can fill up the entire table.

"Which is why a cat would be perfect."

"I'm gone for twelve hours at a time," I go on. "Well, more, if you count my commute to and from work."

"You don't have far to go," Mason quips, leaning back in his chair, beer in hand. He enjoyed watching Mom badger me all dinner about settling down and having a kid before I got *too old*, and he's going to egg Rory on with pestering me over having something to care for. "And cats are easy."

"Then why don't you get one?" I shift my gaze to Mason.

"I'm gone for days at a time, not hours. How could I do that to a poor kitty-cat?" he says, faking innocence. He hasn't been innocent in well over twenty years.

"He has a good point." Rory pushes a little silver figurine in front of me.

"I'm not playing D&D with you, you nerd." I push the figurine back.

"Roll for it?" Rory picks up a twenty-sided die and holds out her hand.

"Fine," I huff and take the dice from her. "Here's to me *not* playing." I roll the dice on the table.

"Two!" Rory pumps her fist in the air. "You're so playing now."

I look at Dean, who's been rather quiet the whole time Rory set up her maps and drawings for a super thrilling game of Dungeons and Dragons. He wants to play as much as I do but is appeasing Rory, which I respect him for.

"I can get you a cat," Rory goes on, giving Mason, Dean, and Jacob miniature figurines as well.

"I don't want a cat," I shoot right back. I like animals and would love a cat or two so the one isn't lonely, and dream of the day I can get a dog of my own, but really, I don't have time. I'm at work more than I'm not, and when I get time off, I tend not to be home.

Because being home all alone is fucking depressing.

"What about a guinea pig or something?" Rory tries.

"You need at least two," Jacob says without missing a beat. "They get depressed when they are alone. It's instinctual for them to be in a herd."

"Then I'll get two," I huff, hoping to shut my siblings up.

"They need fresh hay and vegetables daily," Jacob goes on, slipping right into *Jacob M. Harris, Doctor of Veterinary Medicine* mode way too easily.

"Hey," Mason exclaims, picking up his figurine. "I'm a chick."

"Yeah, you are. You said you didn't want to pick your own character, so I made one for you. Our group needs a druid, so that's what you are," Rory goes on. "I already picked out your name, but you can change it if you want."

Mason cocks an eyebrow, looking at the scantily dressed tiny silver woman. "Can I roll to play with my tits?"

"Ugh," Rory huffs, rolling her eyes. "You're lawful good, so no. Though I wouldn't be opposed to someone killing his character off like right away."

"Sounds good to me." Mason puts the figurine down and leans back again, finishing his beer. "Though it's a little early to hit the bar just yet and that's where I'm going if my character dies." He turns to me. "Be my wingman tonight? Not that I need it, but you do. So scratch that. I'll be your wingman."

"Tempting, but I'd rather be the dwarf-lord of the Shire or whatever the fuck we're playing," I tell him.

"It's more fun than it sounds," Dean presses.

"You wouldn't say that if you weren't sleeping with my sister," Mason grumbles. He sets his now-empty beer on the table and nudges my foot with his. "What do you say? You want to go out tonight?"

I shrug. I'd actually like to go out with Mason, kicking back a few drinks and finding someone to spend the night with tonight. Anything to stop thinking about Chloe.

About the way her white, wet t-shirt clung to her tan skin.

Or the way her smile is exactly like I remembered.

And especially the way she looked at me right before she got out of my car and walked up to her dad's house without so much as a look back.

"We could all go out," Dean suggests, earning a glare from Rory. "After we get through this first adventure. It is early to be going out."

"Maybe," Rory says, looking annoyed. I love my sister, but even she'll be the first to admit she can get a tad dramatic when things don't go her way. "But I'm kind of tired to go out."

"That's fine," Dean says quickly, hand landing on Rory's shoulder. "We can stay in too."

"You can go out," she tells him. "I'd like that, actually. I'll stay with Adam and you can go out and have some fun."

Jacob snorts a laugh. "Sick of him already?"

"Hah," Rory retorts. "No. I'm not at all, but if any of you man-whores would stop and give anyone a chance, you'd get it."

"Get that we'd settle down and then want our wives to leave?" Mason asks, going out of his way to act confused.

Rory just huffs and shakes her head, but I get her. She wants Dean to go out and have some fun because she loves him. She wants him to be happy, even if it means she stays home and takes care of their baby instead of having a carefree night out with friends. She's said before she wishes we were able to spend more time together as a family, and I'm the closest to her and Dean in Eastwood, Indiana, but work keeps me busy and I don't feel like making the two-hour drive from my apartment to their house on my days off.

My phone rings, and I pick it up off the table. Stacey's name flashes across the screen, and I silence the call, letting it go to voicemail.

"I thought you said you two broke up," Rory says, arranging more figurines on her map.

"We did."

"Then why is she calling?" Everyone looks at Rory. "What?" she asks and then shakes her head. "Obviously I know she wants a booty call. But I thought you were done with her. Like *done-done.*"

"Oh, he's *done* her a few times," Mason snickers.

"We are done," I say firmly. "For good. I kind of can't stand her."

Rory opens a wooden box with her dice sets and starts to hand them out to us. "You're just now figuring that out?"

"I couldn't stand her for a while," I admit, sliding the bottle of whiskey Mason put on the table over. Rory also brought pewter goblets for us all to use while playing the game to "get us into character" as she put it.

Someone else I know would love the effort Rory puts into

D&D, and she's actually the person who got Rory into this game in the first place. Rory had to be in fifth grade at the time and came home in tears after one of her friends laughed at her in front of the class because she still watched some sort of kiddie show. I can't even recall the name of the show now, only that it was about magic and dragons.

I blink, and that day flashes before me like it happened yesterday. Jacob and I were throwing a football back and forth and Mason and Chloe were sparring with wooden swords. Chloe was my friend first, but she got along with all of us, and I know Mason had a massive crush on her for most of his teenage years.

Rory got off the bus in tears, running past the four of us. We all went in after her, and once Chloe found out someone was giving her shit for liking fantasy, she took both wooden swords and asked Rory to tell her where the bullies lived.

Never mind Rory's three older brothers were standing right there, ready to fuck shit up. But that's Chloe for you, and my heart swells in my chest at the thought of her protectiveness, both for those she cares about but for not letting anyone make another person feel small for being different or liking something that's not mainstream.

That night, Chloe invited us all to play D&D at her house. I hung out with friends and this girl I was dating at the time. I didn't really like her, but she was handsy and I was a horny teenager. Rory went, obviously, and has been hooked on the game ever since.

"So why didn't you break up with her sooner?" Rory asks.

"She was easy," I shrug. "And I don't just mean sexually. She was familiar and lived nearby. It just worked out well." I pour some whiskey in my goblet and toss it back. "I suppose I wanted to finally end things for a good year before I actually did."

"I get it," Dean says quietly, meeting my eyes in solidarity.

"Routines can be comforting, even when you don't like the routine."

"And that," Mason starts, grabbing the whiskey from in front of me, "is the reason I'd rather be single. No strings, no *feelings*," he says with a shudder.

"I've written your backstory to make you be a helpless romantic," Rory tells him and takes her seat at the head of the table. "Come on, let's get started. Adam might wake up and—"

"And your mom can handle it," Dean interrupts. "He'll be fine."

"I know," Rory says quietly, brows pinching together. My sister has always been good at taking care of things, and being a mom now has put that into overdrive. Rory closes her eyes for a few seconds and then smiles, looking out at us. "Let's begin our adventure!"

"Is this a good stopping point?" Jacob looks at his phone, brows furrowed. "I have an emergency at the clinic."

"Um, I guess so," Rory says. We've been playing for nearly two hours, and I might be having fun, though I don't want to admit it. "Is everything okay?"

"Maybe," Jacob says, rising to his feet. Pluto, one of his rescue dogs, jumps up, panting as he follows behind. "Assuming my patient can get to me in time."

"What happened?" Rory asks, eyes wide as she peers over her folders.

"A dog got hit by a car this evening and the owners just found him."

Rory gasps. "It's still alive?"

"From what I can gather, yes."

"Need any help?" I ask. I know squat about treating a dog, but medicine is medicine.

"Actually, yeah," Jacob tells me. "Until my on-call techs can get in that would be really helpful. The owners are on their way to the clinic now."

The clinic Jacob is referring to sits just yards from his house. We can walk to it, crossing a gravel driveway next to a pasture. Once the local vet in Silver Ridge retired, Jacob took over, and three years later opened his own veterinary clinic in a brand-new building on his own property.

"I'll tell you the amounts of drugs to give," Jacob goes on as we get up. "We'll have to knock the dog out and operate right away."

"I can help too," Rory says, standing and looking from Jacob to me. "I'm an OR nurse, after all."

Mason grabs Jacob's drink and looks at Dean. "Guess we'll have to take one for the team, stay here, and drink."

"You can feed the fawn," Jacob shoots right back. "It'll wake up soon. The bottle is in the fridge. Heat up water and then put the bottle in." He shifts his eyes to Dean, who nods, letting Jacob know he's well aware of how to warm a bottle.

"You need to name him," Rory tells Jacob, talking about a fawn someone brought to the clinic just this morning. I'd be lying if I didn't admit the baby deer was cute as fuck, but it's way too much work for me.

"He's going back to the wild as soon as he's old enough," Jacob reminds our sister. "Naming him makes it harder to let go."

"You're such a softie," Rory teases, smiling as she closes her folders. "No peeking at how the game ends."

Mason rolls his eyes and takes a swig of Jacob's beer. "Don't tempt me."

Dean gives Rory a quick kiss goodbye and the three of us set out, stepping into the night. It's cool tonight, the air still holding onto the chill from the storm. Lights loom up ahead, and the horses in the pasture next to us stir, nickering softly in hopes someone will bring them food. I grew up with livestock and might have been the reigning 4H Champion in the cattle project for three years in a row.

That life is far behind me now, but it comes rushing back fast. Both Mom and Dad were softies, as Rory put it, and couldn't say no when Jacob would bring home an injured animal. When I was in fifth grade and wanted a dog, Dad took me to the animal shelter and we left with three pitbull puppies. We had horses and llamas through my childhood, and in the back of my mind, I assumed I might end up back here whenever I had kids of my own, giving them a similar childhood.

Jacob punches in the security code and lets us into the clinic, flicking on the lights.

"Wow," Rory tells him, looking around. It's the first time either of us has set foot in this new building. "It's gorgeous!"

"Thanks," Jacob says, hurrying to get into the back. Rory and I might not treat animals, but we get it. The rushed panic that's more productive than not. It's like a switch is flipped and you're in emergency-mode. We start prepping the OR, which is similar in more ways than I thought to the operating rooms I'm used to, though it's lacking several machines for obvious reasons.

"Can one of you get that?" Jacob asks when someone knocks on the glass doors at the front of the clinic.

"I got it," I say, carefully setting a set of clean surgical tools down. I'm still in my jeans and a t-shirt, a far cry from what I'm used to wearing when I'm putting my patients to sleep, managing not only their pain but their overall vitals.

Two people stand by the front doors, and a large dog is wrapped up in a blanket, weight supported by both women. I twist back the lock and let them in.

"Thank you so much," the woman rushes out. Her blonde hair is pulled back in a messy bun, and mascara runs down her cheeks from her tears. "Oh, you're…you're not Dr. Harris."

"I actually am," I say, helping the two women inside. "I'm his brother."

"Oh," the woman says, struggling to hold back tears. "Is he here?"

"Yeah, he's getting ready for…" I look at the dog, who looks like some sort of golden retriever mix. Blood is soaking through the purple blanket he's wrapped in, and he's in bad shape.

"Tigger," the woman answers, tears rolling down her face.

"Let me help you," I tell them and take Tigger from her arms, carrying him into the back. Jacob and Rory are in the surgery room. I bring the dog in and lay him on the table. Jacob gets right to work, and I help get the dog put under. The dog has an obvious broken leg and probably a ton of internal damage.

"I can tell you two are brothers," the crying blonde woman says when I come out of the room. Two vet techs responded to the emergency call, and Rory is staying in to assist if need be. "You look alike."

"I'm better-looking," I say with a wink, and she smiles.

"Are you a vet too?" she asks, looking through the window at her dog.

"No, I'm an anesthesiologist."

"Oh, wow. Lucky you were here."

"Things have a way of working out like that. I'm—"

"Sam," the other blonde woman says. She looked familiar right away, but I couldn't place her. "You're Sam Harris."

"Yeah, and sorry, but you are…?"

"Lauren." She brushes her messy hair back. "We went to high school together. I was a grade below you, though." Pausing, she waits to see if it sparks any recognition. I slowly shake my head. "I was Lauren Wallace back then," she says, and the name rings a bell. Lauren Wallace…Lauren Wallace…Lauren… yes, I remember her now. Vaguely…very vaguely.

"Yeah, I got it now. So, uh, how have you been?"

"Good." She smiles again and inches closer. "I've been in Detroit and just moved back and am staying with my sister."

She looks at Tigger's owner. "I got divorced last year," she adds. "So I'm a single lady once again. What about you?" Her eyes go to my left hand. "Anyone special in your life?"

At the mention of *someone special,* my mind goes to Chloe and her rain-soaked hair. She is special, but she's not in my life.

"Sam," Rory calls, coming to the little window. She waves me in, saving me from having to answer Lauren's question. I end up changing into scrubs and assisting with the rest of the surgery, fascinated with both the similarities and differences in a dog versus human surgery.

Dean and Mason are sitting in the waiting room when we're all done, and Rory and I go up front.

"How's Tigger?" Lauren asks, holding her sister's hand.

"Dr. Harris," I say, feeling almost weird referring to Jacob as a doctor when I go by the same name, "said he's stable. He'll be out to talk to you soon."

"Why are you here?" Rory asks Dean.

"We came to check on you," he replies with a frown. "Nice to see you too."

Rory rests her hands on his chest. "You know what I mean. Is everything—"

"Adam is fine," he tells her. "I already called your mom and let her know we got tied up."

"Thank you."

Someone knocks on the front door, making us all jump.

"It's my husband," Lauren's sister, whose name I haven't caught yet, says and gets up. One of the vet techs comes up front at the same time and lets him in, and then waves them back into an exam room, leaving Dean, Rory, Mason, Lauren, and me in the waiting room.

"You still want to go out and get that drink?" Mason asks me and then looks at Rory and Dean. "You guys too?"

Rory shakes her head. "I'm pooped. But Dean, go if you want to."

"Nah, I'll take you home," he tells her, and Rory smiles.

"A drink sounds good," Lauren sighs.

"You're welcome to join us," Mason says without missing a beat.

"I wouldn't want to impose."

"You wouldn't be imposing. At all." Mason waves his hand in the air. "It's been a stressful night. You need to unwind."

Rory catches my eye and shakes her head.

"Oh, I definitely do," Lauren goes on.

"Do you, uh, need to call the mister and let him know?" Mason asks smoothly.

Lauren moves her head back and forth, pushing her hair back again. "There is no mister...not anymore. I got divorced last year."

"You hear that?" Mason's eyes light up way too fucking much. "She got a divorce last year. That must have been so hard for you."

"It was." Lauren lets out a small sigh and leans in. "I came back to Silver Ridge to hopefully get things right this time around."

"Getting a drink is a good way to get the night started off the right way," Mason goes on. "And like you said, you could really use one tonight."

Lauren smiles again, acting like she's thinking it over before she nods. "You're right. A drink sounds so good right now."

"Great." Mason looks at me, mouthing *wingman* when Lauren isn't looking. Sighing, I just shake my head. "What do you say, Sam?" He goes on, purposely calling me out. "You're coming with us, aren't you?"

I open my mouth to say no, that I want to go back to Jacob's and play video games. But he'll be here for a while, staying to check on the dog until the morning. It'll leave me alone with my thoughts, and when I'm alone, I think about her.

"Yeah," I say, regretting it already. I need to go and find someone else to regret in the morning too. "I'll go."

CHAPTER ELEVEN

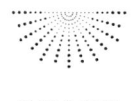

CHLOE

"It happened again," I whisper into the phone, swallowing hard as my eyes dart around the dimly lit living room. She's driving home and it's one of the rare occasions we're actually talking on the phone since she can't text and drive.

"You wrote a creepy scene and freaked yourself out?' she asks with a laugh.

"Yes," I hiss. "And then I heard Balloon scratching on the door to be let out. But he's not here, Farisha! He's not here!'

"There are raccoons all over the forest. That's probably what you heard."

"How can you be sure? Coming here alone was a mistake!"

She laughs and something hits the large living room window, making me jump. Eyes wide, I turn, expecting to see a man with a hook arm or a deranged clown standing next to the glass. Instead, I see several large bugs flying around one of the exterior lights, and some sort of beetle hits the window again.

I let out a breath, shaking my head at myself. I get really into what I'm writing, and being alone in this house surrounded by water and trees reminds me how isolated I am, especially since no one is next-door right now at Wendy's house.

"You need to get out of the house," Farisha says. "Sahil is working tonight. I'm sure he'll give you a free drink or two if you stop by The Cantina." Sahil is Farisha's younger brother who bartends at a bar in downtown Silver Ridge. They have the best margaritas in town.

"That doesn't sound too bad," I muse. "And I already did my makeup for dinner."

"Why did you do your makeup for dinner? I thought you were just eating at home with your dad and Wendy."

"We were at home, and Dad wanted to take photos. I figured I'd put one on Instagram later," I admit, knowing how shallow that sounds. I've grown a thick skin over the years, but if putting on some makeup makes me feel a little better, then I'll do it.

"I'll text him and let him know you're coming."

"Thanks. Give Ally a hug and a kiss for me," I say, missing my goddaughter. She just turned three last month and is the cutest thing ever. Farisha, as well as her husband, teach at Berkeley. We're in the same state but are hours away, so we don't see each other often since it's not like I can hop in the car and make the half-day drive up north easily.

"I will. Have fun, but not too much fun."

"Buzzkill. Night, Rish," I say and then hang up. Stretching my arms over my head, I quickly reread the scene I just wrote, double-check that my document saved, and then go upstairs to change out of my comfy clothes.

I packed rather quickly, and in my haste over-packed, which I usually do regardless. I didn't have time to plan anything out, to stop and think about what I'd need to wear on certain days. I don't like living out of a suitcase and already hung up my clothes in the closet. I pull the hair tie out of my hair as I look through my options, deciding on a black dress. It's simple enough to wear on a casual night out like this, but still adding a hint of date-night sexy too.

My hair air-dried after showering and needs just a bit of

straightening at the top to help tame some of the fly-aways. If my hair wasn't so thick, it would probably curl a lot better than it does, and instead hands in loose waves that make it look like I put effort into my appearance than I actually did.

I grab a pair of dark red stilettos and then change my mind at the last minute, feeling like I'll look like I'm trying too hard if I go all out with the little black dress *and* a pair of killer heels. I trade the heels for sensible wedge sandals.

Without giving myself time to second-guess my appearance, I head out, taking the keys to Dad's Jeep. The air has cooled off after the storm, so I double back into the house to get a sweater, and then have to go around checking the locks before I can go out and come home an hour or so later without freaking out.

"This house has so many windows," I grumble, turning on the upstairs hallway light to make it look like someone is home. Silver Ridge is a small town, but it takes a decent amount of time to get into the downtown area from the lake house since I have to drive all the way around the lake. It's nearing ten-thirty when I pull into the bar's parking lot. The place is packed, though Silver Ridge's definition of "packed" is different than what I'm used to from living in LA.

I haven't been here in years, and it looks—and smells—the same. It's supposedly part of the charm and the reason the owners have hardly done updates over the years. People like knowing what they're coming to, and while it's mostly an excuse to never update lighting or decor, this place is nostalgic for many people, from the locals to the people who come to Silver Ridge on vacation to use our lake and our hiking trails.

There was a time when I wouldn't be caught dead walking into a bar alone. Just thinking about it would cause my chest to tighten and my stomach to clench up. I've gained a lot of confidence over the years, though it didn't come easily, and I still find myself slipping back from time to time.

I'm actually smiling when I step through the double doors,

emerging into the dimly light bar. Sahil is behind the counter, filling beers and talking with his customers. He looks up after he passes out the glasses and waves. I wave back, and he shoos someone away from the bar, giving me their stool.

"Damn, Fisher," Sahil says, coming around the bar to give me a hug. "You look good."

"I'd say the same about you, but that would be a lie," I shoot back, and we laugh. Sahil is five years younger than me and was quite the pain in the ass when Farisha and I were younger, mostly because she got tasked with looking after him when her mom got caught at work, filling out paperwork or coming up with new health protocols for the school.

"Rish said your dad's house is haunted now?" He raises an eyebrow and goes back around the bar. "Or should I say again?"

"There's a good possibility."

"Wouldn't it have had to be haunted before? Unless someone died there recently or something, and as far as I know, there have been no murders in Silver Ridge in over fifteen years."

"Don't jinx it." I pull my hand through the strap of my wristlet purse and put it on the counter in front of me. "And you mean there haven't been any murders that we know of. I stand by what I said before and there has to be at least one body dumped in the lake every other year."

"The lake is pretty populated this time of the year. Wouldn't one end up floating up to the surface?"

"Not if you know what you're doing."

He laughs and reaches below the bar for a glass. "You're so weird, Fisher."

"And you're boring."

We both laugh, and he makes me a cocktail. I take a few sips and turn in my chair, looking out at the patrons, seeing if there's anyone I know. My heart speeds up a little at the thought, and I'm torn either way on someone recognizing me. I love to talk about my books, and I'm so fucking proud of what I've accomplished. It wasn't easy, and I hope my story of refusing to give up after seventy-six rejection letters can give another aspiring writing some hope.

Mrs. Clemmons, my high school English teacher, is sitting at a table with a few of her girlfriends. She has to be nearing retirement now, and her whole face lights up when she sees me. Waving like mad, she turns to her friends, no doubt telling them who I am before getting up. As she weaves her way through the crowd, a blonde woman takes a step back from her friends, who are hanging around a pool table, and accidentally bumps into Mrs. Clemmons. The blonde turns to apologize, and I recognize her right away.

It's Lauren fucking Wallace.

Ugh. Of course she's here tonight of all nights, though it doesn't surprise me she still lives in Silver Ridge. She was Queen Bee during our youth, why give that up? I'm rather proud of myself, though, for not feeling unnerved by the sight of her. She was all big and bad back in middle and high school, but she can't make me feel small, for I've built a successful career on the very things she used to make fun of me for.

"Oh, Chloe!" Mrs. Clemmons coos, coming closer. I smile at her, and then see someone else, someone who *does* unnerve me.

Sam.

The breath catches in my chest and I choke on my words, sputtering to say hi to Mrs. Clemmons. Sam smiles, and I can see his blue eyes sparkle from all the way across the room. He goes around the pool table—the same fucking pool table Lauren is standing next to. He's talking to someone else, and the guy turns slightly to pick his beer up from the table, though I don't need to see his face to recognize Mason.

He hands a pool stick to Sam, saying something that makes Sam give him an annoyed look, which in turn makes Mason laugh. A woman with short dark hair comes up next to Mason, and he slips his arm around her. If he's here with the dark-haired woman, then is Sam here with Lauren?

No wonder he only invited me over for dinner—for a *family* dinner.

"How are you, dear?" Mrs. Clemmons asks, and I tear my eyes away from Sam, forcing a smile. *Act normal, Chloe. Sam isn't interested, not now, not ever.*

"I'm...I'm..." I'm fucking furious, and annoyed as shit at myself for being furious, for still holding onto even a shred of hope that Sam would see me as anything more than his tag-along sister. "Good," I finally spit out. "I've been good. How about you? Are you still teaching?"

"Oh, you remember!" Mrs. Clemmons laughs and brings a hand to her heart.

"Of course! And I remember it was you who told me not to get too hung up on the beginning of a story and I can let the backstory unfold along with character development. That advice definitely helped."

Mrs. Clemmons beams. "Oh my goodness, wait until I tell my students—and yes, I am teaching. This is my last year and then retirement, here I come!"

"That's exciting, congrats!"

She waves her hand in the air. "Not as exciting as you! Just look at you! Books in stores, doing interviews on TV, and having a series turned into a popular show! We are just so proud of you, Chloe."

"Thank you," I say sincerely. "I just followed my dream of being a weirdo." It's something I've said more than once, and Karina has warned me not to use the same line over and over or it will make me sound too scripted.

"Well, it took you far. You even dated that actor. His name escapes me, but he was on those superhero movies."

I nod. "Charles Baldwin."

"Yes, him! Ohhh, my granddaughters just love him. My daughter too. And me," she adds with a laugh.

"He's pretty easy to love," I say back with a laugh. "He's a good guy."

"But you two aren't…"

I shake my head. "No, we're not dating. We realized we're better as friends," I say, going with a line this time Karina has fed me and wants me to use. Because Charles and I are friends, and we all know someday the truth is going to come out, and for Charles's sake, I hope it's sooner rather than later. "And he travels so much for work. *Nightfall* is filmed all over the place. The scenes in the magical forest are all filmed in Turkey."

"Interesting! Do you ever get to go on set—oh look, I'm interviewing you. I'm sure you want to enjoy your evening with your friends."

"It's fine," I tell her, not bringing up that I'm here…at a bar…alone…because a raccoon probably tried to get into the screened-in porch and it scared me. "And yes, I do a lot. The good thing about being a writer is you can write pretty much anywhere."

"Oh goodness, yes. I picked the wrong career path." She laughs again. "How long are you in town? I don't want to impose but school starts next week and the kids would just die if you came and spoke to them."

She's talking about her students, I'm assuming, and that sort of thing is usually set up by Karina for me, but this is home. I don't need special arrangements to go back to Silver Ridge High.

"Probably only a week. I came back to the peace and quiet of Silver Ridge so I can finish my book," I start, leaning to the side so I can look past Mrs. Clemmons at Sam.

He's bent over the table, about to hit a ball with the pool stick. Lauren picks up a beer—Sam's beer—and waits until he's straightened back up to take a sip. She makes a show of putting her lips around the bottle, and damn her, she doesn't spill a drop.

"…the next time you're in town?"

I blink. Fuck. What? "Uh, sure," I mumble, watching Lauren take the pool stick from Sam and bend over, purposely bumping him with her butt. My blood starts to boil...even though I know I shouldn't care.

Mrs. Clemmons claps her hands together and I realize I just agreed to come in and talk to her class. "They're going to love it!"

"Yeah." I try to fake excitement. "Email me details?"

"Of course, of course!"

I grab a napkin from the bar and take a pen from Sahil for a pen to write down my email for her, giving her my personal email account so her message won't get lost. She's so excited she practically skips away.

"You made her night," Sahil says, coming back over and grabbing my drink, topping it off with more vodka and club soda. "What you do, agree to have a quickie in the parking lot?"

"Sex with older women is *your* fantasy, not mine," I shoot back.

"It's a wonder you've never been subject of said fantasies. You're looking pretty old there, Fisher."

"I'd glare at you if it wasn't for all the Botox making me look younger," I joke, and he laughs. "It's nice talking to you again."

"We could talk more often if you came home more than twice a decade."

"I've come home more than that, and shouldn't you be giving your *other* sister the same lecture?" I ask, meaning Farisha. "Though I think having a kid gives her a pass."

"It does, though now that our parents have one grandchild, they won't stop pestering me to settle down. I keep telling them I will once I'm done with school."

"You've changed your major how many times now?" I cock an eyebrow.

"Five. And I'm kind of taking this semester off."

"Oh, right. You should be at school now. You're taking time

off?" I echo. "That couldn't have gone over well with your parents."

"Hell, no. I had to go on three arranged dates to get them speaking to me again."

I laugh and take another slow sip of my drink. Sahil is waved down to the other end of the bar, and I drum my fingers against the worn wooden counter, fighting the urge to turn around and glare daggers at Sam.

That traitor.

Of all the women in Silver Ridge, he has to be hooking up with Lauren fucking Wallace. Letting out a sigh, I take another sip of my drink and turn, casually looking out at the bar. My mistake. Mason catches my eye and a big smile splits his handsome face. He elbows Sam and points, waving to me.

Dammit.

Dammit.

Dammit.

I suck down another sip of my drink and pull the straw out of my mouth too soon and slobber it down my chin. Smooth, Chloe, real smooth. *Confident* by Demi Lovato comes on, and it's like a sign. I quickly wipe my chin, set my drink down only to pick it back up, needing something to do with my hands.

But I'm nervous and what if I drop it? I need to get a fucking grip and have confidence. I look good tonight. I have a successful career. I'm happy. I have no reason to be nervous, even though my mortal enemy from my teen years might be going home with the only man I've ever really loved tonight.

Mason gets to me first, spreading his arms for a hug. I set the drink down, forgetting to be nervous for a few seconds.

"Fish-face," he says affectionately and pulls me in for a hug.

"Fart-breath," I say right back, remembering the stupid nicknames we made up for each other when we were kids. Mason is the youngest of the Harris brothers, and I know he had a crush on me for a few years. There were times when I wished I liked him back, but I've never been one to date a younger guy, and…well…he's just not Sam.

My Sam.

"I heard you were back." Mason gives me a tight squeeze before letting me go, taking a step back. He looks me up and down, not caring how obvious it is that he's checking me out. "Rory might stalk you."

I laugh. "If only all my stalkers were as sweet as her."

"You have stalkers? For real?" The smile starts to fade, and I remember Sam telling me Mason is an FBI agent now. He probably takes stuff like this seriously.

"Kinda comes with the territory. I haven't had anything too bad yet, though, and I'm trying hard not to take it personally. Like, aren't I good enough for you to camp out outside my house for two weeks before you smell so bad joggers find you in a tent made from ripped bedsheets I threw away over a month ago?"

Mason laughs. "That's oddly specific."

"It might have happened to a friend." I swallow hard, eyes shifting from Mason to Sam, who got held up on his way over by Lauren. He stops next to his brother, and my heart thumps like mad in my chest. The stupid thing is going to give me away.

"Chloe," Sam says, and everything in the bar quiets. All I hear is the breath leaving my lungs and my pulse, bounding through my body. "You…you look good."

"Now this time I believe you," I say, shocking even myself at the ease of the words leaving my mouth. "I'm not wet this time." Mason raises an eyebrow and looks from me to Sam and back. "I got caught in the rain," I add quickly, unable to look away from Sam's eyes. He looks good too, casually dressed in jeans and a t-shirt. His hair is still perfectly messy, begging for me to run my fingers through it.

I blink and get a flash of Sam, skin damp from the rain, and I feel the shock all over again. He was the last person I expected to see and seeing him all grown up was almost too much for my system to handle. He's always been fit, but he's filled out, far from the boy I had a crush on.

Sam is all man now, and he looks like a walking heartbreak waiting to happen.

"Who's this?" Lauren pushes her way next to Sam and goes to rest her hand on his arm. He moves away at the last second, making me second-guess if they're actually here together. Lauren plasters a fake smile on her overly made-up face and tips her head as she looks at me, doing a *very* good job of pretending not to remember me.

Mason shoots Lauren an incredulous look. "You don't know who she is?"

Lauren keeps the smile on her face and shakes her head, blonde hair falling over her shoulder. She's still pretty, just as she was before. I never understood how anyone could have such naturally smooth and blemish-free skin like Lauren. She has a lot of makeup on—it's well applied, at least—but I can still tell her skin is just as perfect as before.

"It's Chloe," Sam says, gaze on me. Hearing him say my name sends a shiver through me, and my heart aches at the thought of what might have been.

What *should* have been.

"Chloe," Lauren muses, acting like she has to think back to who I am. "Oh, now I remember you! We went to school together."

"Yep."

"What have you been up to?" Lauren asks, way too chipper.

Mason's brows pinch together. "You're kidding, right?"

"No, silly," Lauren laughs, leaning closer to Sam. He doesn't move away this time, and I hate the tension that fills me when I see her hand brush over his. "Why would I be kidding?"

Mason slowly looks from Lauren to me. "She's famous."

Lauren's eyes go to me again, settling on my breasts for a second. "I don't watch porn," she says and then laughs. Once a bitch, always a bitch, determined to bring anyone else down to make herself feel better.

"I'm an author," I retort, keeping a sweet smile on my face. "But if you're not the reading type, you might not have heard of me."

"Who has time to read?" Lauren laughs. "And I remember now. You have like an ebook or something, right?" She just has to get the final insult in there, and I'm not wasting my time on her. She quickly turns, hair swishing behind her, and puts her hand on Sam's chest.

Suddenly, I'm back in the foyer of the sorority house, tears streaming down my face while Heather Hunt cackles like a madwoman with her hands all over Sam.

"Do you want to get a drink?" Sam asks me, moving Lauren's hand from his chest.

"I, um, I…" I sputter. Getting drinks with Sam is a bad idea. I know it, and he has to know it too, which is probably why he's asking. He might have grown up, but he's still the same playboy who broke my heart years ago. "I already have a drink."

"You'll finish that one eventually." Sam's lips pull into a grin, and he runs his hand through his hair, making me weak in the knees. Stay strong, Chloe, stay strong!

"Maybe."

Dammit. That is *not* what I wanted to say. Thankfully, I'm given a few seconds to recover when the dark-haired woman Mason was with comes over.

"I go to the bathroom and come back to you all gone," she says, and Mason turns, wrapping an arm around her. "I knew you were a sore loser."

"I am not," Mason says back, pulling her hips to his. He doesn't introduce us, and I get the feeling it's because he's not sure what this woman's name is. "Come on, let's play another round."

The dark-haired woman nods and shifts her gaze to Lauren, waiting for her and Sam to follow.

"Go without me," Sam says.

"Get us a table," Mason tells him, whisking both the dark-haired woman and Lauren away, but not before Lauren can give me a final scowl. They leave, and the sounds of the bar wash over me again. Has it always been this loud?

"You're here alone?" Sam closes the distance between us, leaning on the bar. I'm sitting on the barstool again, nervously stirring my drink. Why do his eyes have to sparkle like that? And why couldn't he have shaved this morning? That stubble on his face only draws my attention to his perfectly sharp jawline.

"Does that surprise you?" I ask coyly, surprising myself a bit. Who is this girl being all flirty with Sam fucking Harris?

"It does," he goes on, leaning a little closer, making my heart speed up. "I didn't think you'd be the type to go to bars alone."

"The type?" I put my straw between my lips and take a drink—successfully, I should add. I don't choke or dribble anything down my face this time. "And what type is that?"

Sam smirks. "The type who arrives alone but has no intention of leaving the same way."

One-night stands aren't my thing. The closest I've had to one is sleeping with Martin Miller, a film producer, after our third date. A lot of tequila was involved, and sloppy sex was finished with Martin crying about how much he missed his ex. Such a memorable night, that's for sure.

"Is that why you're here?"

"I didn't come here alone."

I wrinkle my nose. "You came with Lauren?"

Sam doesn't so much as flinch at the mention of her name. "I came with Mason."

"And you intend to leave with him, don't you?"

"It's always been my fantasy," he says seriously, and we laugh, slipping back into that comfortable friendship too easily. I need to claw my way back out to being awkward so I remember not to get ahead of myself.

Sam's eyes are on me, looking at me like I'm a snack and he hasn't eaten in days. I take another drink and put the glass down. I should order something to eat before I sit here, nervously sucking down drink after drink. I'm prone to poor decision making on a daily basis, but my chances of doing something I regret go up one hundred percent when I've been drinking.

"That table will be empty soon," I blurt, right as Sam opens his mouth to say something.

"A table?" he questions, following my gaze to the table where Mrs. Clemmons and her friends were sitting. They just paid their bill and are getting ready to get up to leave.

"Mason asked you to get a table."

"Oh, right. You want to join?"

"Um," I start and grind my teeth together. I want to get something to eat, so it makes sense to go to a table where there's a menu stashed behind the salt and pepper shakers. "Maybe. I am kind of hungry, but I also have the best seat in the house by the bartender."

Sam looks at Sahil. "That's Farisha's brother, isn't it?"

I'm a little surprised he remembered her that easily. "Yeah. Sahil."

"Are you and Farisha still friends?"

"Best friends," I say with a nod. There was a time I considered Sam a best friend too… "She's a professor at Berkeley and has a kid now, so I actually don't see her very often, but we talk all the time." I take another sip of my drink. "Are you getting anything to eat?" I ask him, thinking ordering something to-go will be a good idea. Then I can get out of here before I give into temptation.

"Yeah, I'm always hungry after surgery."

"Has the menu changed much?" The Cantina's dining section is open from four to eight PM, and then limits customers to twenty-one and up after that. "I haven't been here in…gosh…probably six years."

"It's been a while for me too," Sam says. "But I'm going to assume no, other than adding some allergy-friendly options."

I nod and then remember he said he's always hungry after surgery. "You were in surgery? Here?"

"Kind of," he chuckles. "We were over at Jacob's and he had a dog come in after being hit by a car. I helped until the vet techs showed up."

"Oh, well, that was really nice of you. How's the dog?"

"Stable and expected to recover."

"Good." I risk meeting his eyes again and my stomach flip-flops the moment we lock gazes. "So…other than working what else have you been up to?" I bite my lip, a bad nervous habit Karina yells at me for during interviews. I bite hard enough that the pain temporarily distracts me from whatever is making me nervous, but it looks too sexual, Karina says.

"That's pretty much it," he admits. "The trauma center and the gym are more home to me than my actual home."

*Which you share with…*I wish I could will the words right out of his head. His phone rings, and he takes it from his pocket. Looking at the name on the screen, he sends the call to voicemail and puts the phone on the bar counter, face down.

"Not important?" I ask.

"No." He meets my eye again. "What about you? Other than writing and hanging out with celebrities, what do you do?"

"That pretty much sums me up, but with more emphasis on the writing than having a social life." I still consider myself an introvert, but I have fellow introvert friends and we like to hang out hermit-style together. "I have a horse," I add, having to remind myself not to be the crazy cat lady of the horse world. "His name is Spartan."

"You always did like horses."

"I have. So, I spend a lot of my free time at the barn."

"Speaking of horses," Sam starts, lowering his voice. "Here comes a cowboy."

"What?"

He leans in even more. "You should join us before it's too late."

"I just...I don't know. Wait, too late?" I'm sputtering once again. Having drinks with Sam is a terrible idea. He's too gorgeous to be real, and if I didn't see him go through his awkward teenage years—which lasted like ten minutes, by the way—I might think he's a very well-made robot or something.

"What? You don't want to have drinks with me?" He flashes that cocky grin again, knowing the exact effect it has on women. I'm able to get my head to move back and forth, but the words aren't coming out. "It looks like it's either me or him," Sam quips. "I'd say you could talk about horses, but I don't think he's even stepped foot on a farm."

"Who?" I pick the cherry out of my drink and pop it in my mouth. Sam motions across the bar to a guy I can best describe and an obnoxiously overdressed cowboy. His blue plaid short-sleeve shirt is tight, trying to show off muscles that he doesn't actually have, with the top few buttons undone. His tight shirt is tucked into even tighter pants. His shiny belt buckle was bought and not won from a rodeo, I'm sure, and his pointy-toed, snakeskin cowboy boots are so not practical for a day working on the ranch.

The second I flick my attention to him, Cowboy locks eyes with me and smirks. He pushes off against the wall and saunters over.

"It's not too late to join me at the table. It's going to clear out any second now, and I can save you from Clint Eastwood there," Sam says. It's *not* too late, but dammit, I know what one drink with Sam could lead to. I came to Silver Ridge for a break from drama and to focus on my work.

And Sam...Sam is most definitely a distraction—one I don't need. But this overzealous cowboy...he could be distracting enough just for the night. Sam takes a step to the side, moving to an empty space at the bar to order another drink since I'm pretty sure Lauren slobbered all over his beer.

"Calling him that is an insult to Clint. And I don't need saving," I retort and push my shoulders back, offering Cowboy a smile before bringing my drink to my lips.

"Hey," Cowboy starts, stopping at my table. "Did it hurt?"

"Excuse me?" I ask and take a sip of my Dirty Shirley.

"Did it hurt?" he repeats. "When you fell from Heaven?"

Sam snorts, and I do my best not to spit out my drink as I chortle from his over the top cheesy and cliché pick-up line. Carefully setting my drink back on the table, I smile sweetly as I look up at Cowboy.

"Not at all," I tell him. "Because I clawed my way out of the bowels of Hell."

Sam stifles a laugh again, and Cowboy is taken aback for a few seconds before laughing as he hooks his thumb through his belt loop.

"Feisty," he goes on. "I like it." Wiggling his eyebrows. "I'm Dillan."

"Kellie," I say, using the name of my main character.

"It's nice to meet you, Kellie," Dillan says, stepping into the space between Sam and myself. He's a little too close for comfort, and his cologne is sickly strong. "You want a drink?"

"No thanks, I'm good." I hold up my drink.

"Chug that one and I'll get you something stronger." He winks, and I'm not sure what to take away from that. He's being…generous? No, I don't like a stranger coming over here and telling me to chug my drink. Because we all know there's only one reason he's wanting to get me drunk.

"Want to get something to eat?"

"I'm not hungry." I smile politely again and take another sip of my drink just so I don't have to talk.

Dillan leans in. "Want to get out of here?"

"No," I say pointedly, and Dillan leans back, offended.

"Seriously?"

"Um, yeah."

"Prude," he huffs.

Sam straightens up. "What did you just call her?"

"It's none of your damn business," Dillan huffs, looking Sam up and down. Yeah...good luck winning that fight, buddy. "It's between me and the lady."

"And I believe *the lady* isn't interested."

My heart swells a bit in my chest as I watch Sam defend me. If this were a rom-com, he'd punch Dillan, who'd fall dramatically to the floor, and then grab me, kissing me passionately while sappy music starts to play as the camera pans out.

But life isn't like a movie, and me of all people should know that. You're in a constant state of filler scenes, with a happy-for-now sprinkled in here and there. And the cold hard truth is how life goes on past the ending if you're lucky enough to get a happy one, and what once made you smile can cause you to fall apart.

"Maybe *the lady* should tell me herself," Dillan tries, and turns back to me, putting one hand on the bar, leaning just inches from my face. He's drunk, and I can smell the alcohol on his breath. "Come on, let's get out here."

"I said no," I reaffirm. "Now leave me alone."

Dillan hesitates, still hovering over me, and that's all it takes for Sam to grab his shoulder and jerk him back. Dillan immediately takes a swing at Sam, who catches his fist. Not wanting to start a fight, Sam lets him go and pushes him back, but Dillan comes back, both fists in the air. Everything happens so fast, and the next thing I know, my drink is spilled in my lap, Sam blocks another punch and takes hold of Dillan's arm, twisting it behind him. I'd be lying if I didn't say I was impressed. No one has gotten in a real fight over me before like this, and Dillan picked the wrong guy to mess with. Sam could easily beat his ass—and he would if it came down to it.

In a flash, Mason is there, holding up his badge. "Get out before I arrest you," he tells Dillan, who's squinting at Mason's badge.

"You're not a real cop."

"I'm a fucking federal agent." Mason pulls the guy away. "Still wanna test me?"

Dillan grumps and walks away, hooking his thumb through a belt loop again.

"You okay?" Sam asks, grabbing a napkin for me to sop up my wet dress.

"Yeah. Thank you." I press the napkin to my lap.

"Of course. No one messes with you."

I look up and he diverts his eyes, confusing me. A few awkward seconds tick by.

"The table is open now," I say, thankful for a distraction.

"Finally," Mason says. "I'm fucking starving. You're joining us, right, Chloe?"

Lauren and the dark-haired woman, who has to be one of Lauren's friends, come back over. Sam said Mason brought Lauren, but he's been all over the other woman. Whatever, but I don't want to sit there and feel like a fifth wheel.

"Um," I look down at my dress. I'm wet and sticky. "I think I'm going to head home so I can change." Swallowing hard, I look at Sam and my heart hammers in my chest. Nerves prickle along my spine. "I'd love to still catch up, though…if you want to get together and…and…talk."

Sam nods. "I guess we'll catch up tomorrow."

Wait, what? I know I wasn't overly obvious about inviting him over, but I thought the message was clear enough. No, I don't want to sit at the table, but yes, let's *go home* so I can change and talk. Why can I write my characters flirting but fail so miserably in real life at it?

"Oh." I unzip my little purse and put a twenty on the counter, giving Sahil a little wave. I take one last look at Sam's beautiful blue eyes. "Don't worry about it. Tell Rory I said hi."

CHAPTER TWELVE

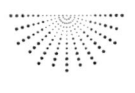

SAM

"What the fuck was that?" Mason elbows me hard in the ribs as soon as Lauren and her friend Paige step away to use the bathroom.

"What?"

"That."

"What is that?" I shoot back, annoyed more at myself than at Mason. I know exactly what he's talking about.

"Have you been doing the drugs meant for your patients and it's caused brain damage?"

"Yes, Mason. I do drugs during surgery. Half my patients are actually awake and screaming."

"I'm honestly a little concerned," he says seriously. "Chloe just invited you to spend the night with her and you turned her down."

"She did not. Chloe and I…we're…we're not like that."

"But you want to be," Mason shoots back. "Don't you?"

I've never wanted anything more in my life, and seeing her again only reaffirms how much I do. She's gorgeous, obviously, but there's so much more to her, and I want to get to know each and every layer of her complexity. Even as kids there was nothing simple about Chloe, and she thought it made her undesirable or too much for someone to handle.

I wanted to *handle* her then, and I'd give anything to handle it now. Chloe is one of the most interesting people I've ever met. She's passionate and driven, but has a heart of gold. We haven't spoken much, so there's a chance I'm wrong here but it doesn't seem like the fame and money changed her, which is impressive on its own. That sort of thing can change a person for the worst.

It doesn't matter how much I want to be more than friends with Chloe, there's no way she'd want to go there with me. I betrayed everything we had between us, and I regret it each and every day.

I should have told everyone to shut the fuck up. To stop laughing at my friend. My *best* fucking friend.

I should have run after her a hell of a lot faster than I did.

By the time I got outside, she was gone, and after half an hour of looking for her, I went back to the house to get my phone. The first call went right to voicemail. I hung up, did shots, and then called again. The world was spinning, and I couldn't get the look on her face out of my head. It wasn't the embarrassment of showing up dressed like she just stepped off the set of *Pirates of the Caribbean*…no, it was the heartbreak reflected in her eyes.

"We're friends," I say, blinking a few times to try to shove the memories back. "Or we *were* friends."

"Why'd you stop being friends?" Mason asks, and we go over to the table. My pulse speeds up a bit, and I wait a beat before answering, seeing if this is Mason's way of testing me. I said we drifted apart. That going away to med school was the reason.

"We went to different schools." I slide into the booth and grab a menu. "She had her own friends and I had mine."

"Yeah, but you two always did and that never made you stop being friends before."

I shrug, concentrating too hard on the menu. I can feel Mason's eyes on me, but he doesn't say anything. He can be a little shit more times than not, but he knows when to stop. Well, sometimes.

Everyone in my family has to know I've had on-and-off eyes for Chloe throughout our relationship. The timing was never right.

"She's single," Mason goes on. Apparently tonight isn't one of those rare times when he knows to shut the fuck up.

"How do you know that?" I look up from the menu and see Mason holding his phone. "Are you internet-stalking her?"

"Doing a quick Google search isn't stalking, plus she posted this on Valentine's Day." He shows me a photo of Chloe dressed like an elf, posing with a gray horse. She looks like something right out of a fantasy movie, ethereal and incredibly sexy without showing a lot of skin. The caption on the photo reads, "The only man I need! The best part is he let me pick out my own V-Day gift. ;-)"

"That was from February. It's August now," I counter. "That doesn't mean she's single."

"She hasn't posted any photos of her with a guy since, and if you look through her history, she tends to post photos of herself with whoever she's dating."

"Give me that." I snatch the phone from Mason's hand, feeling my stomach drop when I see a photo posted in March of Chloe and Charles. It's a throwback, at least, but if they had some sort of bitter breakup, why would she be posting photos of him at all?

She must have been on a book tour for most of April, since there are four photos in a row of her with different gatherings of readers. Most of her photos are either of her with her computer or of her with Spartan, her horse. She wasn't lying about that at least.

"Hey, you." Lauren plops down in the booth next to me and slides over. I tense, silently cursing Mason for inviting her out.

Even if I hadn't run into Chloe, Lauren isn't someone I'd want to hook up with. "Your friend left?"

She literally heard Chloe say she was leaving, and Lauren is just driving the point in.

"Yes."

"Her loss." Lauren wiggles her shoulders and inches closer, looking over at the menu. "What are you ordering?"

"I don't know," I say honestly, and grab another menu from behind the salt and pepper shakers, giving one to her so she stops leaning over mine.

"It's too late to eat anything," Lauren notes, glancing over her menu.

"Too late?" Mason questions.

"I don't eat past eight PM," Lauren tells us. "That's how you get fat."

Paige, who's a curvy girl, jerks her head up, looking at Lauren with wide eyes before turning her head back down, obviously embarrassed. Mason, who's been hoping to hook up with her all night, notices and wraps his arm around her waist.

"Midnight snacking is my favorite." He kisses Paige, and I kick him under the table. "Actually," he starts, wincing from the kick in the shin. "I think some takeout sounds good. We could go back to your place." He wiggles his brows, and I roll my eyes.

"I agree with the takeout," I say. I want to get back to Jacob's and crash on the couch. I close my menu with a sigh, knowing I'm going to have to break it to Lauren that I'm going home alone tonight.

"WHY DID WE AGREE ON BREAKFAST?" MASON GRUMBLES, ADDING a third packet of sugar to his coffee. The whole family is out for breakfast at Silver Café.

"It's nearly ten AM," Dad quips. "I'd argue we're actually eating brunch."

"Whatever it is, it's too fucking early."

"I'm sure being tired has nothing to do with that girl from the bar you went home with last night," I say, bringing my coffee to my lips. Mason glares at me.

"I bet my night was better than yours," he retorts. "At least I got some."

I respond by taking another drink of coffee, because his night was better than mine, and it had nothing to do with Paige and everything to do with me tossing and turning, reliving that night at the party over and over. I hate that I hurt Chloe.

That I missed my chance to tell her how much she means to me—how much she's always meant to me. Finally, when the sun was coming up, I fell back asleep and didn't have a dream at all. I woke up to Jacob's dogs barking at something in the yard, but my head was a little clearer. I feel terrible for what I did to Chloe that night, but it's not like she's still suffering for it.

She's living her best life and is happy. I'm just a blip on her radar, I'm sure. I'll go back to work, back to my old self, and will go a few days without thinking about her. And then a few days will turn into a few weeks and I'll get along just fine. As long as I don't think about her for the rest of the—

"Chloe!" Rory jumps up, bumping into the table and nearly spilling our drinks. "Oh my god, Chloe!"

Chloe's just walked into the café and is alone. She's wearing teal athletic pants and a matching crop top. Her hair is up in a messy ponytail, and she doesn't have any makeup on.

She's beautiful.

"Rory!" Chloe smiles and hurries over, pulling my sister in for a hug. Mom gets up and goes over, hugging Chloe as well.

"Wow, it's almost like you're getting a second chance," Mason mumbles.

"Second chance?" Dean echoes, lifting Adam out of the

highchair. The baby started fussing the second Rory stepped away from the table.

"He's wanted to fuck her since they were kids. Well, teens, to be accurate."

"Don't talk about her like that," I shoot back.

"Ohhh, right." Mason raises his eyebrows and adds more sugar to his coffee. "He doesn't want to fuck her." He tips his head. "If you're not interested...I am. Little Fish-face has really grown up, if you know what I mean."

I go to kick Mason, but he jerks his leg back, expecting it. Rory brings Chloe over to the table so everyone else can say hi and so she can introduce her to Dean.

"This is your baby?" Chloe asks, looking at Adam. "He's adorable!"

"Thanks," Rory gushes. She hasn't stopped smiling since she spotted Chloe enter the restaurant. "He's an easy baby and a decent sleeper. I think I'll have another."

"How's your father doing, honey?" Mom asks Chloe. She turns, angling her body away from me, and talks to Mom for a minute before her name is called at the hostess table to let her know her to-go order is ready.

"What are you doing tonight?" Rory asks, and Chloe hesitates. "We're having dinner before these two losers have to go back to work." She motions to Mason and me. "I know you're super busy, but I would love so much to catch up!"

"Bring your father and Wendy," Dad adds, and I'm not surprised he knows Chloe's dad is dating someone. Gossip spreads fast in a small town.

"Um, they're on vacation. I'm hiding out at the lake house to try and finish a book."

"Can you spare an hour for dinner?" Mom asks hopefully.

Chloe's cornered, and I know her well enough at least to know she doesn't want to make anyone feel bad.

"Don't force her," I say, trying to be supportive of Chloe but everyone glares at me. And this time Mason kicks me in the shin.

Chloe flicks her eyes to me, and something sparks behind them. Something I haven't seen before…something I can't quite place.

"Yeah," she says with a smile. "I can spare an hour or two."

CHAPTER THIRTEEN

CHLOE

What the hell is wrong with me? I don't like pain. I go to great lengths to avoid it. Sometimes I take Advil before settling down for a writing sprint because I know my back will hurt from sitting still for hours on end. I avoided the dentist for an impressive three years without getting another cavity because I was scared the one I needed filled would hurt. I might be stupid, but my tiny human brain can at least process that pain is bad.

So why the hell did I agree to go to the Harris Farmhouse for dinner tonight?

"Ughhh," I huff to myself and take off my shoes, closing the front door behind me. I set my bag from Silver Café on the counter and go upstairs, trading my workout clothes for a sundress. I couldn't sleep when I got home from the bar last night and stayed up taking my frustrations out by getting lost in my story. I wrote nearly five thousand words before I fell asleep on the couch in the living room.

I woke up, got dressed, and had every intention of going for a run. But then I got distracted with Instagram and decided to record some little video clips of the lake to post to my stories.

Fast forward twenty minutes, and I "ran out of time" to work out and instead ordered breakfast.

It's hot and sunny out again, so I grab my sunglasses and a big floppy hat along with my bag of takeaway and go down to the dock, sitting on the edge with my feet in the water as I eat. My plan today is to eat and write until it's time to go to the executioner, aka the Harris family farm.

Fishing boats slowly drift by, and everyone waves. The Sunday fishing crowd is made up of mostly older men, and I'm certain none of them know who I am or are fans of *Nightfall*. It's peaceful out here, making me realize how much I missed this place. My house in LA is up on a hill, with thoughtfully placed trees to make my lot as private as possible from my neighbors. I have "ocean views" if I climb up on top of my roof and jump up an extra twenty feet or so to see over said trees. It's quieter than I expected LA to be, but it's not like this.

Right now, I don't hear a single car horn or sirens. There's no smog hanging over the lake, and the homeless population is definitely lower here in Silver Ridge.

My mind wanders to me moving back here. I left partly for the opportunities presented to me, but also so I could avoid seeing the man who broke my heart. He's not here, though, we would run the risk of occasionally running into each other. But Spartan would love the trails here and jumping through snowdrifts.

Moving wouldn't impact my writing really at all. If anything, I might get more work done here since there's less to do. I take another bite of bacon, thinking way too much into this. I have friends in LA, not the best friends, but friends I feel comfortable with and who don't judge me when I'd rather stay home and play D&D than go out clubbing. They might judge me for showing up at a housewarming party in last season's shoes, though, instead.

Swishing my feet in the water, I peer down, always a little afraid someone is going to grab me and pull me under. The water is rather shallow at this part of the lake, thanks to a dry summer. If someone was lurking beneath the surface, they'd have to be hiding in the seaweed to stay out of view.

Freaking myself out, I pull my feet from the water, wipe sweat from my forehead, and eat the rest of my pancakes and bacon. I planned to only have half and then eat the rest for lunch, and I feel sickly full by the time I'm done.

After half an hour of sitting at my computer feeling like I'm going to fall asleep, I drink a third cup of coffee and give up when that doesn't do the trick. I lie down on the couch, expecting to fall asleep quickly since I was having a hard time keeping my eyes open while writing. Of course, the coffee kicks in now, and I'm getting anxious.

I get up, stretch, and change back into my workout clothes. A run will get my blood pumping and adrenaline flowing, which is vital when I'm writing the fight scene that is coming up in my manuscript. I pull the hair tie from my hair, flip my head upside down, and try to smooth out my ponytail the best I can. Then I grab my headphones, phone, and head outside, leaving through the front door. I double-check that the deadbolt is locked so I won't worry about serial killers sneaking inside while I'm out. I took the key from Dad's keyring and then realize the workout pants I'm wearing don't have pockets. I could slip the key in my bra, but it's hot, I'll be sweaty, and that's just really uncomfortable. Instead, I hide the key on Wendy's porch. If anyone finds it, they'll assume it's for her house.

Turning up my music, I start off jogging down the road, not stopping until I reach the entrance to the trail in the woods. It's cooler in the shade, and I slow, not too worried about burning calories but more about clearing my head and feeling more awake when I get back to the house.

The trails are fairly busy today, and I'm sure the picnic shelter is full. I pick up the pace again, wanting to get ten thousand steps in, which I haven't done in a while. The trail forks, with one direction taking you to the picnic area and the other going along the side of the lake. It's a popular trail for birdwatchers, and more and more bald eagles have been returning every year, according to Dad.

The trail has eroded a lot since I last walked it, and you'd fall and roll down a steep hill before splashing into the lake. Well, that's if you're lucky. I slow and look down at the rocky shore, which is another reason this is the "quiet part" of the lake. There are lots of rocks hidden just below the surface of the water, and when the water level is higher than it is now, you don't see them until it's too late.

Thinking I see a bald eagle, I inch to the edge of the path, narrowing my eyes as I squint into the sun. Opening my camera on my phone, I hold on to a tree and lean forward to get a picture of the eagle.

My music is still blaring in my ears. I can't hear what's going on around me, but I sense someone behind me. I jerk my head to the side and am startled to see Sam standing just inches from me. I jump, drop my phone, which pulls my headphones out of my ears and start to slip down the steep hill.

Sam lunges forward and grabs me around the waist, effortlessly pulling me to him. My hands land on his shoulders, and he spins me around, putting me safely back on the trail. My breath leaves my lungs in a huff, and my lips part as I try to process what just happened.

"Are you okay?" Sam asks.

"I'm…I'm…" I'm tight in Sam's embrace, his large hands still clasped around my waist. His skin is warm beneath my fingers and sweat glistens on his tan skin. He's shirtless, wearing only athletic shorts. I thought Sam was muscular before, but seeing him without his shirt…this is doing bad, bad things to me. "Are you stalking me?"

"I—what—no. You should be thanking me."

I inhale, breasts pressing against Sam's firm chest as I breathe. I'm fine, steady on my feet. I should push him away.

He should let me go. Yet we're both standing here, neither wanting to make the first move and separate.

"Thanking you for sneaking up on me?" I try.

Sam's fingers press into me. "I was calling your name. You shouldn't have your music so loud you can't hear anything around you."

He's right, I know. "I was lost in thought."

"You're not very graceful."

"And you're not very..." My words waver. I can think about a hundred things Sam is *very* in some ways right now but am at a loss for what he's *not*. I close my eyes in a long blink. "Thanks." I slide my hands down Sam's chest, feeling every ripple of muscle beneath my fingers. "You're sweaty."

"It's hot outside." He releases one hand from my waist and brings it up, gently brushing a renegade curl out of my eyes.

"Yes...hot. Out. Outside." There aren't many people who can make me go nonverbal, but Sam is one of them. My pulse was already pounding, and I swear my asshole of a heart is going to give everything away. Sam's hands are on me, and things are still very PG right now, yet my body is craving more.

"You're working out again?" he asks, and I have to think to get what he's asking. Right. He saw me this morning in workout clothes.

"I didn't end up running this morning," I start. "I put my workout clothes on and then, um, got food instead."

Sam chuckles, lips curving into a smile. "That sounds like you."

I nod and my fingers brush over the waistband of Sam's pants, causing butterflies to take flight in my stomach. What is wrong with me? I stand this close to Sam for a few seconds and I'm back to my old schoolgirl self, nervous and pining for a man I'll never have.

"It's purposely misleading," I go on, unable to stop myself from rambling. "I could be hungover and looking like shit, but people will think I just worked out really hard and give me the benefit out of the doubt."

"I like the way you think." He's looking right into my eyes, and I realize my hands are still awkwardly hovering over his crotch, though he doesn't seem to mind.

"You were working out," I say and bring my hands to his biceps, wanting the excuse to touch him again. "Do you run a lot?"

"Not as much as I should. I mostly lift."

"I can tell." I sink my teeth into my bottom lip, biting down hard, and not thinking about how Sam could interpret it. He deeply inhales again and starts to lean in. My heart jumps—is he going to kiss me? I've dreamed about his lips on mine so many times. Wished for it. Prayed for it. Hell, I even tried to cast a love spell on him when I was thirteen. I quickly un-cast it, afraid of him fake-falling for me and then the spell wearing off and realizing it was all a sham.

A group of women come down the trail, talking and laughing loudly. Sam and I break apart, and it's only then I realize I was holding my breath, too afraid to breathe.

"I'll get your phone," Sam rushes out and moves down the steep hill with grace. He's in incredible shape, and I could watch him scale down hills like this all day long. He climbs back up just as easily and hands me my phone. My fingers brush over his and I wish I was back in his arms, having him look at me like I'm the only thing that matters in the world.

Now that the moment is over, he steps away, diverting his eyes.

"Thanks," I say as I wind the cord of my headphones around the phone.

"I'm surprised you don't have cordless earbuds," Sam notes.

"Oh, I do. This is a testament of how antisocial I am," I start, smiling as I talk. "I like to go to coffee shops to write sometimes and usually have my hair down, hiding the earbuds. This way people know I'm listening to music and won't try to talk to me."

Sam runs his hand through his already messy hair and laughs. It's not fair how good he can look after a run. When I run in the heat like this, my cheeks are flush and I have sweat *everywhere*, which I'm suddenly very aware of.

"Do you want to cool down with me?" Sam asks. "Or did you just start your run?"

"I'll walk. I didn't really set out to run today but more to clear my head."

We start down the trail, going back the way I came.

"Everything all right?"

"Yeah." I nod. "I got a little stuck on the chapter I'm writing. It's so frustrating when the words won't come to me."

"That would be frustrating. Did coming out here help?"

Seeing you half-naked and glistening with sweat certainly did. "I think so."

"It's not going to rain today," Sam notes after we walk a few paces. "Though right now rain would be nice."

"Yeah, it would be nice. I wish the lake wasn't so warm."

Sam nods in agreement. "It feels like bathwater."

I look at Sam, heart rate picking up speed again. We shared a moment back there, I'm sure of it. And I want that moment to happen again.

"A cold drink sounds good too," Sam notes, quickly stealing a glance at me.

"It does."

"Want to go grab a drink?"

I turn my head, taking another look at his muscular chest. "Now? Isn't it a little early for drinks?"

"I actually meant lemonade or something," he says with a laugh. "Though it's never too early for drinks," he teases, playfully elbowing me.

Laughing, I shake my head. "Lemonade actually sounds good."

We walk a few more paces. "We can go to Sunset Tavern," Sam suggests. Sunset Tavern is one of the newer restaurants in Silver Ridge, and it caters to the tourists vacationing here in the summer. Like Silver Café, it's along the lake, but on the opposite side. The same people who own Sunset Tavern own Sunset Marina, which is the only place to rent jet skis and boats from if you want to take one out on the lake.

Locals to Silver Ridge don't typically go to Sunset Tavern. The food is on the expensive side for what it is, and the owners have gotten a bit snooty over the years. It's a shame, really, because the rooftop bar has an amazing view of the lake, and it can be entertaining to sit up there and watch boaters go by.

"Yeah, I'd like that a lot."

"Did you walk here?" Sam asks.

"I did, and I'm guessing you didn't. Where are you parked?"

"The east parking lot."

It's the same lot he was parked in the day it rained, and we're a decent walk away from it. Not that I mind. We walk in silence for a few minutes, but it's peaceful and not awkward. Though it's hot out, it's a gorgeous day, and the sound of nature surrounds us.

"I didn't realize how much I missed the woods before," I muse. "It's so peaceful."

"It is. Living in Indy and then Chicago has made me appreciate small-town life so much more than I did before. Everyone was so eager to get out of here."

"They were, and I was one of them," I say, not sure if I'm admitting something new to Sam or not. I was on the fence about leaving when I graduated high school. Part of me longed for a fresh start and an adventure, typical of seventeen and eighteen-year-olds, I know. But another part didn't want to leave Dad alone, and I felt guilty enough going away to college.

"Do you like living in LA?"

"Overall, yes. It has its downfalls, I'll admit, but the weather is amazing and my publicist is there, so it works out really well. Plus the network studio headquarters are close by, so when I go to sit in on any sort of discussions, I'm right there."

"That would make things easier." We walk a few more paces. "If you weren't writing, do you think you would have ended up there?"

I think about it for a second. "I don't know. I was itching for a change, but I didn't make the move to LA until I got the screen option for *Nightfall*. I don't even know what I'd do if I wasn't a writer." I look at Sam with wide eyes. "I'd have to get a real job."

He chuckles, and damn, that man is so gorgeous when he smiles. "You have no idea what else you'd do?"

"Hmmm..." I think for a moment. "I'd be a paleontologist."

"Really?"

I nod eagerly. "And I'd be a really good one, who'd find something that would enable me to co-fund a dinosaur theme park, but I'd be like really in touch with the dinos. So when the T-Rex breaks free of her enclosures, she picks me up with her tiny little arms and puts me on her back before she reigns hell on earth and eats everything in her path."

"I'm sorry to break it to you," Sam says, stopping and putting his hand on my shoulder. "I don't think that's what paleontologists actually do."

"Dang it." I love the way his large hand feels against my skin. "That's the second-most disappointing thing I've ever heard."

"What's the first?" He slides his hand down my arm.

"The people who wear old-fashioned clothes at the start park are volunteers through the Park Department. They're not paid to dress up and cook homemade apple pies on a wood-burning stove. If they were, I'd be all over that job."

"That would be a low-stress-level job. I might even do it."

"You could be a nineteenth-century doctor, traveling around with your leather doctor bag. Tell the people you don't like their ailments are caused by demons so they're families kill them in their sleep."

He laughs again. "Did they really do that?"

I shrug. "Maybe? I'm making things up, though I do know demons were to blame for things they couldn't understand back then."

"Can you imagine living like that?"

I shake my head. "I'd have been locked up or burned at the stake years ago. I'm way too independent and weird to have been born even fifty years ago. Though I sometimes think I would have thrived if I lived in a *Lord of the Rings* type of time and setting."

"Oh, for sure."

We laugh and keep talking about what life would be like if we lived in fantasy worlds, both agreeing I'd lead some sort of rebellion and Sam would end up being the one burned at the stake, accused that his claims of science and medicine are actually witchcraft.

Sam puts his shirt on when we get to his car, and I pull my hair out of my ponytail, wishing I had a brush. I do my best to rake it out with my fingers before getting in the car, throwing the loose strands that came out into the wind. It's a wonder I'm not bald with how much hair I shed every single day.

We give the car a few seconds to air out before getting in. Sam turns on the vented seats and puts the air on full blast. The radio is on and connects to Sam's phone. Tom Petty starts playing, taking me right back to the days when Sam drove me home from school.

The parking lot is pretty full at Sunset Tavern, even though they only opened an hour ago. The hostess looks at us like we don't belong, and I suppose we do look a little out of place for a "nice" restaurant since we're both sweaty and dressed in workout clothes. There's no dress code or anything here, though, and my Lululemon workout pants probably cost more than the average patron's entire outfit. She holds up her finger, giving up the "one moment" signal, and looks back down at her phone, grinning at whatever she's typing. We move closer, and I see she's on Instagram—her personal Instagram, so I can't even justify her as managing the restaurant's social media accounts.

I'm not one to flaunt anything in anyone's face, but I hate seeing someone scoff like this. What gives this hostess the right to look at anyone like they're *less than* and not good enough for her time of day? I can shrug this off, knowing that I'm not what she thinks, and I'm sure Sam can too. But there are others whose day will be ruined by being treated so rudely. They might have fragile self-esteem to begin with, and having someone act like you're beneath them hurts.

A family comes in behind us, and the mom is nicely dressed in a pink sundress. Her daughter who looks to be about four or five is wearing a matching dress. They look so freaking cute, and their infant son is coordinating with the dad. The mom has a designer purse hanging from her shoulder and the hostess looks at them with a smile.

"Hi, how many?" she asks, and the mom looks at us, a bit confused.

"I think they were ahead of us."

"Yes," Sam says pointedly. "We were." He looks at me, resting his hand on my arm. "Unless you want to go somewhere else, Chloe. I know you're short on time since you have to work on your next bestselling book." He says it on purpose, I know, and I love this slightly petty side of Sam.

"You're Chloe?" the mom behind us asks. "Oh my goodness, I thought you looked familiar. Russ, this is Chloe Fisher, the girl who wrote the *Nightfall* series! Her photo is up in City Hall!"

The hostess's face pales when she realized how incredibly stupid she was to stereotype us based on how we look. I turn, smiling broadly, and chat with the mom for a minute. She has a worn copy of the first book of the series in her car and sends her husband outside to get it. I sign it, take a photo with her, and then link my arm through Sam's as we're led to our table.

"Sorry if that embarrassed you," he tells me once we're seated. We're on the rooftop, and only two other tables up here are occupied. Most people had enough sense to eat inside in the air conditioning today. We get a table along the balcony railing, with a green umbrella in the middle, giving us shade from the hot sun. "Maybe it was just me, but that hostess was bitchy."

"Oh, she was, and it didn't. It's weird coming back here, though. I promise I don't get recognized like this anywhere other than Silver Ridge."

"Everyone loves a success story."

"You're successful."

"I am," he agrees. "But it's not the same."

"It's not at all." I open the drink menu, debating on getting a spiked lemonade for a second. It's way too hot to drink alcohol, and sitting here with Sam is intoxicating enough. "You're saving lives. I'm just writing about fictional people."

"When you put it that way, I do sound awesome."

I lean back in my chair, trying to stretch my shoulders. My bad posture all night paired with almost falling down a ravine has created a knot in my muscles. Sam's phone rings, and he silences the call again, but not before I catch the name on the screen.

"Who's Stacey?" I ask.

"My ex. We've had an on-and-off-again thing for a while," he admits, looking right into my eyes. "I ended things for good a few months ago."

"Should I be sorry?"

"Nah, not at all. I don't want to sound heartless, but I never had high expectations for the two of us."

"That does sound a little heartless."

"We got along fine," he goes on. "But there was never…never…"

"A spark?" I ask, heart skipping a beat as our eyes meet. Sparks are flying over here, threatening to ignite. Or at least they are for me.

"Yeah, I guess you could say that."

"So, you're single now?"

"I am." He closes his drink menu. "What about you? Are you with anyone?"

My last public stint with Charles was two years ago. I've gone out on dates since then, and dated Aaron for three months before things fizzled out. "Single as well."

Sam looks at me for a few seconds, gaze so intimate it makes me blush.

"What?" I finally ask.

"Remember that promise I made you?"

My mouth goes dry. Of course I freaking remember that promise. It was my first day of high school and the day had gone to hell by lunch. Sam swooped in and saved the day. He drove me home, told me I wasn't undateable like I thought… and promised he'd marry me if no one else would.

"We're both over thirty. You're single. I'm single. Why not see where things go?" Sam grins, and my heart flutters.

"Just like that?"

"Sure. Why not?"

I swallow hard. All I've ever wanted was to *see where things go* with Sam, but this…this feels contrived. It's not the way I saw things going down, and I feel like I'm at an obvious disadvantage here. He had to have known the effect he had on me back in the woods, and he is more than aware of how incredibly good-looking he is. Add in that he's all grown up and a successful doctor now…and he's a heartbreak waiting to happen.

"I…I…" I don't know what to say. How many times did I wish for just one chance with Sam? I was so sure that one chance was all I'd need to have him fall in love with me, to see me the way I see him. But this? This feels more like convenience—for him. Sunlight bathes his handsome face, causing the light blue specks in his eyes to sparkle. I should say no, that this is a bad idea. That this is only to end in heartache and pain for me.

But I can't.

Because what if it doesn't? What if things were to work out and I'm left wondering *what if* for the rest of my life if I did turn him down? The unknown is more torturous than any mistake I might make, and if Sam ends up being one, then he'll be my favorite mistake.

He reaches out and puts his hand on mine. "How about we go out for drinks after dinner?"

"It's Sunday. Is The Cantina open on Sundays now?"

"I don't know, but I doubt it." Sam slowly trails his fingers down my hand. It's nearly ninety-five freaking degrees out today and I'm sitting in direct sunlight, yet that man just sent a shiver down my spine. "I could always bring a bottle of wine over and we can sit by the lake while we drink it."

Damn you, Samuel James Harris. That sounds wonderful.

"It's been a long time, Chloe." He gently flips my hand over and traces his fingers along the vein on the inside of my wrist. "We have a lot to…to talk about."

"Yeah." I quickly bob my head up and down. "T-talk…we should talk."

"I've missed you," he says, and I can't help but wonder if he really has. He tried contacting me for weeks after the incident at the party, until Farisha blocked him from my contacts. I got a new phone the next year when I went off Dad's network plan, so he didn't even have my number to call after that even if he wanted to.

But I've had a social media presence for years now, and my email is very easy to find on my website. My assistant handles all the emails sent to my "author address" and she definitely would have flagged a message from a former friend if Sam had tried to contact me that way.

"Mh-hm," I squeak out, nodding once again. I'm getting hotter by the second, which has nothing to do with Sam's hand on my wrist, long fingers still tracing the visible veins. Long fingers I'm imagining somewhere else.

"So what do you say?" He leans back, taking his hand off me and making me miss his touch immediately. His lips curve into another cocky grin, confident enough to be sexy but not arrogant. "Should we make good on that promise?"

CHAPTER FOURTEEN

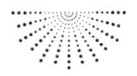

SAM

"You can't be serious?" Chloe shoots back, making me think I've laid it on too thick. I don't want to run away to the nearest chapel, but I am desperate for any reason to be with Chloe. I'm terrified she's going to jerk her hand back and tell me there was a good reason she moved away and never looked back. I've dodged relationships over the years, knowing no one could ever hold a candle to my Chloe, connecting more on a physical level.

It's what I know. It's what I'm good at. And I'm certain Chloe will enjoy it. I want more with her, but this is the only route I know to go.

Chloe blinks several times, long lashes fluttering over her pretty green eyes. A warm breeze blows in from the lake, messing up Chloe's already messy hair. "You want to get married?"

"Well, no," I start.

"But that was what the promise was, was it not?"

"We don't have to start with marriage," I say back.

"What do you want to start with?" Her eyes are wide, and before I get the chance to answer, the waiter comes over to take our orders.

"I'll, um, I'll…" Chloe's flustered and it's so fucking adorable. "I'll have a strawberry lemonade, please."

"Same for me," I say. I'm flustered too but internalize it better than Chloe. Acting under pressure comes with the job of being a doctor, especially at a trauma center.

"Can I interest you in an appetizer?"

"Um, sure," Chloe says, head bobbing up and down.

"Did you have anything in mind?" the waiter asks after a few seconds pass by.

"Artichoke dip," I rush out. The waiter nods, smiles, and says he'll be right back. "I hope you still like it."

"I do," Chloe says, voice a little breathy. "I'm surprised you remembered."

"I remember a lot about you."

She smiles, cheeks reddening. "Your mom made me artichoke dip every Friday for years."

"And you would eat it with apple slices instead of chips. Want me to ask for that instead?"

"No, it's fine, though that does sound good."

"I'll ask when he brings our drinks out."

"Thank you."

Stacey calls again, and I send the call right to voicemail. What does she want? It was clear things were over between us, and she didn't seem all that bothered by it.

"Your ex seems to really miss you," Chloe notes, leaning back in her chair. "Did it end badly or something?"

"No," I tell her honestly. "We were never serious, and to tell you the truth, I think she was seeing someone else at the end."

"I'm so sorry," Chloe says.

"We weren't exclusive." Well, not that time at least. We'd been exclusive in the past, but it never lasted long. Technically, Stacey and I were broken up before I called her over that night, and we had a long talk in the morning, clearing everything up. It wasn't the painful conversation I braced myself for, which really drove in how little the relationship meant to us in the first place…and that maybe Rory was right about Stacey being a gold-digger all along. "It's not a big deal." I wave my hand in the air.

"But she keeps calling. Maybe you should answer and let her down easy. Again."

Well, this is a first. The woman I've had eyes on for years is right in front of me. She's single. I'm single. The timing is finally right. But she's encouraging me to talk to my ex? I don't know what the right answer is here.

Talk to Stacey and risk Chloe thinking I have baggage?

Blow Stacey off and have Chloe think I'm the same asshole of a guy who hurt her in college?

"If she calls again, I'll answer," I tell Chloe. "Though I'd rather talk to you."

"Good," she says with a laugh. "Because it would be really awkward if you didn't."

"Yeah, that would be."

The waiter comes back with our drinks and says the dip will be right out. I ask for apple slices, and after a quizzical look, he nods and says he'll see if that's possible. Chloe grabs her drink and gets up, going over to the balcony railing. Shielding her eyes from the sun, she looks out at the water. I wait a beat, not sure how the conversation got so off course, and follow suit.

"It's a nice view," she says when I stand next to her.

I'm looking at her when she talks. "It's beautiful."

She puts her lips around the straw and takes a drink. "And this is very sweet. That's a lot of sugar."

I try mine. "Fuck, that is."

"I sweated out all my water on that run and now I'm drinking sugar with a splash of lemonade," she laughs. "Good thing I'm not diabetic."

"It's good, though, isn't it?" I take another sip. "I don't drink anything but water very often."

"Why not? No judgment," she adds quickly. "I'm just curious."

"I try to be healthy. Keyword there is try. I put a lot of effort into working out, and a big part of that is your diet."

"You've better than me," she laughs. "I need to get back to eating healthy and working out regularly."

I use her own words as an excuse to look her up and down. "You look fantastic."

"Thanks," she says, blushing slightly again. "I started running and doing yoga and actually stuck with it. I refuse to diet, though. I like food way too much to restrict myself, but I know the importance of being healthy. It might help in the event I...I..."

She doesn't have to say it. I know where her mind is going. *If I get sick like my mother.* The cancer wasn't detected until it had spread through most of her mother's body, and the treatments made her even weaker. It was awful, watching Mrs. Fisher deteriorate before our eyes, but even worse to watch Chloe's heart break apart bit by bit every day.

I did the best I could to pick up the broken pieces and put them back in place.

Until I single-handedly shattered it.

Taking a minute to look out at the water, I turn and admire Chloe. I want to apologize and let her know I've regretted that night at the party every day of my life. I want to tell her I've dreamed about her. I've missed her so much it hurt. I've hated how things ended between us, and I'd do anything to go back.

"Chloe," I start and lean on the railing next to her, drink in one hand.

"Yeah?"

"I—"

"Sam?" someone interrupts. "Sam Harris, is that you?"

Chloe and I both turn and see a woman walking toward us. Pink streaks her pale blonde hair, matching the long dress she has on. She's familiar, yet it still takes me a minute to place her as one of my former girlfriends. Chloe, however, recalls this woman right away.

"Tiffany," she says, with just a bit of question in her voice. "Tiffany Henson?"

"It's Miller now," she says and shows us her left hand. "I've been married for eight years already, gosh, I'm old!" Tiffany, one of my many high school girlfriends, comes over, slowly shaking her head. "How the hell are you?" she asks, looking from me to Chloe and back. "Chloe, right?"

Chloe smiles and nods. "Yeah, that's me."

"I love your show. And I'm sorry if I was ever a dick in high school," Tiffany spits out easily. I just need to come out and say it too, but I need Chloe to know I mean it.

Chloe shrugs. "It's water under the bridge now. We all did—and said—things we didn't mean when we were teenagers." She flicks her gaze to me, and I can't help but wonder if she's talking about our pact. "How are you?"

"I'm good! Teaching at the elementary school, which I love. My youngest just turned three two days ago. My sister is in town" —she motions to a woman at a table behind her— "and we snuck away from a quick sister outing before she has to head back to the city this evening." She angles her body toward mine. "I know what Chloe's been up to, but what about you?"

"I'll let you two catch up," Chloe says quietly and goes back to the table.

"I'm a doctor," I say, watching Chloe unwind her headphones from her phone. "In Chicago."

"Wow, good for you. I always knew you were smarter than you let on."

Chloe holds her phone up to her mouth, talking into it.

"Uh, thanks?"

Tiffany laughs. "I mean that in a good way. You were so caught up in being Mr. Popular then, not that I blame you. I was too." She shakes her head. "Gosh, what were we thinking? Talk about being young and dumb, right?"

"Right. I did a lot of dumb things, that's for sure." My eyes go to Chloe again. She brings her phone to her ear, listening to a message. She must send voice messages via text the same way Rory does. We all tease her and say she's too lazy to text, yet hates calling. But she might be onto something because it *is* much easier.

"You did something right." Tiffany smiles and follows my gaze to Chloe. "You're a doctor and you two are finally together."

"What?" I blurt, blinking in the bright sunlight.

Tiffany presses her lips together and looks at me dubiously. "Like you guys were fooling anyone. I should go before my sister takes off without me. It was really good seeing you again, Sam. You look good." She smiles. "And happy." Her eyes go to Chloe again. "I can see why."

"Yeah, it was nice seeing you again, Tiffany," I say, and my heart skips a beat in my chest when I turn back to Chloe. She's talking into her phone again, and looks up. She stops talking when she sees me looking, and smiles.

Fuck.

I wasn't fooling anyone then…and I'm tired of trying to continue to fool myself now.

CHAPTER FIFTEEN

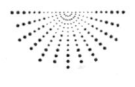

CHLOE

I need someone to pinch me.

No, really. I might offer the couple over there, clearly on their first date, twenty bucks per pinch because I'm having a good time with Sam—a *really* good time with Sam. We're talking, just casually talking, and it feels so good to hang out like this again. I forgot how easy he was to get along with, and now that my heart has settled back into my chest it almost feels like old times.

Almost. Because I know for certain Sam wants to sleep with me, and I can't get that out of my mind.

"We still have a few weeks left," I tell him, putting my empty glass on the table. "It's not too late to buy a costume online and go."

"But getting the time off work," Sam starts, and I laugh, knowing he's full of shit. "That might be tricky."

"Bullshit," I laugh. "You just told me you get several days off every month, and that always includes a weekend. You're just scared."

"I am not," Sam counters.

"Then put on some tights and come to the Renaissance Faire with me."

"What are you wearing?" Sam's blue eyes glimmer and warmth rushes through me yet again. I take a slow breath and purposely look away from Sam, needing a quick second to recover. Things are surreal right now, and I've never been so confused while having this much fun before in my life, and that includes the time Charles and I accidentally ate edibles thinking they were plain gummy bears.

"Depends on the theme of the day." The waiter comes over and refills my water glass and takes the empty bowl of artichoke dip, which was good, but nowhere near as good as the dip Mrs. Harris makes.

"There are themes of the day?" he asks with a chuckle.

"Don't laugh!" I playfully nudge his hand, which is on the table near mine. "And yes, there are. Here, I'll show you." I grab my phone and scroll through photos. "Not every day is themed, but there are a few themed days a month."

"A month? How long does this fair go?"

"From Fourth of July to Labor Day. But only on the weekends, which really isn't that long."

"I suppose not. And you go every year?"

I shake my head. "Only if I get back this way. The one in California runs at a different time." I hold out my phone, showing Sam a photo of me with a few of my LA friends at the Ren Faire in California last year. We're all dressed like belly dancers with matching outfits.

"Fuck," he mutters under his breath, and I don't think he intended for me to hear. "You look good here, Chloe. Really good. Do you still, uh, have that outfit?"

"I did, but I forgot to pack it this trip."

"Darn."

"Right?"

We both laugh, and I lean back, letting out a heavy breath. I've had to pee since I got here and have really had to pee for the last fifteen minutes or so. I didn't want to say so to Sam for some dumb reason, but it's either excuse myself to do a very human thing and use the bathroom or risk peeing my pants, which would—in the end—be much worse than just telling him I have to pee in the first place.

"I'll be right back," I say, pushing my phone and glass to the middle of the table. "I have to use the bathroom. Don't dine and dash on me."

"I'll do my best not to," Sam says with a wink as I walk away. My shoulder aches again, and I stretch my arms out in front of me, trying to get rid of the charley horse that's now plaguing my back. I make a face and reach behind me with one hand, trying to massage the knot out of my muscles.

The bathroom is on the first floor, and I'm glad I'm in gym shoes and not heels as I hurry down, and am thankful for no line when I get in, going right to a stall.

"Oh, hey, Chloe," someone says when I'm done with the toilet and go to the sink to wash my hands. It's Tiffany, Sam's old high school girlfriend.

"Hey, Tiffany."

She's at the sink next to me and just finished washing her hands. She shakes the water from her fingers and grabs a paper towel from the basket on the counter. "You are so pretty."

"Thanks," I say back, and take a look at my reflection. I'm in my favorite workout outfit today, and my hair, which is damp from sweating, hangs in natural waves around my face. Usually, I don't like my reflection without makeup, but maybe the lighting in here is really good—or really bad—and it's hiding my imperfections. "You are too."

Tiffany lets out a snort of laughter. "You don't have to lie. I gained a lot of weight since my last baby." Her words slur a bit.

"I didn't notice," I say honestly. "You look happy, though, and that's just as important, if not more than looking good."

"True, and I am happy." She gives me a goony smile. "Thomas is a good guy." She must be talking about her husband. "And such a good dad."

"I'm happy for you." I bring my hands back, letting the automatic water shut off.

"And I'm happy for you."

Assuming she's talking about my success with my writing, I smile. "Thanks. It wasn't easy, but I'm glad I didn't give up."

"If anyone could change his playboy ways, it's you."

"Wait, what?" I grab two paper towels and ball them up, drying my hands.

"Sam," she says with a laugh. "He was such a man-whore back in high school, and from what I heard, he was in college too."

I blink a few times, trying to piece things together. "You think Sam and I are…together?"

"Aren't you?" She looks genuinely surprised.

"No."

"Oh. Could have fooled me."

My mind is still whirling. "What do you mean if anyone could change him, it would be me?"

"I saw the way he looked at you, and that's part of the reason I was such a bitch. I was jealous of you when I was dating Sam."

"The way he looked at me?" I echo, still not following along because it just doesn't make sense. Until maybe an hour ago, I was under the impression Sam looked at me as a strictly platonic friend. And now this confuses me even more. Though maybe…maybe he wasn't hinting at meaningless sex. Maybe it *would* mean something to him.

"You're really not together?"

"No. We're just friends."

She raises a hand up to make air quotes. "*Just friends.*" She gives me a big wink. "Right. Just friends who are boning."

"We—we're—we're not boning."

"Your loss," she says with a snort of laughter. "Don't tell Thomas I said that." Turning to look in the mirror, she frowns.

"I have to take the pink out of my hair before school starts. I like the pink."

I saw the way he looked at you. I want to press her for more details because I'm *that* pathetically in love with Sam. Though hearing her remind me how much of a playboy Sam was—and probably still is—is a good thing. I'm hopelessly in love with the idea of what could be. It would be easy to have him pull me under his spell and feel something he doesn't.

"It was nice to see you again," I tell Tiffany. "Have fun with your sister."

"You too," she says. "With Sam." She gives me a big wink, and I walk out, head spinning.

I'm so confused.

He reminded me how I was so much like a sister and then turned down coming home with me the other night. But I *know* he was giving off vibes in the woods, and he just brought up our silly pact and he definitely wasn't hinting at waiting until the big day to have sex.

What. The. Fuck.

One thing is for sure: I need to avoid whatever the hell it turns out to be. Sam and I are only in town together for a few more days. I can keep things PG between us. How hard can that be?

Hot, humid air slaps me in the face as soon as I step outside, going back up to the rooftop bar. The ache in my shoulder comes back with a vengeance, and I try rolling my neck to loosen it up. It just makes it worse. I go up the last step and slow, looking at Sam. All I can see is the back of his head right now. He's leaning against the back of his chair, relaxing and looking at the lake. A light breeze blows in, rustling his hair. Hair I very much want to run my hands through.

Dammit, that's not helping the whole *hate the player, not the game* situation.

"Hey," Sam says when I get back to the table. My throat tightens and my heart swells.

"Hey." I go back to my seat at the table, reaching for my phone. "I ran into Tiffany in the bathroom. I think she's drunk." It would explain the crazy things she was saying…that Sam looked at me like he loved me.

"At one in the afternoon?" Sam looks at his watch. "It's one-thirty, if that makes it any better."

I laugh. "It's five o'clock somewhere, right?"

"Very true. Do you need to go home and write before dinner? I already paid, so we can leave whenever you're ready."

"Thanks, and yeah, I do." I roll my neck again. "Even though the thought of sitting at my computer is painful."

"Because of the writer's block?"

"I wish. I have terrible posture when I'm writing, and my shoulders hurt because of it." I pick up my water. "I think I'll live."

"I think so too." His eyes settle on me, looking at me as if he's mentally undressing me. "Want to get out of here?"

"Yeah, it's hot on the roof."

"It is. The lake is looking better and better."

"Jumping in sounds so refreshing." I take a drink of water and get up, following behind Sam. He holds the door open for me and takes my hand as we walk down the wooden dock, heading back to the parking lot.

"Shit," I say. "I left my phone on the table."

"I'll go get it." Sam gives my hand a squeeze, and my stomach does that stupid flip-flopping thing again. A smile takes over my face as I watch him jog back in, and a voice in the back of my head—which sounds a lot like Farisha—yells at me not to get ahead of myself. Sam wants sex, and I know myself. I don't do casual sex. I've tried the no-strings thing and it doesn't work for me. Sex isn't as enjoyable for me without emotion, and the few times I did attempt a causal relationship, I got attached and hurt when the guy easily moved on, taking it personally even though I braced myself for it from the start.

I let out a breath and go to the edge of the dock; I look

down in the water and watch little fish swim about. Sam has always been my white knight, swooping in to save the day. I'm no longer a damsel in distress, and I'm more than capable of defending myself now. I need to remember that and hold on to my resolve. But…fuck…just the thought of Sam slowly undressing me gets me wet.

"Twice in a row," a woman says, startling me a bit. It's Lauren, and she's with her sister. I can't recall her name, only that she was two grades ahead of us and bitchy and judgmental like Lauren. It must run in the family. "I'm starting to think you're following me."

"Well, I was here first, so if anyone was being followed, it would be me," I say back. Lauren laughs and comes to a halt, putting her hand on her hip. "I'll admit I'm impressed. First you went to a bar alone and now you're here—alone."

"I'm not alone." Right on cue, Sam comes out of the restaurant with my phone in his hand.

"You're here with Sam?" Lauren spits.

"Yeah, I am."

"Figures." She smiles smugly. "I fully assumed he'd try again after he struck out at the bar. Though I made sure to take care of him."

"Come on, Lauren," her sister urges. "I'm hungry."

"Good seeing you again, Chloe." Lauren wiggles her fingers in the air and walks past, smirk on her face, and says something to Sam as he passes by. I can't be mad at Sam for hooking up with anyone last night, even if that person was Lauren Wallace. We're not in a relationship, and he owes me nothing. I could have gone home with anyone last night and he couldn't say boo about it.

And if anything, this proves that whatever Tiffany was talking about doesn't matter. Maybe Sam really did look at me *that way* when we were younger, but it doesn't matter now. He's living his best life, and it's not fair for me to hold that against him because I want him to live that best life with me.

But it does mean I have to remember that Sam has always been a player, and I've always accepted that. I've stood back and watched him date girl after girl, all the while wishing one of those girls was me. I know what he wants, but he's going to have to get it from someone else. It's tempting not to let this opportunity pass me by, but I have to stay strong. I have to remember: Once a player, always a player.

And Sam has brought his A-game.

CHAPTER SIXTEEN

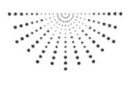

CHLOE

"Are you okay?" Sam asks after I re-tried the hidden key from Wendy's porch.

"Yeah," I rush out. "My shoulder just hurts." It's a lame excuse for me being rather quiet on the car ride to my dad's house, but it's all I can come up with right now. I spent most of the drive reminding myself I can't be mad at Sam. I can't consider him hooking up with Lauren another betrayal. He doesn't seem to remember Lauren was a raging bitch to me in high school. I think only Farisha and my dad knew the extent of her bullying. I never hid things from Sam—except my love for him, of course—but I didn't go rushing off to tell him a rundown of the mean comments Lauren said to me throughout the day.

"Maybe take an Advil or something."

"I can do better." I unlock the door and step inside. Sam follows, and I'm wishing I could uninvite him over. Okay, I don't. But I should. I take my shoes off as I walk and end up tripping over my own feet. Sam dashes forward and catches me. His hands, already familiar with the curve of my waist, go right back to where they were only an hour or so ago.

He pulls me to him, crushing my breasts against his chest.

He's warm against me, and desire floods my body. Would it be so bad to give in and let him rock my world just this once?

Yes, Chloe, it would be bad. Terribly bad.

"Careful." Sam's deep voice rumbles through me and my lips part. Somehow my hands end up hooked around his neck, and he tightens his hold on me, pulling me so our hips brush against each other. I can feel the bulge of his cock through his athletic pants, and suddenly I'm getting weak in the knees.

"At least there wasn't a ravine to fall down this time," I say, voice all breathy.

"I'm glad I was there to catch you."

"Y-yeah." Wide-eyed, I lock gazes with Sam. My heart is racing and I'm starting to sweat again. I swallow hard, now worried my breath smells like the artichoke dip we just devoured.

Because I think Sam Harris is going to kiss me.

Then his phone rings, and he takes one hand off my side to fish it out of his pocket.

"Stacey again?" I ask, not wanting to be nosey, though I am a nosey person.

"No, it's my mom."

"Oh, well, you better answer it."

"I can call her back." Sam silences the call.

"What if it was important?" I slowly slide my hands to his chest, wishing he'd take his shirt off again.

"Then she'll call again and then I will answer. She's probably calling to ask what I think you'd like for dinner. They're all pretty damn excited to have you over."

"It's been a while since I've had a family dinner with you all."

"It's been a while since I've had one too." We're still in the foyer, and Sam sets his phone on the entryway table. His hand goes back to my waist and he flicks his eyes to my lips. If he kisses me, I'm done for. All it will take is a millisecond of him pressing his lips against mine to make me grab his hand and pull him into my bedroom.

But nope. I need to be strong, and the longer we stay like this, locked in each other's embraces, the harder it's going to be. I suck in a breath and move back, taking my hands off Sam's shoulders.

"I'm, uh, going to find some…something."

"Something?" Sam chuckles. "That's specific."

I just bob my head up and down quickly and go into the kitchen, opening the cabinet next to the microwave. It's full of medications, sunscreen, and bug spray. The thing is organized chaos, and if there's ever an apocalypse, Dad has his own mini-pharmacy right here.

Sam leans against the counter watching me. His gaze on me is intimate again, and I can feel my resolve slipping away beneath my feet. "I know they're in here somewhere," I mutter. "Dad never throws anything out." I rustle through old pill bottles. "Ah-ha!" Smiling, I grab what I was looking for.

"Are you sure you should be taking expired muscle relaxers?" Sam asks, crossing his arms over his chest in a way that I so don't notice his muscular biceps bulging against the sleeves of his black t-shirt.

"Are you sure you should be telling me what to do?" I retort and struggle to untwist the childproof lid.

"Well I'm a doctor, so when it comes to taking medication, yes. I should be telling you what to do, and taking old medication isn't smart."

"Touché," I say with a forced smile, eyes narrowing. The last thing I need is Sam fucking Harris judging me. "It's easy to forget you actually got accepted and then graduated from medical school."

Sam laughs and plows a hand through his thick brown locks, messing them up in a way that looks way too fucking good on him. On anyone. His lips pull into a half-smile and his eyes meet mine. "With honors," he adds. "Don't forget that I graduated with honors."

"Who'd you have to sleep with to get that?" I spit back, working hard to keep my composure. I will not crumble…I will not crumble…

"Whoever I damn well wanted to," he says with a shrug. "Though that had nothing to do with my exceptionally good grades." He parts his lips, tongue darting out to wet them. He knows exactly what he's doing, and I wonder if this is a game to him, seeing how easily I'll cave and fall back on our pact. He doesn't want the night to end in marriage, no way, but he wants to get what he couldn't before.

Me, naked in his bed. And dammit, I really want that too.

"Let me," he says, closing the distance between us, and cups his hands around mine. It's then I notice all over again just how grown up Sam has become. Where once stood a boy stands a man, and he's *all* man now. He was always athletic before, but he's filled out, thick with pounds of muscle. The boyish, playboy charm still sparkles in his eyes, but it's peppered with something that alludes to experience, something that promises he knows his way around a woman's body and he never disappoints.

"These expired seven years ago." He holds up the bottle. "If you're that desperate, let me prescribe something for you."

I let out a breath and bring my hand to my shoulder, pressing my fingers into my stiff muscle. It's really not that bad; nothing a trip to a good massage therapist wouldn't cure. Yet there's nowhere to get a decent massage in Silver Ridge, evidence perhaps that I've grown too used to my cushy and very extra LA lifestyle.

"Or," Sam goes on, deep voice like gravel as he sets the pills down on the counter, "I could do this." He takes a step back and brings his hands to my shoulders, gently massaging them. His large hands are warm against my skin. Deft fingers work right into the knot above my shoulders blade, and some of the pain immediately leaves me, only to be replaced by a different kind of pain. It's not physical, and it's rooted in a deep longing for something I'll never have.

One that will only get worse the more he touches me. My eyes flutter closed and a beat passes before I can even suck in the air to speak.

"Mhhh," I breathe. "That feels good."

"You have a knot." Sam presses a little harder, moving his fingers in a circle. "Right here." He presses two fingers deeper into my muscle, and I let my head fall forward.

"You slouch when you write?" he asks, sweeping his fingers across the base of my neck, moving my hair over my shoulder.

"Yeah," I say, fighting to find my voice. "I try not to but then find myself practically leaning over my desk an hour or so into working. I got a posture brace but never wear it."

"Maybe you should start." He pushes two fingers into my muscle and slowly works out the knot. "Your back is very tight."

That's not the only thing that's tight. Sam lets his other hand drop down to my lower back, gently running his fingers over my skin. Sam flattens his hands over my back and slowly drags his fingers down, and a soft moan escapes my lips. He leans in, moves my hair to the other side of my neck, and slips his fingers under the strap of my bra, going back to working out the knot. The tension leaves my shoulders almost immediately, but the room is filled with a different kind of tension.

Tension I have to break before it breaks me.

"Thanks," I blurt and move away, ripping his hands off me like a band-aid. "I'll, um…um…take some Advil." I squeeze my eyes closed for a second and dread turning around. But then Sam's phone rings again.

"You should go see if it's your mom again," I rush out, turning. We stare at each other for another second, and then he nods, going into the foyer to get his phone. Needing to get up and do something to shake the sexual frustration that's now plaguing me, I follow him. "Is it her?"

"No, it's the trauma center," he tells me. "I have to take it."

"Of course," I say and hear him answer the phone as "Doctor Harris" which does bad things to me all over again. I go into the kitchen for a glass of cold water. I should just dump it all over myself or at the very least down my pants.

Grabbing two glasses, I fill them both with ice water and set them on the counter, listening to Sam talk about medications to whoever he's talking to. A minute later, he's back in the kitchen. I motion to the water.

"Thanks," he says and picks up the glass.

"Everything okay?"

"Yeah." He takes a long drink. "I asked to be updated on a patient while I was away."

"I hope it was good news."

He takes another drink and shakes his head. "It was expected news. One of our patients is being brought out of a medically induced coma, and he's not showing much brain activity."

"I'm so sorry."

"Thanks." Sam looks out the window, visibly bothered by the prognosis of his patient.

"It has to be really hard to see your patients like that," I say gently, running my finger down my water glass, following a drop of water that's rolling down.

"It can be. I knew what I signed up for when I took the job at the trauma center. Some patients stick with you more than others. Kids are the worst to see in those situations, especially when the trauma is the result of abuse."

"I can't even imagine." I shudder. "But you're saving people."

"That's the goal." He takes another drink and looks out at the lake. I can see the stress of his job weighing down on him in that moment, and I want to take it away. He *has* grown up and changed, yet I still can't throw caution to the wind because *I* haven't changed.

At least not when it comes to my feelings toward Sam.

"I, um, have a lot of writing to do before dinner."

Sam looks…I'm not sure—hurt? Disappointed? "Right. That's the whole reason you came here. Want me to pick you up later?"

"I can drive. I don't want to make you go out of your way."

"I'll gladly go out of my way for you." That cocky grin comes back to his face. "And get out of the house for a while. I forgot how chaotic it is with everyone there."

"I miss that chaos."

"It's back with a vengeance with my nephew there."

"He's a cute baby."

"Of course he is. He's related to me." And that's the Sam I know. We laugh, locking eyes once again. "So…I'll be back at five?"

"Yeah. I'll be ready." Without looking away from Sam, I bring my glass back to my lips and end up clinking it against my teeth. There's a reason taking a drink on national TV gives me anxiety. I set the glass down and walk Sam to the door. "Thanks for, um, not letting me fall into the lake."

"I'll always catch you, Chloe." He tucks my hair behind my ear and pulls his keys from his pocket. Please stop being so perfect. My heart—and libido—can't take it. He grins and then turns, going outside and right to his car. He looks back at me before he gets in, and I close the door once he slips into the driver's seat.

"Holy fuck," I pant, leaning against the door. I grab my phone and call Farisha.

"Hey, lady," she says when she answers. "You okay? You never call."

"I haven't figured out if I'm okay or not. Sam just left. I also haven't listened to your messages yet."

"Sam left your house?"

"Yeah," I say and go into the living room. I don't talk on the phone often, but when I do, I tend to walk around the entire time. "I need you to be honest with me."

"I always am."

"Should I have no-strings sex?"

"With Sam?" she asks incredulously. "You're joking, right?"

"I thought you were all for sexual freedom." I open the French doors that lead to the screened-in porch. It's hotter than balls out here today. I switch on the fan and pace around the room.

"I am, but having so-called 'no-strings' sex only works when there are no strings. You've been in love with Sam since you met him. Where is this coming from?"

"We ran into each other again and he's giving me major fuck-me vibes, plus he brought up that stupid pact we made when we were kids. But instead of getting hitched, he wants to fuck. I think. I'm still pretty confused."

"All the more reason not to sleep with him, Chloe."

"I know," I sigh. "And I think he hooked up with Lauren Wallace last night. Gross, right?"

"Super gross. But why do you think that?"

"I got lucky and saw Lauren two days in a row and she said she *took care* of him. I don't know. She's always been a liar."

"She has, and she's still jealous of you. She'll take any chance she can get to make you feel small. She's a textbook bitch," Farisha reminds me. "And that's almost literal since I use her as an example of toxic women in my lectures. Now circle back to Sam. He brought up the pact and offered to sleep with you?"

"Not like that. He brought it up and was all flirty and then we came back here. He was rubbing my back and—"

"Whoa, whoa, whoa. Why in the world was Sam rubbing your back?" she asks.

"I was complaining about my back hurting and was going to take old muscle relaxers, but he said he's help rub out the knot instead."

"Rub out the knot...sure."

I let out an exasperated sigh. "I'm so confused. I like him, obviously. He's beyond gorgeous, and I know sleeping with him will be amazing. But..."

"But you'll get your heart broken even more if you have meaningless sex with him, Chloe."

"Well, send me leg-closing vibes tonight. He's picking me up to have dinner with his family at five."

"He's picking you up? Don't you have a car there?"

"Yeah, I have my dad's. I thought it was nice of him to offer to pick me up."

"So he can take you home, duh."

"Shit. I didn't think of that." I open the screen door and go outside, walking down the stone path to the dock. "There were times, though, when I swore there was something more between us."

"You guys have a long history, and honestly it used to surprise even me you two never got together. You know I liked Sam. He's a good guy who was there for you whenever you needed him...until he wasn't."

"Yeah," I sigh again. "It'll be nice to see his family again. Rory is here with her baby."

"Have fun over there but be smart. You probably shouldn't drink. You get frisky when you're drunk."

"I thought you liked that."

"Oh, I do. But you're not in the safety of my home tonight where we can wake up in our undies wondering what the hell happened."

I laugh. "Good times."

"Be careful. I love you and don't want to see you get hurt. Again."

"I don't either. Thanks, Rish. I miss you."

"Miss you too."

We end the call and I go back inside. Farisha is right, and I'm so thankful I have a friend like her who will lay down the truth even if it's not what I want to hear. Though when it comes to relationships, I have a tendency to do the opposite of what's good for me.

And there's probably a good chance that's exactly what will happen tonight.

CHAPTER SEVENTEEN

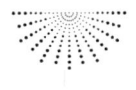

SAM

"Where have you been?" Mason looks up from his phone, half-eaten sandwich in his hand.

"I went for a run," I say, taking off my shoes.

"Bullshit you were running the whole time."

"What, afraid you can't keep up?"

"I could outrun you any day," Mason shoots back. Rory comes into the kitchen holding Adam and gives me a pointed look.

"Don't start," she warns.

I take Adam from her, bouncing him gently in my arms. He reaches for my nose, smiling.

"Start what?" Mason asks, taking another bite of his sandwich.

"You know," Rory says, opening the fridge.

"No, I don't."

Rory rolls her eyes. "You're stupidly competitive, and it's annoying."

"I am not," Mason spits back. "Okay, fine, I am. So where were you?"

"Running, that whole time. Blindfolded and uphill both ways. Barefoot too."

"Hah-hah," Mason snickers. "Hilarious. Next time you want to actually workout, let me know."

"What, are you going to go cut down trees or something? With an ax like a real man," Rory retorts.

"Yeah, that's a good idea." Mason stuffs the rest of his sandwich in his mouth. "But with chainsaws."

"That is not a good idea for a doctor." Rory grabs her leftovers from breakfast this morning. "Gotta protect the hands."

"Why, it's not like he's a surgeon," Mason says with his mouth full.

"Next time you're not breathing and need a tube inserted down your throat, remember it's not that important if I have steady hands or not."

"I bet you use that as a pick-up line, don't you?" Mason leans back. "I would."

"Gross," Rory says under her breath.

I take a seat at the island counter, still holding Adam. "Where's Dean?"

"Helping Dad fix the fence out back. They should be done soon. But now I'm curious…where were you?"

"With Chloe," I say, knowing those two words are going to raise a lot of questions. Rory freezes, hand midway in the air to turn on the microwave, and gets a big smile on her face. "Calm down. We just had drinks and caught up a bit."

And then I don't know what happened. I thought we were on the same wavelength. I thought I had read her right. Maybe I was wrong. Maybe Chloe doesn't want to be more than friends…if we can even be that at all after what happened.

"You should date her," Rory says.

"We're just friends," I press and hold Adam up so he can see out the window. "Friends who haven't seen each other in a while."

"Sure you are," Mason and Rory say at the same time.

"We are."

"Don't you want to be more?" Rory presses, and I want her

to stop. I don't want to snap at my sister, but I don't want to be asked questions that make me uncomfortable either. Of fucking course I want to be more than friends with Chloe. And I thought Chloe wanted more too. Fuck. Am I that off my game? Or am I just that pathetic when it comes to Chloe, clinging desperately to anything she throws my way, hoping and praying she might feel the same.

I've changed, and I want her to know that. I'm not the same lost young adult who didn't know his place in the world. I've grown up a lot since the night of the party, and that was my sobering moment that made me realize how much responsibility for my life I hadn't yet taken. I was in med school, on my way to becoming a doctor, yet still coasting along carefree, living for me and me alone.

Losing her hurt more than anything I've ever experienced, and knowing I hurt her in the process just about killed me.

"We're friends," I say, giving Rory a *please stop* look. "Don't make her feel uncomfortable when she's here tonight."

"I won't say anything to her," Rory promises. "But how cool would that be if you dated Chloe and then I got to go to premieres of *Nightfall*."

"That's the real reason you want me to date her, isn't it?"

"Of course not, but it would be cool, wouldn't it? I like Chloe, and I like how she never took shit from you—from any of you. She was a huge influence on me when I was younger, and without her, I wouldn't be the nerd I am today. And you don't have to worry about her being a gold-digging whore like your last girlfriend. Chloe makes a lot more money than you. If anything, you'd be the gold-digger whore."

"Way to be subtle, sis," Mason chuckles. "But if Sam wants to be a trophy husband, he needs to get in better shape."

"Fuck you," I say, narrowing my eyes as if I'm actually angry. I'm in the best shape of my life right now. "I didn't go through twelve years of schooling just to be a trophy husband."

"Your loss. I'd take Chloe up on that offer any day."

"Adam and I are glad you chose the path you did instead of being a trophy husband," Rory says. "I wouldn't have met Dean if you hadn't gotten me a job in Eastwood."

"You got that job because you're a good nurse," I say, and Rory smiles. "All I did was let you know of the opportunity."

The microwave beeps and Rory takes her food out and comes over. Adam reaches for his mom and starts fussing

"I just want to eat one meal in peace," she sighs.

I stand up, rocking Adam to help calm him down. "I'll distract him."

"Thank you. I think he needs a diaper change too—kay, bye!" She turns and I shake my head but take Adam into the living room to change his diaper. I lay him down on the blanket spread out on the floor.

"You and Chloe are really just friends?" Mason comes in and sits on the couch. He has another sandwich in his hand.

"Yes."

"And you don't want to be anything more?"

I unsnap Adam's onesie and put the clean diaper underneath him before undoing the dirty one. "She lives in LA," I say, giving him a non-answer and trying not to let myself think too much into it. If Chloe doesn't want anything more, then I'll have to accept it and do everything I can to make sure she's happy. I'd rather have her in my life as a friend than not in my life at all, no matter how much it'll hurt to stand by the sidelines and watch her with someone else.

"You wouldn't want to do the long-distance thing then. Yeah, I get that." He turns the TV on, and I finish changing Adam. I hold the baby against my chest as I take the dirty diaper into the bathroom to throw away.

"Do you want to do tummy time with him?" Rory asks as I walk by.

"Sure. Is the playmat in the living room?"

She nods. "It's in the pack-and-play. He likes the one with the mirror and the fish."

I get things set up and sit on the floor with my nephew. Mason is flipping through different crime documentaries on Netflix. "So, you're not going to make a move on Chloe tonight?"

"No," I say, getting annoying at my siblings for pestering me. Enough is enough already. I don't want to have to blurt out the truth to get them to shut the hell up.

"Then you won't mind if I do, right?"

"Hilarious," I deadpan.

"I'm serious," Mason goes on. "You wouldn't mind? You've seen her. Damn, she's hot."

I look at Mason, not sure what the fuck he's trying to do. Though I'm confident if Mason did make a move on Chloe she'd laugh and think he was trying to be funny. There's no way she'd take him seriously. Hell, even I'm not taking him seriously.

"Isn't she?" he goes on.

"Yes," I say, remembering standing in the kitchen with my hands on her back. Her hair felt like silk against my fingers and her skin was soft and smooth as I massaged her shoulders. "She's attractive. She's always been attractive."

"Yeah, she has. Hey, remember that summer after her freshman year of college? We took the boat up to Lake Huron for the weekend, and Chloe wore this pale pink bikini." His eyes are on me, and I know Mason well enough to know he's trying to get a reaction. He can be an asshole like that. Lucky for him, Mom comes home with groceries and has him help put stuff away.

She's in a panic about the house not being clean enough for Chloe to come over, and we all do our best to appease her and pitch in with the cleaning. Chloe was the least judgmental person I ever knew, and from the little time we spent together, I think it's safe to say she still is, which is impressive, really, considering how much her life has changed.

"Mom," Rory presses at half-past four. "The good china is going overboard."

"I agree," I say, not wanting to wash any more dishes. "Chloe's excited to see everyone. She's not even going to notice the dishes."

Mom's standing in the dining room, looking at the table. She bought a new centerpiece today as well. "You're right. Chloe is just like family. It's just been so long since we've seen her."

I feel everyone flick their eyes to me, hoping I'd give some sort of a better explanation than just the standard "we drifted apart." Mom turns her attention to me. "You should have invited her over sooner."

"I haven't seen her in ten years."

"You could have called."

I did. And she never answered. "I'm going to go get her now."

"Already?" Mom jumps back into action. "Did anyone clean the upstairs guest room's bathroom?"

"She's not going to go in there," Dad says, patting Mom's shoulder. "And it was cleaned before the kids arrived."

"Fine, fine." Mom lets out a breath and turns to me. "Drive slowly, please."

"I'll take the long way," I tell her, and I actually will. I told Chloe five, and it only takes about twenty minutes to get to Chloe's dad's house since I have to drive around the lake. "Both times." I get my keys, wallet, and phone from the junk drawer where Mom stashed them and go outside. It's still hot as fuck out, and another storm is on the horizon, making the air even more sticky than it was before.

I stop for gas on the way and get to Chloe's house just a few minutes before five. She comes outside when I pull into the driveway. I put my BMW in park and get out, meeting her halfway on the sidewalk.

"Hey, Sam," she says with a smile.

"Chloe," I breathe, fighting to find my voice. She looks absolutely beautiful in the blue dress she's wearing. It hugs her curves and shows off just enough of her breasts to be a constant distraction tonight, I'm sure. Her hair hangs around her face in loose curls, and her eyes look greener than before. "You look beautiful."

Her smile widens. "Thank you, kind sir."

My heart flutters in my chest, and I want so fucking badly to grab her, pinning her body between mine and the car, and kiss her breathless.

"Did you get a lot of writing done?"

"Enough to make me feel productive," she replies. "I saw that it's supposed to rain all day tomorrow. I'll hole up on the screened-in porch and plan to knock out a ton of words."

"Do you make an outline?" I open the car door for her and go around.

"Not really," she tells me as she pulls the seatbelt over her body. "My editor likes to review it, so I give her a super rough one. It's a waste of time for me to make anything more than a rough outline. I change things too much."

"That's interesting. You probably get asked this all the time and you're wanting me to shut up, right?" I back out of the driveway.

"I don't mind," she assures me.

"Good, because you're going to be bombarded with questions as soon as you walk through the door."

"I can talk about writing and horses all day. Be warned: I can get pretty talkative."

I steal a glance at her. "I think I can handle it."

She looks out the window, watching the scenery pass by. "Have you run into anyone else since you've been back in town?" she asks after a few minutes tick by.

"No, but I haven't really left my parents' house much."

"Same. The few times I have left, I've run into you. Funny, isn't it? We go years without talking and it's like I can't avoid you." She turns, and I can feel her eyes on me. Slowing at a stop sign, I take my eyes off the road for a second to look at her. "I think you are stalking me."

"I was going to say the same about you. I was at the bar and Silver Café first. You showing up after I was already there means you're the stalker."

"Hah, that's the same thing I said to Lauren today."

"Lauren?" I question.

"The girl from the bar...we saw her at Sunset Tavern."

"Oh, the chick Mason went home with. Maybe? He was with her friend when I left, but I wouldn't be surprised if he brought them both back with him."

"You left without Mason?" she asks, eyes going wide.

"Yeah, I'm not his keeper."

"And you went back to your parents' house?"

I shake my head. "Jacob's. I had to check on the dog."

Chloe smiles and lets out a breath. "That's really sweet. And if I was stalking you...would you mind?"

"If *you* stalked me? I suppose it would depend on the reasoning."

"So I could kidnap you, lock you in a dark basement, starving you so your skin gets all baggy and I can cut it up to make a quilt."

"I would expect nothing less."

"I'd sell your organs on the black market too."

"Make sure you get top dollar. I like to think I'm rather expensive."

"You are, though I might have to knock a few thousand off due to your old age."

"Please," I retort. "I'm only two years older than you."

"I know, I know...I'm getting old too. At least I don't look like it."

"And I do?" I laugh.

Chloe reaches over and messes with my hair. It sends a shock through me and I grip the steering wheel tightly. "Nah.

You don't have any grays yet. Though it's so unfair guys are 'sexy' and 'distinguished' with salt-and-pepper hair and women are shamed."

"Are people really as superficial in LA as TV shows make them seem?"

"Yes and no. It depends on where you are and what crowd you're running with. Anyone in the film world is always worried about their looks but mostly because the media will criticize them and it can be a hard pill to swallow."

"It would be, and I would not enjoy public criticism. At all."

"Lucky for you," she starts. "There's little to criticize."

"Thanks for the ego boost."

"Like you need it." She's smiling at me, and I start to get a weird feeling in the pit of my stomach. It's not something I'm used to, and I don't like it, not one fucking bit.

"Wow," Chloe says when we pull onto the gravel driveway of my parents' farmhouse. "It looks the same."

"Are you getting emotional?" I tease.

"Maybe," she says back with a laugh. "But it's just like old times."

It hits me then, that *that* is exactly what's causing the bad feeling. It is just like old times. Old times where I'm stealing glances at Chloe, counting down the days until she turns eighteen so we can be together, because I was so sure everything would magically work out by then.

It's just like old times, when Chloe will go home, alone. I don't want it to be just like old times. And I won't let it. I'm going to do whatever it takes to make Chloe mine.

CHAPTER EIGHTEEN

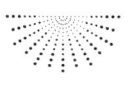

CHLOE

"It's so good to see you!" Mrs. Harris pulls me in for a big hug. Sam and I just stepped into the farmhouse and Mrs. Harris bombarded me just like Sam warned she would. Mrs. Harris really stepped in when my mother died, and losing contact with Sam meant not talking to his family anymore either.

"You too."

"It's been way too long." She gives me a final squeeze before letting me go. "You're even prettier than I remember. You look like your mother." Mrs. Harris blinks away tears, and I have to blink several times to keep from tearing up as well.

"Dinner smells amazing," I tell her, looking at the spread of appetizers on the counter. "I hope you didn't go through too much trouble."

"It's never trouble for you, dear." She smiles.

"Hey, Chloe!" Rory whispers, coming into the room holding her sleeping baby. I flash her a big smile.

"Hey," I say back, just as quietly. "He's so sweet."

"He is, but my arm is falling asleep and I have to pee," Rory chuckles softly.

"I'll take him," Sam, who's standing behind me, offers. My

ovaries threaten to explode when I see Rory gently hand off the sleeping infant to her oldest brother. Sam rocks the baby, keeping him sound asleep.

"Everyone is outside," Mrs. Harris says. "Michael is outside grilling the steaks. The boys are all out there too." She turns and checks on the sweet potato fries she has in the oven.

"Do you need any help with dinner?" I ask.

"Oh, no, but thank you." She picks up another glass dish that's on the counter and puts it in the oven. "I'm just keeping things warm now. Would you like anything to drink? Sam, why didn't you offer her anything to drink?"

"Seriously?" Sam mumbles, looking at the sleeping baby in his arms. We've only just walked in the house. Sam hasn't even taken his shoes off yet.

"I'm good for now," I say.

"Help yourself to anything, dear," Mrs. Harris says. "I think things are mostly in the same place as they were before." She turns and looks at Sam, smiling. "You need to have one of your own."

"I'll get right on that, Mom," he says dryly. Rory comes out of the bathroom and takes the baby back from Sam.

"Mom, I'm laying him down. Please do not go get him." She looks at me. "We're trying to get him used to napping in his crib at home. He hates it."

"Good luck."

"Thanks. I'll be right back. I'm so excited you're here!"

"Want to go outside?" Sam asks me.

"Yeah, it'll be nice to see everyone else." We go through the kitchen to get to the covered patio out back. "What's Rory's husband's name again?"

"Dean."

"Right. I remember now. And you all approve?"

"We do. Dean and I were friends before he started dating Rory, actually, which helped."

"Oh, for sure. So that's how they met then? Through you?"

"I'll gladly take credit for arranging things," he says with a smile as he reaches for the sliding glass door.

"I never took you as a matchmaker," I laugh. Sam holds the door open for me and I step out. Jacob, Mason, and Dean are sitting at the patio table, and Michael, who I still call Mr. Harris, is standing by the grill. The smell of the steaks makes my mouth water.

"Hey, guys," I say with a wave.

"Chloe, hey!" Mason says back. "Grab a drink and join us."

Sam rests his hand on the small of my back, and the heat from his fingers goes right through me. I remember all too well how good those fingers felt, massaging my sore muscles only hours ago. And I know how good those fingers will feel if he —*stop it.*

"Whatcha drinking?" I ask, looking at a bottle of brown liquid on the table. The label is turned away from me and there are several shot glasses on the table.

"One-hundred-and-thirty-seven-proof rum," Dean says, reaching for the bottle. "It's, uh, interesting, that's for sure."

"That sounds disgusting," I laugh. Sam pulls out a chair for me and goes over to a cooler next to the grill, getting two bottles of water before coming back and sitting next to me. "Thanks," I tell him and twist the cap off the water.

"Want to try some?" Mason asks, picking up an empty shot glass.

"One-hundred-and-thirty-seven proof," I echo, making a face. "You know what? Why not." I look at Sam, a smile playing on my lips. "If I try it, you have to try it too."

Sam mirrors the apprehensive look on my face but grabs a shot glass. Mason fills each of the shot glasses halfway. Sam lifts his in my direction.

"Ready?"

"No," I laugh and clink my glass with his. I down the rum without gagging but cough as soon as it slides down my throat. "Holy shit," I say, and everyone laughs. "That is strong." I trade my shot glass for my water and take a big drink.

"Want more?" Mason asks, giving the bottle a little shake.

"I should say no," I laugh. "But I'm kind of intrigued."

"It's better than the peanut butter whiskey," Jacob tells me, popping the top off a beer. "Which is shit too."

"That sounds disgusting."

"It's not as bad as it sounds," Sam tries to convince me.

"Says the guy who ate peanut butter sandwiches every day for lunch for four years in a row."

He shrugs. "I like peanut butter."

"To be fair," Jacob goes on. "You have to try it before you judge it."

"I have had pumpkin spice whiskey," I say. "Which was terrible. I don't even like pumpkin spice coffee." I take the bottle of rum from Mason and take off the cap, pouring just a tiny bit in my shot glass. I haven't eaten since Sam and I shared an appetizer at Sunset Tavern, and I know this super strong booze will hit me hard and fast even though I only had half a shot. Farisha made it a point to warn me not to drink, and I have a tendency to overdo it sometimes. I get to feeling good and don't want that buzz to wear off.

I bring the shot glass to my nose and sniff. "It smells like something I'd clean my bathroom counters with."

"It's probably strong enough to disinfect," Dean jokes.

Mason takes the bottle back and fills up his shot glass, drinking it slowly. "It'll keep me from getting sick then."

"It doesn't work that way," Sam tells him.

"Damn."

The sliding glass doors open and shut, and Rory and Mrs. Harris come out onto the patio. "Are the steaks almost ready?" Mrs. Harris asks.

"Just about." Mr. Harris flips them once more. "Chloe, how do you like your steak?"

"Medium rare," I reply.

"Good answer," he says with a wink. "Rory still likes hers well done."

I gasp. "That ruins a perfectly good steak."

"That's what I've told her."

"I don't like my meat to be bloody. I overcook chicken too," Rory admits and then looks at Dean, eyes sparkling. "At least he doesn't mind."

Dean smiles right back at Rory, and they look so in love it's adorable. "Hey, if you're cooking me dinner, who I am to complain."

"Smart man," Mrs. Harris says with a wink. It's nice to see Rory's husband fit in so well with the rest of the Harris family. I remember Rory complaining about how overprotective her brothers were when she was a kid, and how if there was an off chance she were to get a boyfriend, her brothers would just scare him away.

"Chloe," Mrs. Harris starts. "Tell us all about being an author. What's life like in LA? Do you get to go to the set when they're filming your show?"

Sam nudges my foot with his under the table, giving me an *I told you so* glance.

"LA is nice," I start, and Rory grabs a chair and comes over to the table. Sam scoots his chair closer to me, making room for his sister to sit next to Dean. I can feel the heat coming off of him in waves, and my breath hitches in my chest. "The…the weather is the best part."

"It doesn't get cold there at all?"

"Not really. The temperatures can drop at night in the winter, but it's nothing like here."

"You were smart to go to the west coast," Rory says, checking the camera to the baby monitor. "But it's really expensive out there, isn't it?"

"It is, and adjusting to the prices differences took me a while. A 'good deal' on food or something there is expensive here."

"Do you go out with celebrities all the time?" Mrs. Harris asks.

I shake my head, pushing my hair back over my shoulder. It's hot out still, and having my thick hair hanging down my neck is a sure way to start sweating. "No. I'm home a lot. Or at the barn with my horse. Though right now he's recovering from an injury, so I haven't been able to ride in a few weeks."

"What happened?" Jacob asks. Right, he's a vet. Sam brings his arm up to pick up his water bottle and his skin brushes against mine. We were so close to combustion standing together in my kitchen, all it will take is one little spark to start the fire again.

"He slipped on wet grass. We were worried it was a stifle injury, but thankfully it's not."

"That's good. Those can be hard to make full recoveries from."

I nod and am thankful to talk to Jacob about horses until dinner is ready. We all move inside into the air conditioning.

"Do you want red or white wine?" Mrs. Harris asks me.

"Whatever you're having is fine with me. I'm not too picky when it comes to wine," I say, and Mrs. Harris smiles and goes with a bottle of red wine. Sam hands me a plate and motions for me to go in front of him to get food.

"Where should I sit?" I ask when we get into the dining room.

"Next to me," Sam says, eyes meeting mine. His gaze lingers for a few seconds, and then he turns, setting his plate on the table. I put my plate down as well and then turn to go back into the kitchen to get my drinks. I assume Sam is doing the same, and I almost walk right into him. I stop short and his hands go to my waist, fingers pressing softly into my skin.

My lips part and I tip my head up, meeting his gaze. He's wearing a dark blue shirt today, matching the color of his eyes perfectly.

"I thought you might fall again," he says.

"I...I might have. These floors are quite uneven."

"I was thinking slippery."

"Yeah. I'm not wearing socks," I ramble. Sam slides one hand from my waist to the small of my back and turns his gaze from my eyes to my lips. The floor creaks behind him and I jerk back, moving fast and whacking my hand on the back of a chair.

How he's able to get me turned on that fast with hardly touching me is a talent only Sam can possess.

"Do you want wine?" he asks.

"Yeah, like half a glass," I say, remembering Farisha's words. I'm not drunk from the little bit of rum, but I feel my head buzzing even more now that I had Sam's hands on me again.

"Is this any good?" He looks at the label of Pinot Noir.

"I'm not familiar with that vineyard, but I'd say it depends. Pinot Noir is a dry wine, but it has low acidity which makes it smooth to drink."

"Look at you." Sam pours wine into a glass for me.

"I went to a wine tasting a few months ago with friends. We spent a weekend in wine country and tried to act cultured. That little tidbit about Pinot Noir is the only thing I remember. I made the rookie mistake of drinking the entire glass given to me instead of just sipping it. I was the only one out of our group who didn't puke in the vineyard, though."

"You had me fooled." He slides the glass to me and pours a little bit for himself. "Pretending to work out when you're really being lazy and acting like you know about wine."

I take a sip of the Pinot Noir and give him a wink. "I'm all about the illusion of having shit together."

"You mean you don't?"

I let out a snort of laughter and turn, going back to the table. The others join us right after, and everyone bombards me with questions, just like Sam warned. I really do enjoy talking about writing and everything that goes along with it, especially when the people I'm talking to won't pick me apart about it later. Or at least, if they do, they won't post about it on social media, tagging me in every single critical post. And it's another good distraction, because every time I look at Sam, I see him shirtless and sweaty, like he was in the woods. And if I catch his gaze, I swear he's mentally undressing me in his mind.

"The most important thing," Mason says, finishing his third —fourth?—beer, "is if the rumors are true."

I reach for my own wine glass, heart jumping. "What rumor? There are a lot of them." I smile nervously, feeling Sam's eyes on me. What would he think if he found out I was in a fake relationship for years? I'm standing my ground with him on the basis that I'm not a "one-nighter" and I don't do meaningless anything. The fake relationship wasn't anything, though, but I'm not betraying Charles by saying so.

"The rumor that Cardi B is going to make a cameo next season."

I let out a sigh of relief and suck down a mouthful of wine. "Oh. I hadn't heard that one yet," I laugh and set my glass down. "Next season has already been filmed, but I do love her. If she did make a cameo, I would probably die."

"So you don't have much control over the series?" Mrs. Harris asks.

"No. I'm lucky I have the control I do. Basically, I sold the rights to my series to the network. They're in charge of everything, but my agent was able to have it written into the contract that I'm a 'consultant,' and since the series was so popular before the show, the producers know the importance of sticking with the original plot."

"Holy crap," Rory says. "It's so amazing."

"Nah," I say, waving my hand in the air. "I just got lucky."

"The *Nightfall* books are good," Rory counters. "Kellie is the most relatable character ever, even though she's a badass witch with powers."

I always feel weird when the conversation takes a turn like it does. "I just wrote what I wanted to read. I never realized how many other people wanted to read it too." I take another drink of wine and go through another round of twenty questions while we finish dinner.

And then the chaos Sam warned me about rains down on the household: Jacob tries to leave to go check on the animals at the clinic, but Mrs. Harris presses for him to stay for dessert, all while baby Adam cries hysterically and won't let anyone but Rory console him. Mason and Mr. Harris get into a political debate, and something spooks the chickens, causing them to squawk so loud we can hear it inside the house. Thinking it might be the fox Mrs. Harris spotted a few days ago, Sam and Dean run out to deal with it.

Not wanting to get drawn into talking about politics or side with anyone—though I agree that Mason is right—I go upstairs with Rory and help her get Adam bathed and changed.

"I'm really glad you came over," she tells me, checking the water in the bath before putting her baby in the little blue tub.

"Me too," I say, getting the baby shampoo out of the diaper bag for her. "I can't believe so many years went by without seeing you all."

"It's weird when you think about it." She dips a soft blue washcloth into the water and gives it to Adam. He can hardly hold on to it, but it distracts him while she washes his fat rolls. He's so chubby it's adorable. "You were like my sister and then you just weren't there anymore."

"I'm sorry."

"I don't blame you," she rushes out. "Sam said you all lost contact, but I know something...something more had to have gone down."

"Yeah, but it was a long time ago. And speaking of time... you're married with a kid. That's insane."

She laughs. "It kind of is. I really thought I'd end up alone."

Hah. I know the feeling. I've always loved Rory like a sister, and I'm happy for her. She and Dean are perfect for each other.

"I could have told you that was not going to happen."

Rory puts her hand on Adam's chest and looks at me, smiling. "I feel like I owe you so much, Chloe. You inspired me to be confident in who I am, even though I did inherit your nickname."

"Which one?"

"Creepy Chloe. They called me Creepy Rory."

My brows pinch together. "That doesn't have a ring to it like Creepy Chloe does."

"Right? That's what I said!" She laughs and shakes her head. "I've embraced it, though, just like you said."

"Good," I say, rocking back on my heels. "Being weird made my career. Literally."

"I try," Rory tells me, rinsing Adam clean. "Though I might have tried a little too hard before and it didn't end well."

"Hiding who you really are never does." I take the towel off the rack and unfold it, getting it ready for Rory to use to dry off Adam.

She gets him dressed in cute puppy-print PJs. Things are much calmer when we get downstairs. Sam is coming back into the living room from the den, carrying a stack of board games.

"You guys still do game night?" I ask, a smile coming to my face. Mr. and Mrs. Harris used to basically force it upon the boys growing up. They'd have dinner and then play some sort of board game. It was something I used to do with Mom and Dad, before Mom got sick, of course. And then after Mom died, I'd spend a lot of my weekends either here or with Farisha while Dad worked. I never realized how hard that had to be on Dad back then, and I never felt like I was displaced or struggling. I felt included here, like I belonged, and being with Sam made everything better.

It still does, which is stupid of me to think, I know. I want a relationship with Sam, and he's interested in one thing and one thing only.

"If we're all here like this, there's no way Mom will let us have dinner and then not play a game." Sam sets the games on the coffee table and sits on the couch, patting the cushion next to me. Rory takes Adam outside to find Dean, who was finishing up helping their dad fix a fence, and I cross the living room to take a seat next to Sam.

Mason gets there first and plops down in the middle of the couch. "Want to be on my team?" he asks me.

"I, um, I…sure." Sitting next to Mason, I look at the games on the table. "What are we playing?"

"I don't care as long as we make it a drinking game," Mason says.

"How do you make Clue a drinking game?"

Mason picks up the game and turns it over, reading the back. "You can make everything a drinking game. Candyland is a good one. Take a shot whenever you pass over one of those squares that has a candy on them. Sip a drink when you get a double-square card."

"You sound like you've played a lot," I laugh.

"It's been a while. Speaking of drinking, want to try the obscure flavors of whiskey?"

"Yeah, I'm kind of curious, though peanut butter whiskey still sounds disgusting."

Mason nudges me with his elbow. "Don't knock it till you've tried it."

"I'm open to trying just about anything once. I've discovered I've enjoyed quite a few things I thought I wouldn't otherwise like that way."

"I'm sure you have." Mason stands and holds out his hand, helping me up off the couch.

"Sam, you coming?" I ask.

"Nah, he's lame," Mason rushes out and ushers me out of the room. The whiskey is already out on the counter along with two shot glasses. Mason pours a little bit of the peanut butter whiskey in my shot glass and fills his up.

"To old friends," he says, holding up the shot glass.

171

"To old friends," I echo. Sam walks into the kitchen, coming up behind me. Mason moves closer, looks into my eyes, and flashes a flirty smirk.

"And to trying new things...things you wouldn't have before."

CHAPTER NINETEEN

SAM

The little shit was serious.

He's putting the moves on Chloe, right in fucking front of me. She looks a little confused as she taps her shot glass against his, and gags when she tosses the whiskey back. She and Mason both burst out laughing, and Chloe waves her hand in front of her face.

"That's terrible! Oh my god!" She's still laughing and turns around to go to the sink. She rinses her shot glass and fills it with water, taking a drink.

"Now that we've gotten the worst out of the way, try this one." Mason unscrews the lid to a bottle of peach vodka.

"It's probably not a good idea to be mixing types of alcohol like that," I say.

"Told you he's lame," Mason huffs, and I glare at him, still in disbelief he's hitting on Chloe. It was an unspoken rule between the three of us that we never made moves on a chick one of us liked.

"He's right." Chloe's eyes go to mine. "I shouldn't mix booze like this, and I had wine with dinner. I don't want to get drunk or feel sick or anything."

Mason puts his hand on top of hers. "Hey, if that happened,

you know I'd take care of you." That's it. He crossed a line. I storm over, ready to put a stop to whatever the fuck he thinks he's doing.

The garage door opens and the rest of the family comes in.

"You're drinking without me?" Dean asks and looks at the choices of alcohol on the counter. "Never mind."

"I tried the peanut butter whiskey," Chloe says. "Jacob was right. That strong rum was much better."

"I could get that," Mason offers, and Chloe shakes her head.

"I'll pass for now and will stick to water. Or kombucha tea, but I'm guessing you're all out."

"I don't even know what that is."

"It's fermented tea that's supposed to be good for you." She shrugs. "I don't think any of the health benefits have been proven yet, but I swear I've been healthier since I started drinking it. I used to get a cold every few months, and I haven't been sick since December. That's a record for me."

"You're not going to counter that with medical facts?" Mason looks at me.

"I don't see an issue with drinking tea daily," I say, and Chloe and I both move closer to each other. It's instinctual for me to be near to her. "But tell me your essential oils work better than modern medicine and we might have an issue."

Chloe laughs. "I have a few friends who would argue that. All with peer-reviewed articles to back up their claims, and by that, I mean viral Facebook posts." Her eyes meet mine. "I can see how frustrating that would be for a doctor. I get annoyed enough when horses whinny and rear in movies. They don't really do that."

"Right?" Jacob agrees. "It's annoying."

Dad shakes his head. "Between the four of you, we can hardly make it through any medical, animal, or law enforcement shows without someone pointing out how wrong something is."

"There's certain jurisdiction that has to be—I'll stop," Mason says, and everyone laughs. I'm still glaring at him.

"Let's get started," Mom says, waving everyone into the living room. My phone rings as soon as I'm seated next to Chloe. I turn my wrist, looking at my Apple watch to see who's calling. If it's the trauma center, I'll answer. If it's anyone else, I won't.

"Stacey?" Rory says out loud, letting the whole room know who's calling me. "Again?"

"She must really want to talk to you," Chloe adds. "This is the second time she's called you today, isn't it?"

"You're still talking to Stacey?" Mom echoes.

"I'm not." I hit *decline*. Talking about my clingy ex is the last thing I need right now. I sit back, arm brushing against Chloe's. "What are we playing?"

"What about that picture game?" Rory suggests. "The one where you draw something and then pass it to the person next to you and they have to write what they think it is."

"That sounds fun," Chloe says. "But I'm a terrible artist, which I'm guessing is part of the fun."

"It is," Rory assures her, and Mom passes out the game pieces. We get started and play for a solid half an hour, laughing so hard at some of the drawings our sides hurt. Everyone is having a good time and, dammit, I wish it could be like this all the time. We play one more round and then stop for dessert since Rory wants to try to get Adam to bed soon.

Mom made apple pie, one of Chloe's favorites when we were kids. We crowd around the dining room table again to eat, and then Rory and Dean go upstairs to get Adam asleep. Mom, worried about her chickens, has Dad go out to make sure the fox isn't back and has Jacob come with her to check that none of the chickens got injured.

Mason, Chloe, and I are in the kitchen, and I bring my plate over to the pie to get a second piece. "Do you want any more?" I ask Chloe.

"I do!" Her eyes light up and her smile splits her pretty face. "Even though I shouldn't, I'm trying to cut back on carbs." She pats her stomach like she has weight to lose, which couldn't be further from the truth. I don't like a woman who's all skin and bone. Everyone likes to eat, and denying such a primal thing is a turn-off. I, for one, am not going to deprive myself of anything when I want it.

Well, anything besides Chloe.

"One night of indulgence won't hurt a damn thing," Mason says, taking a seat next to Chloe at the island counter. "Giving in to what you desire is good for you."

Chloe blushes and looks down, slowly shaking her head. She opens her mouth to say something and then her phone rings. "Oh, that's my agent's ringtone. If she's calling on a Sunday night, it has to be important." She hops off the barstool and goes to her purse, fishing out her phone. "I'll be right back," she tells us and slips out onto the patio to talk in peace.

"What the fuck are you doing?" I round on Mason.

"I told you, I'm making my move on Chloe. She's smoking hot, and since you're not emotionally invested, she's fair game."

"She's not a game to be played."

"If you like her, then admit it and I'll back off." Mason holds up his hands. "But since you already said all you want is to be her friend, why do you care?" His eyes pierce mine, testing me. "We both know that's not true, and I can't stand here and watch you strike out again and again."

"Fuck you."

"You should be thanking me."

"For hitting on Chloe? No fucking way."

"Admit it," Mason goes on. "You want to be the one fucking her tonight."

I open my mouth only to snap it shut.

"Your loss. Her tits look fucking fantastic in that dress." He holds his hands up. "I bet they feel even better."

Anger boils inside me, both at Mason for being a shithead

just to be a shithead, and to hear someone talk about Chloe that way. I swing my fist at him, not actually wanting to punch my brother. Mason blocks my arm as I expected him to and tries to kick my feet out from underneath me. I grab him, trying to pull him down instead.

"I don't want to hurt you," I say through gritted teeth.

"Hurt me?" Mason rams us forward into the kitchen table. "Go ahead and try." He puts his foot between mine and knocks me off balance, but we both go down. "Admit it!" He tries to pin me down, a typical move he always did in our youth. I dodge out of the way and go to stand back up, but he grabs me again, wrestling me back to the ground. "Admit it!" He swats at my face. Now that we've started the fight, we're going to end it, though neither of us wants to actually injure the other. But like hell, I'm just going to roll over and submit.

"Admit what?" I say through gritted teeth as Mason knees me in the gut.

"That." He swats at me again. "You." Somehow I get his shoe and start smacking him with it. "Love her!"

The fuck? He knows I'm in love with Chloe? This whole thing was a show just to piss me off, forcing me to admit it. My own brother fucking played me, and I'm not sure yet if I should be mad. Mason takes advantage of my hesitation and knees me in the stomach again, and I hit him once more with his shoe.

"Boys!" Mom's voice rings out around us. "What the hell is going on?"

I let Mason's shoe fall from my grasp and look up and see—shit—Chloe.

CHAPTER TWENTY

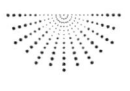

CHLOE

"Hey, Vanessa," I say when I answer the phone. I close the sliding glass door behind me and am surrounded by the sounds of the night. "Is everything okay?"

"Yes, and I'm so sorry to bother you on a Sunday night," she starts. "I got a quick question for you before I pursue this any deeper."

"Pursue what?" I walk along the patio, looking past the white picket fence at the barn. The lights are on, and I can hear voices coming from inside. I know Mrs. Harris still has chickens, but I'm not sure what other farm animals they have now that the kids are grown.

"I went out to dinner tonight and just happened to strike up a conversation with a producer. Of course you came up, and to make a long story short, they're interested in getting you involved in an upcoming show. They're putting a twist on medieval legends, based on a book written thirty years ago that ended on a huge cliffhanger. The author died before he got to finish it. Basically they want to say *the writer of the Nightfall series* is continuing the plot as well as tweaking the original to be up to today's standards of equal representation."

"Holy shit."

"Yep," she laughs. "It's nothing formal at all at this point, but before I go forward at all, I wanted to see if it's something you'd be interested in. It would require you to meet in person, probably weekly if not more. I know that takes time away from your novels. And if this does go through, they want to start in January."

"Wow. That would be an incredible opportunity." I look out at the woods behind the barn. It would tie me to LA, and I was just thinking about actually coming back home. For good. "Okay, I'm kind of interested to see the formal offer or contract or whatever, but not sold on saying I'm actually interested. Sorry for the non-answer."

"Don't be. It was a lot to dump on you, and trust me, it was not what I was expecting to take away from dinner tonight. I'll get back to the network and we'll go from there. How's your write-cation going?"

I unlatch the gate and step into the dewy grass. "Good. It's been nice to get away, and I have the entire day by myself to write tomorrow. I'm feeling very inspired too."

"Great. Enjoy your night and give me a day or so to get something more concrete about this to go over with you. Take care."

"You too." I end the call and am about to turn back inside when the barn doors open. I wave, not wanting to freak out Mrs. Harris or anything, and end up walking back inside with them. I wipe my feet on the mat outside the garage door and follow behind Jacob. I'm going slow as I open up Vanessa's email.

"Boys!" Mrs. Harris exclaims, and I jerk my head up to see Sam and Mason on the ground in what at first looks like a fight but is more of a comical squabble. "What the hell is going on?" Mason has one arm locked around Sam's legs, and Sam is holding Mason's shoe. It drops from his hand and they both scramble up.

"He started it," they say at the same time, pointing to each other. I cock an eyebrow, looking from Sam to Mason.

"I don't care who started it," Mrs. Harris goes on. "Just stop it."

"You know I would have whooped your ass if I wanted to," Mason quips, and Sam narrows his eyes.

"You never could before."

Mason swats Sam on the back of the head.

"I have horse tranquilizers in my truck," Jacob says.

"Maybe you should get them," I whisper.

Mr. Harris sighs and walks into the kitchen, going to the sink to wash his hands. "I thought you two grew out of this."

"Mom did say she wanted things to be just like they were when we all lived here," Mason grumbles and goes back to the counter, getting another piece of pie.

"Did your agent have good news?" Sam runs his hand through his hair.

"Yeah." I go back to where I was sitting before, next to Sam. "A producer at a popular streaming service wants me to help them write a show. I don't know any more details other than that."

"Ohh, how exciting!" Mrs. Harris coos.

"Maybe?" I shrug. The more I think about it, the less I want to do it. I like writing novels where I can work from my house and control everything in my book. I don't have to get a room full of others to agree with me, though having a team to help me write would be nice when I get stuck on something. But having to go into an office…that's not really my thing.

"I'm going to head out," Jacob says. "It was really good to see you again, Chloe."

"It was good to see you too."

Mrs. Harris gives Jacob a hug. "Tell Rory and Dean I said bye."

"Are you ready to go home?" Sam asks me, and my heart flutters, remembering his offer to drink wine by the lake in the moonlight.

"Yeah," I say, talking with my heart and not my head. "Do you think Rory will be down soon?" I fiddle with my hair, wrapping a curl around my finger. "I want to say bye before I leave."

"She should be," Mrs. Harris says.

"How long is she staying in town?" I ask.

"She's leaving Wednesday evening. You're not sure when you're leaving yet?"

I shake my head. "I don't really have to go back anytime, though I do miss my horse. He's getting loved on by the little girls at the barn, so he's more than fine."

"It must be nice to work anywhere you want," Mrs. Harris says.

"It is. I definitely don't take it for granted."

The stairs creak and Rory and Dean come down. "Success!" Rory cheers quietly. "He hardly fussed at—" She's interrupted by the baby crying. "Son of a bitch."

"He's your son," Mason starts. "So does that make you the bitch?"

"Hilarious," Rory replies dryly. "I'll get him."

"We're gonna head out," Sam says quickly before his sister goes back upstairs. I get up from my chair so I can give Rory a hug goodbye.

"It was so good to see you again," I tell her. "We should get lunch before you leave."

"I brought my dice sets," she tells me, pulling me in for a tight hug. "We could play D&D over lunch."

"Ohhhh, yes, please!" I step back and look at Dean. "It was really nice to meet you."

"Oh, Sam, before you leave, let me show you what Archer and I got for our league this year," Dean says.

I assume they're talking about some sort of fantasy sports league, but whatever it is, Sam gets excited and goes into the living room with Dean. Mrs. Harris gives Rory all of a minute before going up to "help" with her grandson, and Mr. Harris huffs about her being overbearing and goes into the living room as well, leaving me alone with Mason, who's on this third piece of pie already.

"What were you and Sam fighting about?" I ask, debating if I should get more pie too. I never had the second piece like I wanted.

"Nothing," he says and shoves a forkful of pie into his mouth. "Just horsing around like we used to."

I nod and look at my phone, reading the email from Vanessa over again.

"Can I ask you something?" Mason puts his fork down on his now-empty plate.

"Sure."

"You and Charles...it was never serious, was it?"

"What makes you say that?" My heart skips a beat and I instantly panic, thinking back to everything I said during dinner. I didn't say anything that gave it away, did I?

"It's my job to analyze people, and I'm good at it."

"So you analyzed my relationship with Charles?"

"Not on purpose," Mason says. "It's kind of a habit now. And from what I saw, you two were never really in love."

I look at Mason, feeling entirely too exposed. "What gave it away?" I ask quietly.

"It's the way you look at him, or rather the way you *don't* look at him."

"That doesn't make any sense," I rush out, heart skipping a beat. I can't fool Mason. Hell, I can't even fool myself.

"It does," Mason goes on slowly. "Because I've seen the way you look at someone when you are in love with them."

My throat tightens. "Yeah, and who would that be?" I finally spit out.

Mason tips his head towards me and gently nudges me with his elbow. "We both know the answer to that."

Right on cue, Sam comes back into the kitchen. Our eyes

meet and butterflies take flight. Mason is right, and now one more person knows the truth.

I'm in love with Sam. If only he could love me back the same way.

CHAPTER TWENTY-ONE

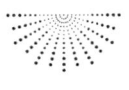

SAM

"It's beautiful out," Chloe says quietly, and I pause before looking up at the star-studded sky. I'm standing just inches from her, having come around the car to open the door for her to get inside. It's cooled down a lot from the heat of the day this afternoon, but not so much that it's uncomfortable to be outside. I love nights like this when I can be out in sweatpants and a hoodie, covered up enough to keep from getting eaten alive by mosquitos without breaking out in a sweat.

A soft breeze rustles Chloe's hair, and I reach out, not even thinking, and tuck her hair behind her ear. I get zapped with an electric shock when my fingers grace over her flesh, and Chloe jumps slightly.

"Maybe you're a merman." She reaches up and puts her hand over mine.

"What?" I ask with a chuckle.

"It's something from a made-for-TV movie I used to watch when I was a kid. He shocked people when touched them."

"I think I remember that one." I flip her hand over and lace our fingers together. Stepping in close, my heart is in my throat. I could tell her now, put it all out on the line, and see what happens from here. There's a chance it could all crash and burn around me, but there's a chance it won't.

And I need to take it.

"Should we get going?" She pulls her hand out of mine. Is that an unspoken answer to my question?

"Yeah. It's, uh, getting late." I bring my hand back and run it through my hair, needing to calm my heart and my dick down. Chloe holds my gaze for a second and then turns, opening the door and getting in the car.

"Fuck," I mumble to myself as I go around the car. No one has ever made me unnerved like Chloe does. When it comes to women, I'm always calm, collected, and never strikeout.

But I've never cared like this before. Chloe has always been everything to me, even if I didn't see it. Losing Chloe once hurt bad enough. Losing her again, knowing that she never wants to be anything more than what we are now…it will fucking destroy me.

"Do you mind if I roll my window down?" she asks as we pull out of the driveway.

"Not at all. We can open the sunroof too."

"I'd like that." She turns, smiling, and reaches up to push the button to open the sunroof at the same time I do. Her fingers slide over my wrist and—dammit—just that little bit of feeling her skin against mine sends a jolt through me. "Sorry."

"It's okay." I press the button and the glass slides back. "I don't get to use this all that often."

"In California, you would." She gathers her hair in her hand and moves it behind her back, keeping it from blowing in the wind.

"For sure. You don't get much rain there, do you?"

"No, we go through drought seasons, and it seems like every year gets worse. The wildfires came really close to my house two years ago. It was terrifying."

"I can't even imagine."

"I was more worried about Spartan. I camped out at the

barn for four nights, too scared to leave him and the other horses. We kept a really close eye on everything, of course, and had emergency plans to load up the horses and drive to another barn miles away. Thankfully, it didn't come to it."

"I think I'd rather take the snow and cold over fires."

"It's a trade-off, but it's not like fires happen regularly, like snow here in the winter."

"True, but snow doesn't burn your house down or risk killing you from smoke inhalation."

She gives me a pointed stare. "Thanks. As if the thought of another fire didn't scare me enough already. Want to remind me about earthquakes too?"

"I was going to save that one until right before you fall asleep. That way you can lay in bed wide awake worrying about being buried alive in rubble."

"You're late to the party. I've already had that nightmare over a dozen times."

"Then I'll remind you how you're more likely to be robbed after a natural disaster."

"I need to find my own island to live on—and don't even talk to me about tidal waves," she says, and I laugh. I turn off the rural road my parents live on and get on the main road that runs through downtown Silver Ridge. We have to go around the lake to get to Chloe's dad's house, which adds a bit of time to our drive.

The actual town of Silver Ridge looks big on a map because of the lake, but population-wise, it's a small town. I felt claustrophobic here in my youth, which is almost humorous now considering I live on the sixth floor of my apartment building in downtown Chicago.

Chloe sticks her hand out the window, feeling the air as we speed down the road. She lets go of her hair, letting it wildly fly around her face for a few minutes, a smile on her face the whole time. When I slow to go through the few blocks of Silver

Ridge's downtown, she closes her window halfway and combs her hair with her fingers.

"Are you cold?" I ask, seeing the goosebumps on her arm.

"I get chilled easily."

"It's like eighty degrees out."

"It's seventy-six," she corrects, pointing to the temperature displayed on screen. "You're off by a whole four degrees. And I thought you were supposed to be good at math since you're calculating how much medication to give someone."

I laugh. "You mean you don't want a rough estimate next time you're put under?"

"Next time?" She shakes her head. "I've never had surgery."

"You're lucky then."

"I've been tempted to get cosmetic procedures done, but I'm more scared of being put to sleep than anything else," she admits.

"You don't need anything cosmetic changed on you," I tell her. "And that's actually pretty common. A lot of patients are more nervous about going under anesthesia than whatever surgical procedure they're having done. Their concerns are valid, but as long as you're going to a credible and accredited hospital, you'll be fine."

"I'll ask you for recommendations when I'm old and needing a lift." She brings her hands to her chest, giving her breasts a squeeze. I grip the steering wheel tight, fighting to keep my focus on the road.

"I'll happily help." Chloe closes her window the rest of the way, and I turn the music on. We're nearing her dad's house now, and I need to mentally prep myself to man the fuck up and tell Chloe how I feel.

Or show her. I've always been better at show than tell.

"Do you still want to sit by the lake?" she asks almost timidly.

"If you want me to." I lock the car and shove my phone and key fob in my pocket.

"I do. Come in with me first. I need to get a sweater."

"But it's seventy-six degrees," I tease.

"Seventy-five now." She gets the house keys from her purse. "It's sweater weather for me now. Also, the mosquitos are pretty bad out there at night. I should get us a blanket instead. Something lightweight but that will keep the bugs away."

"That's a good idea."

She takes her shoes off, uses the bathroom, and then motions for me to follow her outside, grabbing a blanket from the living room on the way. We leave through the screened-in porch and walk down a little cobblestone path that leads to the wooden dock.

"Does your dad do much fishing?" I ask, seeing the boat tied up. A jet ski is on the other side, neatly covered to keep safe from the weather.

"I think he and Wendy mostly drift around the lake with Balloon, their dog."

"Balloon?"

"He came with the name and my dad couldn't bear to change it." She sits on the dock, slowly dangling her feet over the edge.

"Are you still scared of dark water?" I ask, taking my own shoes and socks off.

"I might still have a slight—"

I give her a gentle nudge, pretending to push her into the water. She yelps and grabs onto me, holding on for dear life. I laugh and wrap my arm around her waist, pulling her close.

"Not funny, Samuel!"

"No one calls me that, you know."

"I do when I'm mad." A smile plays on her face, blowing her cover for acting pissed. She laughs and rests one hand over my chest. My heart is thumping away in there, and she has to feel it.

"I guess I should make it up to you then."

Moonlight pours down on us, reflecting off the glossy

surface of the lake. "Y-yeah." Her breath leaves in a huff, and she straightens up, taking the blanket and draping it around both our shoulders.

"It's really peaceful out here, isn't it?" She apprehensively dips a toe in the water. Her hand is next to mine on the dock, and I intertwine our fingers.

"It is. I haven't seen Silver Lake at night in years. Almost makes me wonder why I left."

"Did you think you'd end up back here?" Chloe plunges her other foot into the water, and I move so my feet dangle over the dock as well. The water is warm but feels good.

"Willingly?" I ask.

"Yes."

"For a while, yes. And then I realized my options would be limited. There's one small hospital here and no trauma center."

"Do you like working in trauma?" she asks.

"Most of the time. You were right to call working in trauma traumatizing. It can wear on me some days. But it's exciting, and every day pushes me to be the best doctor I can be. Every patient that comes in is in a life-or-death situation."

"You could work at a plastic surgery center instead."

"A buddy from med school does that now. He's in Miami and loves it. No holidays or weekends. Pretty much everything is pre-scheduled, and you don't have too many late nights."

"Did you always want to be an anesthesiologist?"

"Actually, no. I was interested in oncology." I pause, but don't have to go on for her to know what made me want to go that direction. I was with her, comforting her, holding her hand and giving her a shoulder to cry on as her mom lost her battle with cancer. "I was matched with anesthesiology, and there was an opening for my residency at the hospital I wanted, so I took it."

"That's interesting."

"I love it now, and if you ever need someone put in a coma, I'm your guy." I let go of her hand, and she stiffens slightly. I tip my face up to the starry sky and put my arm around Chloe, pulling her close. Her whole body relaxes once she's in my embrace. "What about you? Did you think you'd end up back here?"

"I did. It was home. It still feels like home…well, kind of. I was eager to get out, though I never thought I'd end up in California."

"Where did you think you'd end up?"

"Chicago. It's a big city but not that far away. For some reason, I was all about experiencing city life."

I chuckle. "I get that. It was exciting to finally go to a big city in college. I thought it would be night after night going out and living it up, but med school sucks the social life right out of you. Residency is even worse."

"Who needs a social life when you're hooking up in the janitor's closet with your extremely good-looking fellow doctors?"

"Do not get me started on that." I turn my head down, looking into her eyes. "You know it's not…" I trail off forgetting what I was going to say. Chloe is so fucking beautiful, and sitting here with her feels so right, so natural.

My heart jumps, and I don't think. Just act. I bring both hands up, cupping her face.

And then I kiss her.

The entire world fades around us, and the only thing that exists, the only thing that matters, is Chloe. It should have been this way all along. I push my hands up, moving her hair back. Chloe leans in, kissing me back just as passionately. The blanket falls from my shoulders as I move closer to Chloe, needing to feel more of her.

Eyes closed, I rest my forehead against hers.

"I'm such an idiot," I breathe, hands still in her hair.

She jerks back with a slight gasp. "Because you kissed me?"

"Because I didn't kiss you sooner." Her eyes get glossy, and we fall together again. I lean back, bringing Chloe with me. Her body presses against mine. Warm. Soft.

Perfect.

Her thick hair falls like a curtain around us. I cup her face, kissing her harder. My tongue slips past her lips, and I bring one hand down, resting it on the small of her back. She hooks a leg over me and moves on top. Her dress is ridden up around her waist, with her hot core hovering right over my hardening cock. She widens her legs and sinks down on me, rocking her hips to purposely feel me against her. It's hot as fucking hell and we're still fully dressed. I gather up her dress and find the tie in the back.

"Sam, stop," she says suddenly as I pull the bow undone.

"Okay." I take my hands off of her right away. "What's wrong?"

"I…I…" She's still on me, hands planted on my chest. Her brows push together and her bottom lip trembles. Did I say something wrong? Upset her?

Push her past where she wants to be pushed?

Fuck, I never meant to upset her, and hurting her is the last thing I ever want to do.

"I'm sorry," she says and scrambles off me. Her feet get tangled in the blanket and she almost falls. I shoot up and catch her before she drops into the water. "Thank you, again."

"Of course, Chloe. I told you, I'll always catch you."

She looks away, eyes brimming with tears.

"Chloe, what's wrong?" My own heart is in my throat, bracing myself for the worst.

"I…I can't do this."

And the worst is exactly what I get.

CHAPTER TWENTY-TWO

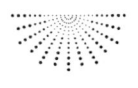

CHLOE

"I...I can't do this."

The look on Sam's face just about does me in. But I can't. I have to stand my ground or that momentary look on Sam's face will be on mine for months, if not years. Or forever. Because it's been over ten years since I've gazed on this man's gorgeous face and I'm still just as in love with him as ever.

"Then we don't have to," Sam says gently and takes his hands off me. I miss him right away. "I'm sorry. I thought you... I'm sorry." He's flustered and confused, and I can't blame him. Because I do want to keep kissing him. I want him to undress me and fuck me until I'm screaming his name. I take a step back and blink away tears. "I really didn't mean it was idiotic to kiss you," he rushes out.

"I know," I say quietly. "And I agree you were an idiot for not kissing me sooner, because I really like you kissing me." Dammit, I do, and desire for him swirls deep inside me, but I have to fight it. I have to stay strong. "I just...I can't."

"I'm confused," he says slowly.

"I...I..." Shaking my head, I look out at the lake as a tear rolls down my cheek. Sam gently rests his hand on my shoulder.

BACKUP PLAN

"What's wrong, Chloe?" he asks.

My bottom lip quivers and I suck in a breath. I just need to say it. Get it out there so I can finally move on. "I've been in love with you since the day we met." My words come out strangled, and I fight against tears. "When you promised you'd marry me if we were both over thirty and single, I knew the only way that would happen was if you exhausted all your other options and you had to fall back to me as your backup plan." Another tear rolls down my face. "You were always my first choice."

Sam's hand slips from my shoulder, and I know this is it. The moment he tells me sorry, that he cares but doesn't want anything serious and the joke is on me—again. His brows pinch together and his lips part. A moment passes before he says anything, and I don't dare take a breath in that time.

"You would never be my backup plan," he says, and runs his hand down my arm, taking my hand in his. "Because I've been in love with you too."

The whole world stops, and I'm not sure if I heard him or if I'm bordering on delusion, so I don't get my heart broken—again. I open my mouth to speak, but no words come out. Did he just—no, there's no way—but maybe…

"What?"

Sam pulls me close, wrapping one arm around me and cupping my face with his other, gently turning my chin up to look at him. "I love you, Chloe. I have for a while, and seeing you again made me realize just how much of an idiot I was for not saying anything sooner." He puts his lips to mine, needing to kiss me before going on. "I fucked up before, but I'm not going to anymore. I love you, and I want to be with you if you'll have me. I'm sorry for standing there like a drunk idiot the night of that party. I went after you, but you were already gone. If I could go back and change things, I would." He rests his forehead against mine, and I fasten my arms around his neck. Sam has never been a share-your-feelings type of person and hearing him confess everything sends pulses of electricity right through me.

The lake gently laps against the dock, and the sounds of the night ring out in a chorus around us. My heart is beating away in my chest, and more tears fill my eyes. This is everything I've ever wanted: Sam, telling me he loves me. Hearing him confess his regret over the past, and how he wants a future with me.

And now I'm doubting even more than this isn't a dream.

"Chloe?" Sam whispers after a few seconds tick by and I say nothing.

"I...I think you need to pinch me."

"Why?"

"To make sure this is real."

He tips my chin up. "Can I do this instead?" He softly kisses me, leaving me wanting more the second his lips move off of mine.

"Yeah, that works too, but I think you need to do it again. Just to be sure."

He smirks. "Just to be sure." We kiss again, but this time it's anything but soft. Sam holds me tightly, crushing my breasts against his chest. He kisses me with fervor, hands wandering all over my body.

Suddenly, he breaks away, taking a fistful of my hair. He looks at me like I'm the only woman in the whole damn world, like if he doesn't have me now, he won't survive much longer. "I love you," he breathes. "I needed to say it out loud again."

"I love you, too." I rake my fingers through his thick dark hair. "I've loved you since the moment I met you."

He kisses me again, running his hands down my body. One hand pushes between my thighs, and the other gathers the hem of my dress, balling it in his hand. The wind picks up, blowing in warm air from the lake. My eyes fall shut and I inhale deeply, desire flooding through me. My breath comes out a little ragged, and my entire body begins to tremble.

Sam's tongue pushes past my lips and he parts my thighs,

stepping in closer. His fingers brush over my core, and my knees threaten to buckle. I hold on to him tighter to keep from falling. He's already undone the tie at the back of my dress, and he continues to kiss with as he brings one hand to my back, feeling for the zipper.

Something splashes nearby in the lake, but it does little to distract us. Sam stops kissing me, looking into my eyes as he slowly undoes the zipper of my dress. He's doing it on purpose to tease me, and if he keeps taking his damn time, I'm going to shove him down on the dock and climb on top. I've waited years for this, wanting and loving him in secret.

I need him. Now.

Sam gets the zipper down and moves his hand up, slipping it inside my dress, fingers settling right over the top of my ass. I run my hands down his chest, stopping at the waist of his pants. My breasts rise and fall with my rapid breathing, and I desperately try to undo Sam's belt.

"Patience," he tells me, deep voice rattling right to my core. "We have all night." He grabs my wrist and pulls my hand away. "I'm going to take care of you first." He spins me around, gathering my hair in one hand and puts his lips to my neck. I lean back against him, feeling his cock hardening against me. He kisses and sucks at my neck, sending pulses of pleasure right through me. He lets go of my hair and sweeps his hand down my body, slowing down as his fingers pass over my nipple.

I've always known Sam's no stranger to a woman's body, and tonight is not going to disappoint. I just hope I'm good enough for him, to make him feel as good as he's going to make me. I'm far from a virgin, but don't have the experience Sam does. I don't enjoy sex when I'm lacking an emotional connection, and it's hard to connect with anyone when you're in love with someone else.

But now, that man I love is loving me back, and I know it's going to be fucking spectacular.

Sam gently nips at my neck and brings his hand down

between my thighs. I gasp when his fingers go over my clit, covered only by the thin fabric of my panties. I rest my head against him and part my legs at his urging.

Laughter floats over the lake and I open my eyes, startled to see a boat. Right. The rest of the world still exists. I'd forgotten all about it. Sam either doesn't notice or doesn't care. His fingers dance over my entrance again, feeling how hot and wet he's making me—and he's hardly even touched me.

"Should...should we go inside?" I whisper, afraid if Sam stops touching me I'll combust before we make it into the house. Without saying anything, he spins me around, kisses me hard and then picks me up. My legs go around his waist, and I cling to him, kissing him as hard as I can as we stumble our way to the house.

Somehow Sam manages to open the gate with me still in his arms, setting me down only when we get to the door leading to the screened-in porch. I make a desperate reach for the latch, missing it twice before I can push the door open. We tangle together again, desperate to peel each other's clothes off. My dress is hanging off one shoulder now, and Sam takes one step back, looking at me in the pale light.

"Take it off," he tells me, and my breath hitches in my chest. Normally, I'd be shy to be on display like this in front of anyone, but not Sam, not with the way he's looking at me like he needs me as much as I need him. I push one strap of my blue dress down my arm and slowly move to the other side, letting the other fall. I hold it up at my chest, waiting a beat before letting the dress fall to the floor in a whoosh.

"Fuck, you're gorgeous," he tells me, struggling to restrain himself. He runs his eyes over me, letting me know exactly what the sight of my body is doing to him. I've had men look at me with desire and hunger before, but never like this. Sam wants me in an obvious way, but his want is more than physical, and this is the first time I've ever been intimate with a person in such a way.

Sam closes the distance between us and puts his lips to mine. The heat pulsing through me intensifies, and I'm afraid I'm going to explode. I wrap my arms around Sam, opening my mouth and deepening his kiss.

Both of Sam's hands go to my ass. He gives it a squeeze and I'm very aware that the only thing keeping us apart is the thin lace of my black panties. He brings me to him, and I fasten my arms around his shoulders.

In a swift movement, he spins me around, pressing my ass against his hard cock. He urges my legs apart and runs his hand down my stomach, slowing when he gets to the top of my panties. My breath leaves me, and Sam puts his lips to my neck. I lean back against him, not sure how much longer I can stand this. He's hardly touched me and I'm basically melting right here on the floor, wanting him more than I've ever wanted anyone.

He's moving slow on purpose, somehow able to control himself, and inches his fingers down. I hold my breath, desperately waiting for him to give me more. He sucks at my neck and curls one finger over my clit. My lips part and a moan escapes me from that small movement. He moves his finger back, rubbing me again, and it feels so fucking good.

And then he lets go, stepping back so suddenly I almost fall. I start to turn but Sam is already there, hands clasping around my waist. He pushes me forward and I stumble back, holding onto him as he pins me between his body and the wall.

"Chloe," he breathes, and hearing him say my name is one of the most erotic moments of my life. "Touch yourself. I want to watch."

Okay, now *this* is the most erotic moment in my life. I swallow hard, unable to take my eyes off of Sam's. He puts his lips to mine and takes my hand, moving it between my legs. With our fingers together, I rub my clit. Sam takes his hand off of mine and steps back, watching me touch myself.

My lips part and I arch my back, resting my head against

the wall. I let my eyes fall shut, but can still feel Sam's gaze on me. I bring my hand up only to push it back down, inside my panties. A growl comes from deep inside Sam's throat, and he comes to me again, pulling my hand from my panties. He presses himself between my legs as he kisses me and runs his hands down my body again.

I can feel his big cock through his pants, and it sends a thrill through me. I've never been with a man this large, and I know it's going to destroy me in the best way possible. My hands go to his pants again, fumbling with the button. Finally, I pop the button right as Sam kisses me, and his cock forces the zipper down. He groans when I touch him, taking in the sheer size and girth of that thing. There were always rumors about Sam being well-equipped, but having him against me like this is intimidating.

I push his pants down as we make out, Sam's hands exploring my body. He steps out of them and drops to his knees, mouth going to my core. His breath is hot against me, and I gasp as a shiver makes its way down my spine. He looks up, gaze promising what's to come, and kisses my stomach.

Slowly, he slides his fingers under the sides of my panties and rolls them down, letting them fall when they get past my knee. He kisses his way down my thigh and lifts up one of my feet, taking my underwear off so now it's just hanging around one leg.

Then he widens my legs and dives right in between, mouth open. His tongue lashes against me once, but then he stands up, leaving me quivering before him. He kisses me, hand going between my legs. This time, I won't let him tease me. I can't handle any more of it.

I grab his wrist, keeping his hand between my legs. He works his fingers, rubbing my clit and then pushing two fingers inside me, finding the spot that brings me right to the brink of orgasm. He moves his lips to my neck, figuring out fast that I'm a sucker to be kissed in that spot.

"Don't you…you dare stop," I pant.

"What are you going to do if I do stop?" he whispers right back, rubbing my clit again. My entire body is tingling, so close to coming.

"I'll…I'll finish myself while you watch and then send you on your way."

"Damn," he croons and nips at my skin. He speeds up his movements, and only a minute later, my legs are shaking as the orgasm ripples through me. I cling to him, legs no longer working, and let my head roll back again the wall again as pleasure rolls through me. My pussy spasms around Sam's long fingers and my ears ring. Before I can open my eyes or even form a coherent thought, Sam picks me up and grabs my beach towel and spreads it on the floor. He lays me down on it and goes right between my legs.

Holy fuck.

I'm still reeling from the first orgasm as he dives in between my legs, licking and flicking his tongue over my already-sensitive clit. I'm almost on overdrive, and don't know if my body can handle another—oh fuck. Yes, yes it can.

I put one hand on Sam's head, tangling his hair between my fingers. He alternates between licking and sucking my clit, and it doesn't take long before my mouth falls open and my body shakes from the intensity of another orgasm. I gasp for air as the world spins around me. Sam moves over top, kissing me softly.

My eyes flutter open and shut, needing to look at Sam's handsome face. I've imagined this day for years…wondering if actually sleeping with Sam would be as good as I hoped it would be. And tonight he's proven that it's even better.

But he hasn't even fucked me yet.

"Where's your room?" His voice is low, heavy with want, and rattles right through me.

"Up…upstairs," I pant, and he scoops me up, strong arms holding me against him. He knows there's no way I could get up and walk right now, and he effortlessly carries me up the stairs.

"First door," I tell him, and my heart, which was finally slowing down, starts to speed up again as I think about Sam pushing that big cock inside of me. He lays me down on my bed, and I suck in a breath, pushing up on my elbows.

He pulls his shirt over his head, dropping it on the floor. The outside lights dimly light the room, giving me just enough to admire Sam's muscular body.

He moves between my legs, and I bend one leg up. "You are everything, Chloe," he breathes and puts his lips to mine. I reach down, pushing at the elastic of his boxers. He helps me strip him bare, and now we're together with nothing in between us. "I never should have waited to tell you I love you."

He lines his cock up with my entrance and kisses me, waiting just a beat before pushing inside. I cry out from the tight fit. Moving slow at first, he pushes all the way in and then slowly pulls back only to thrust in again. He repeats it over and over, fucking me harder and faster with fluid movements.

"You are so fucking hot," he pants, pushing his cock in balls deep. I open my mouth to tell him that he is too, but I'm overcome with pleasure again and my words turn into a loud moan. I've never come from penetration before, and I've had some very eager contenders swear they'd be able to make me.

The orgasm comes from deep inside, spreading through me like wildfire. My pussy contracts around Sam's cock. My toes tingle and I see stars floating above us. Sam's breathing becomes ragged and he pushes his cock deep inside me, holding it there as he comes.

Holy. Shit.

The world is spinning. My heart is racing. And Sam told me he loves me.

He kisses my forehead and slowly pulls out, lying next to me and wrapping me in his embrace.

"I love you, Chloe Fisher," he says, voice still breathy. "I've loved you for years. I needed to say it again."

"I like hearing it. And I love you, too."

He pushes up on one elbow and brushes my hair back. "I'm sorry for being such an idiot before. I never should have let you run away."

"You shouldn't have, but I forgive you. We were young. I'm not going to hold it over your head forever."

"Good." He smiles and kisses me again. My heart is racing and I'm sure it's going to be that way the rest of the night. I slip away to use the bathroom and clean up, hurrying to get back to bed and next to Sam. He spoons his large body around mine and slowly drags his fingers up and down my arm. I want to stay awake and soak up every second of this moment. Things finally fell into place, and I know there are still details to work out, but for right now, everything is how it should be.

"Good morning."

My eyes flutter open, and I turn my head up, looking at Sam. I'm still enveloped in his arms.

"Morning," I say back, voice thick with sleep. I stretch out and roll over, resting my head on Sam's chest. "You were right."

"I usually am, but I'm gonna need you to specify this one."

"You're an idiot." I splay my fingers on his bare chest. "We could have been doing this for years."

He pulls me closer and kisses my neck. "We'll have to make up for it."

"Mhhh," I moan, agreeing with him. "But let me pee first." My eyes flutter shut, and I lie there for another few seconds before finally forcing myself up. I can feel his eyes on me as I walk butt naked out of the room and into the bathroom. I clean myself up as fast as I can, quickly brush my teeth, and run a comb through my hair.

Sam isn't in the bedroom when I get back. Clanking dishes echo from the kitchen, and I smile as I grab a pair of sleeper shorts and a tank top. I get dressed and go downstairs, finding Sam by the coffeepot. Two mugs are out, and the smell of coffee fills the air. He's wearing just boxers, and his hair is even messier than usual. I smile, feeling all hot inside since I know his hair is messy due to how much time he spent between my legs last night.

"I could get used to waking up like this," he says, pushing off the counter and coming over to me. He wraps me in his arms and kisses me, slow and gentle at first. He moves one hand up, balling my hair in his fist and pulls my head to the side, lips going to my neck. He remembers exactly how much I like it.

I slip my hand inside his boxers, wrapping my fingers around his cock. I pump my hand up and down, and then push him away, dropping to my knees.

"Fuck," he groans as I pull his boxers down and take his cock in my mouth. One hand lands on the top of my head, taking a tangle of hair in his fist. I start slow, sucking and licking my way up and down his big dick. Then I take him in my mouth again, sure I'm going to gag when I try to fit that entire thing in my mouth. I impress myself with my lack of gagging, and Sam certainly seems to enjoy it.

He stops me right before he comes and pulls me up. Kissing my neck, he reaches inside my shorts.

"You're wet already," he breathes, breath hot on my skin.

"You make me wet," I groan back, pussy begging for more. He runs his finger over my clit, and I let my eyes fall shut. "Take me upstairs." Unable to break apart, we stumble our way through the kitchen and end up falling together on the living room floor.

The large floor-to-ceiling windows are right next to us, and if anyone was out on the lake today, they could see inside. But that doesn't matter. The only thing that matters is Sam and getting him naked and on top of me.

And then inside of me.

He strips me of my sleeper shorts and moves over me. I reach down and grab his cock, rubbing the tip against my clit. I'm already turned on, already close to coming. And so is Sam.

Holding himself up on his elbows, he kisses me right as the orgasm ripples through me. My center contracts wildly, and without waiting for the climax to subside, Sam pushes that big dick into me. It sends another jolt to my core, and I cry out.

"Fuck me hard," I pant, feeling another orgasm building on top of the other he just gave me.

Sam delivers, and I come hard the second time, just moments before he does. Both breathing hard, Sam rests his head on my forehead, holding himself there as his cock pulses inside of me.

"Yeah," he pants. "I definitely like this morning routine."

I run my hands over his muscular back, ears still ringing from that intense double orgasm. "Me too. It's a good way to start the day."

"The best." He kisses me and slowly pulls out, reaching down for my shorts. I get up, going straight to the bathroom to pee and wipe myself up. Sam's boxers are in the kitchen, and the coffee is done when we both get back in there the second time.

"Want to take that outside?" I ask, watching Sam pour two cups full.

"If you do, yeah." He sets his cup and takes me around the waist again, looking into my eyes.

My body is still humming, and his words only add to it. I've been floating on cloud nine since last night when he told me he loved me. Throw in the amazing, best-I've-ever-had sex, and it's not surprising why I'm still hovering with my feet off the ground.

"I have to go back to Chicago tomorrow," he says and suddenly I'm crashing onto the ground. He plants a kiss on my forehead and gets both mugs of coffee. "I work on Wednesday, so I'll need to get a good night's sleep tomorrow night." We slowly make our way to the screened-in porch.

"You work twelve-hour shifts, right?" I ask, remembering him mention it during dinner last night when he and Rory were talking about life in the OR.

"Yeah, but I can easily get stuck at the trauma center for longer." He takes a sip of coffee. "I shouldn't say stuck, that makes it sound like a bad thing."

"Even I don't want to work any longer than I have to," I tell him and go out the screen door. "And I can work while day-drinking on the couch."

Sam chuckles. "Lucky."

"Oh, I know. How do you get held over at work?"

"Sometimes surgeries take longer than we expected, or someone will come in right before it's my time to leave. I don't just stop as soon as the clock hits seven."

"Makes sense."

We left the blanket on the dock last night, and I give Sam my coffee so I can shake it out and then fold it for us to sit on. I dangle my feet over the water, not as scared to stick them in since it's not dark out.

"I work Wednesday through Friday this week and then have Saturday off and am on-call Sunday evening," Sam starts. "I don't know if you're able, but I want you to come for the weekend."

I just took another drink of coffee and turn, looking at him before I can answer.

"If you want to," he adds and puts his coffee down. "I meant what I said, Chloe. I regret not making things right between us just as much as I regret not telling you how I felt from the start. I know you're in LA and I'm in Chicago." He pushes my hair back. "But I want you in my life."

Setting my coffee down next to Sam's, I loop my arm through his. "I want to be in your life too." My heart speeds up, and I rest my head against him. "And I'd love to come be with you this weekend."

"I can't promise you'll have time to write." He flashes a grin. "I already know I won't be able to keep my hands off you. Like I said, we need to make up for lost time."

"We do." I tip my head up, squinting in the sunlight. What happened to the rain I was promised? "It sucks that we're finally together and you have to go to Chicago and I have to go to LA."

"But we are together…as we should be," he says firmly, and my heart melts. "We'll figure things out because there's no way in hell I'm letting you get away this time."

"Oh, like you let me go last time?" I tease, pushing myself up so I can kiss him. "Luckily, I can travel frequently. I'll come to Chicago this weekend and maybe you can come to LA the next time you're off?"

"Yeah," he says, cupping my face to kiss me again. "I get two or three days off in a row at least twice a month."

I don't like the thought of only seeing each other only a few times a month. I've been toying with the idea of leaving LA and coming back to the Midwest for a while now, but it took us over fifteen years to confess our feelings for each other. I'm not going to so much as hint at moving in together yet.

"When I get days off like that, I'll come to LA," he goes on. "And you're welcome to come stay with me any time you want. Knowing you're there when I get off work would be so fucking nice."

"I will most likely be naked, waiting for you with a home-cooked meal."

"Now you have to come stay with me."

"As soon as I get this book finished, I'll have more free time," I tell him.

"Oh, right. You need the day to work, don't you?" He puts his arm around me.

"I should spend the day writing."

He smooths my hair back. "I'll go then so you can work. I'd like to take you out to dinner tonight."

I smile. "I'd like that too. What are you going to do today?"

"I don't know. Mason is leaving tonight, so I'll probably hang out with him, Rory, and Dean."

"It's nice you guys get to see each other every once in a while. Tell them I said hi, and I guess I'll be seeing them again…soon."

CHAPTER TWENTY-THREE

SAM

"He's home!" Mason shouts as soon as I step into the house. He's sitting in the kitchen, eating the rest of the pie, and snickers when both my mom and Rory come practically running into the room. "I almost had to call in a favor and report you as a missing person."

"I was worried," Mom exclaims. "You didn't say anything about staying elsewhere last night." She holds up her hands. "I know, you're an adult, but I was expecting you home."

"Sorry. I didn't think about it." I put my keys and phone on the counter.

"Where were you?" Rory asks, doing a terrible job at hiding her excitement. She knows exactly where I was last night. Not playing into her excitement, I look at the leftover biscuits and gravy on the stove. I'm fucking starving.

"I was with Chloe," I say as I get a plate from the cabinet. Thinking about her sends a rush through me, and I have to stop myself before my mind wanders back to her soft lips.

"About fucking time," Mason says with his mouth full.

"What?" Mom and Rory say at the same time.

Rory runs over, taking the plate out of my hand. "You're serious?"

"Yes. I was with Chloe last night," I say and try to take the plate from her, but she snatches it back.

"But *how* were you with her?" Rory presses, and I raise an eyebrow.

"You want to know details about last night? Like how we—"

"Ew, no!" Rory gives me the plate back. "Are you together now? Please tell me it wasn't a one-night kinda thing."

"It wasn't. And yes, she's my girlfriend now," I say, and Mom joins in on the excitement.

"I always hoped you two would get together," Mom coos. "I just love Chloe! And she's so pretty and successful and—" Mom gasps. "She lives in LA! You're in Chicago. What are you going to do? Certainly one of you is going to have to move. Have you talked about the future? That'll make it difficult when you get married and have kids and—"

"Mom," I cut her off. "We haven't talked in detail yet. She's been my girlfriend for less than twenty-four hours. I'm not going to talk about marriage and babies yet, and I know she won't either."

Mason gets up to put his empty plate in the sink. "It's about damn time you two hooked up," he says, clapping me on the back. "You should have twenty years ago."

"I'd hope not," Mom counters. "Sam would have been fourteen, which would make Chloe twelve." Mom looks at me and smiles. "I'm happy you have a nice girlfriend who we know isn't after your money."

"That's always a plus." I fill my bowl with food and stick it in the microwave. "Where's Dean?"

"Dad suckered him into helping with another project at the office," Rory says, sitting at the table next to Mason. Dean's a contractor, and Dad was all too excited to have a "professional" help him finish the million projects he started over the years. "He should be back soon. Why? Do you want to double date?"

"I was thinking more along the lines of just us hanging out. Chloe has to work on her book before she can do anything."

"I'd like that." Rory smiles. "It's supposed to rain, want to see a movie?"

"Sure," I reply, not even knowing what's playing. No matter what, time is going to go by slowly. Adam starts fussing, and Mom rushes to get him. The microwave beeps and I grab my bowl, which I warmed up too much on accident, and join my siblings at the table.

"You can thank me now," Mason says. "I knew you needed a push."

Normally, I'd give him shit before giving in, but not today. Because I am so fucking thankful. "I did, so thanks for that."

"Am I missing something?" Rory asks, looking up from her phone.

"No one but this dumbass missed it," Mason says, but Rory still looks confused. "Last night he was still saying he didn't have feelings for Chloe. Which we all knew was bullshit."

"I wondered from time to time," Rory confesses. "But I didn't want to get my hopes up. I've always wanted a sister!"

"Don't you have like a million sisters-in-law?" Mason asks.

"I have four," Rory replies, rolling her eyes. "And Quinn is going to be so excited! She loves the *Nightfall* series. Have you told Archer yet?" she asks me. Archer is one of my closest friends, who I met during residency. He's a surgeon, and we ended up in the OR together more times than not. We shared an apartment during the final years of residency, and he's married to Dean's sister, making him Rory's brother-in-law now.

"You're acting like I proposed," I say, getting annoyed. "Calm down."

"Fine," Rory huffs. "Just don't fuck this up. I like Chloe."

"I won't now that you said so," I say sarcastically and take a bite of my breakfast. Though Rory has nothing to worry about. There's no way I'm fucking this up.

"Chloe?" I call, pushing open the gate. I texted her to let her know I was on my way. She said she was on the screened-in porch writing and said to come around. Not wanting to startle her, I call her name again as I walk up to the porch. The sun is just now starting to set, and my heart speeds up and my dick jumps when I see her sitting on the couch on the porch, computer in her lap. She's wearing headphones and can't hear me.

I wave, trying to catch her attention before pushing the door open. She looks up right as I'm lifting my arm in the air and smiles. She pulls her earbuds out of her ears and closes the computer, putting it on the glass coffee table in front of her. She strides over, and we meet in the middle. I wrap her in a tight embrace.

"Fuck, I missed you." I put my lips to hers, losing myself in her kisses.

"I missed you too." She stands on her toes and rakes her fingers through my hair. My eyes fall shut, and I grip her tight around the waist, pressing her hips against mine. It rained on and off most of the day, lowering the temperature drastically from yesterday. Light rain was just starting to fall as I walked around the house, making it perfect porch-sitting weather.

"Did you get a lot of writing done?"

"Yes, a ton." She leads me to the couch. "I was very inspired, for some reason."

We sink onto the couch together; it's surprisingly comfortable for an outdoor piece of furniture.

"Oh yeah? What inspired you?"

She raises her eyebrows and shifts her gaze to my lap, licking her lips. "Your dick." God damn, woman.

"Just my dick?"

Nodding, she straddles me. "Yep. Might as well put a bag over your head next time you fuck me."

"I'd be okay with that."

She laughs and leans in, breasts in my face. She's still wearing the tank top and shorts she was wearing earlier, and her hair is still slightly damp from the shower. I move my hands up her back and press my fingers into her shoulders, massaging her stiff muscles.

"Does your back still hurt?"

"A little. I was all hunched over writing today."

"Here," I say, urging her to relax against me so I can rub her back.

"Mhhh," she groans. "That feels good." She lazily hooks one arm around my shoulders and rests her head against me. I'm the one massaging her, but it does feel good. Having Chloe in my arms like this is how it's meant to be, and I know it was nothing short of kismet for us both to be here at the same time.

I sweep one hand down Chloe's back, fingers slipping under the elastic band of her shorts. Chloe rocks her hips, pressing her hot core against me. My cock starts to harden, and she moans again, lifting her head up. I push her hair back and kiss her.

"I could use another dose of inspiration," she says coyly and moves off of me, looking at my lap as she wets her lips. "Take your pants off."

I undo the button of my pants, and she pulls them down to my ankles. I kick them off, along with my shoes. Chloe watches, a hungry smirk on her face. She pushes me back and sticks her hands inside my boxers, slender fingers wrapping around my thick cock. Slowly, she moves her hand up and down, and her soft skin against me is almost enough to make me come right here and now. She inches closer, leaning over so I get a clear view of her breasts, and circles her thumb over the tip of my cock. It feels so damn good.

With her free hand, she pushes me back. It's a tight fit with both of us on the couch, but Chloe doesn't stop jerking me off. My eyes flutter closed as I reach down for her hand, wrapping my fingers around her wrist. She releases me and I sit up, taking her back in my arms. She moves on me again, sitting up so her breasts are in my face. I bend my head down, burying my face in them and then look up, needing to kiss her.

I go to lay us down and we almost fall off the couch. I grip Chloe tightly, pushing her back onto my lap and then stand up, carrying her inside and up into her room. I kiss her the whole way there, tripping once up the stairs, but neither of us can break apart. I need to push my cock into her tight pussy. It'll destroy me all over again, and I'm more than okay with it.

We fall onto the mattress, with Chloe beneath me. She curls her legs around me, rubbing herself against my cock. I stop kissing Chloe only so I can undress her, and she lifts her ass off the bed to make it easy to pull her shorts off. She's not wearing underwear, and that alone is so fucking hot.

The glistening top of my cock is sticking out of my boxers, and Chloe reaches down, groaning as she spreads the wetness down my shaft. "I need you," she pants, pumping her hand up and down faster and faster.

"I need you too. Now," I growl and take both her hands, pinning them above her head. Her eyes flutter closed, and her body trembles with anticipation. I move over top of her, kissing her hard. Chloe wraps her legs around me again, and the tip of my cock rubs against her clit. She moans, and I almost give in, pushing my cock inside of her and fucking her senseless.

Instead, I hold myself over her, kissing her once more. She rakes her fingers down my back, grabbing the hem of my shirt and pulling it over my head. I strip her of her tank top and trail kisses down her body, taking my time when I get to her collarbone. I lift my head up for a second, admiring her perfect tits. I remember a time in high school when she confessed feeling insecure because she didn't have big boobs like some of the other girls in her grade. I thought she was crazy then, and she had no idea how hard it was to sit there and have her talk about her breasts. It took an enormous amount of self-control not to stare at them, and even more so to casually tell her she's fine, that as long as there's enough to fit in my hand, I was more than happy.

Cupping them both in my hands, I bend down again, kissing my way to one of her breasts, and flick my tongue over her pert nipple. Chloe squirms, tightening her legs around me. Teasing her nipple with my tongue, I slide one hand down between her legs. Moving slow on purpose, I circle the entrance to her pussy. She's so fucking wet already.

Her hands are on my back, and her nails dig into my skin as I rub my finger over her clit, getting her worked up in just seconds. My cock is rock hard now, begging to push inside of her. She wants it too and feebly pushes my boxers down.

In a swift movement, I pull away and dive down between her legs. I want to taste her again, to lick up every last drop she gives and feel her pussy contracting wildly against my face. Chloe rests one hand on my head, sitting up just enough that she can steal a glance at me. I flick my eyes up at the exact same time, and knowing she's watching turns me on even more. My cock aches and I know it'll take just one touch from Chloe to make me come.

Without wasting any more time, I put my mouth over her, tongue lashing out against her clit. She moans loudly and hearing her pleasure almost does me in. Damn, she tastes so fucking good. I keep working my tongue, and Chloe squirms against me, desperate for a release. I slide both hands under her ass and lift her off the mattress. She hooks one leg over my shoulders, and I can feel her whole body tense up. She sucks in a breath and I know she's about to come. Keeping my mouth against her, I lower her back onto the mattress and slip a finger inside, going right to her G-spot. I press against it, and it pushes Chloe over the edge.

She cries out loudly as the orgasm ripples through her. I keep my mouth on her, not stopping until she's writhing in pleasure, pushing me away because she can't physically handle any more. Both her hands go to the top of my head, and I slowly move away, wiping my mouth with the back of my hand.

Chloe's cheeks are flushed, and it's so fucking hot to know I'm the reason for it. I'm the one who made her come so hard there's a wet spot on the bed now. Her eyes are still closed, and she's breathing hard, breasts rapidly rising and falling. I move back on top of her, pulling my boxers down before I settle between her legs. She needs a few seconds to recover, so I kiss her forehead and brush her hair out of her face.

Chloe inhales deeply and opens her eyes, looking right at me. Then she puts her lips to mine, and knowing she can taste herself on my lips does me in. I can't wait any longer. I need her.

Now.

I guide my cock to her entrance and kiss her again as I push inside. She holds me tight against her, bending her legs and rocking her hips along with mine. I could come right now, and I grit my teeth, not wanting to finish until she comes for the second time.

Thankfully, it doesn't take her long, and the second I feel her pussy tighten around my cock, I let my head drop against hers and push in balls deep, coming harder than I ever have before. We're both panting, and I slowly pull out, moving to the side and wrapping my arm around her.

"I came inside you three times," I pant, hating that I'm killing the moment, but the thought suddenly dawns on me. I've spent the last several years fucking a lot of women, trying to fill the void in my heart that only Chloe could fill, but in all those times, I was always very careful to practice safe sex.

"I'm on birth control," she tells me, voice still breathy. "I have been for years." She runs her fingers up and down my arm. "I get really bad cramps and it helps. I have super light periods now, which I'm thankful for. And you probably don't want to know that."

"If I'm having sex with you, you can talk about your period."

"That is fair." She lifts her head off my chest and smiles. "So then it's okay for me to tell you too that I'm going to get up and pee because I don't want to get a UTI."

I playfully smack her ass. "And as a doctor, I approve."

She gets up and hurries to the bathroom, returning just a minute or two later. The bed isn't made, and she settles in it, snuggling under the blankets.

"I never got dressed for dinner," she says, looking up at me.

"It wouldn't have mattered since I undressed you anyway."

"Good point." She traces her fingers up and down my chest. "I was going to and do my hair and makeup, but I was really into what I was writing and thought I'd have more time, and well…I'm kind of a procrastinator."

"I remember." I smile and kiss the top of her head. "You can blame it on being an artist now, right? Artists are allowed to be flakey."

"Well, good," she laughs. "Because I can be from time to time. Not flakey like you can't depend on me, but flakey like I lose track of time really easily and forget about things."

"I'll remind you. I'm good at remembering things and have three alarms set in the morning because the thought of being late to work gives me anxiety."

Chloe laughs again. "We're a good fit then."

"Yeah." I tighten my hold on her. "We are."

"I don't want you to leave."

"I don't want to leave either…but we need to talk about it. We're hours apart…you're okay with that, right?" I ask, almost afraid of her answer. I finally got her back in my life—the right way. I'm not going to lose her again.

She lifts her head off my chest. "Yes, I'm okay with it. It will be hard, but very much worth it."

"It will." I run my fingers up and down her arm, feeling

sleepy now myself. There's no fooling ourselves: long-distance relationships suck. Starting a new one, long-distance sucks even more. But she's right: it's worth it. We're both able to travel relatively easily, Chloe more so than me, but when I'm not at work I'll happily take off to LA since there's nothing in Chicago holding me back. "We'll figure it out," I promise her. "Nothing is going to keep us apart."

CHAPTER TWENTY-FOUR

CHLOE

It was harder than I thought to say goodbye to Sam. He stayed the night on Monday, and we were together until he had to go back to his parents' house to say bye to his family and get his things. I spent the rest of Tuesday writing, missing him already. We only have a few days until we see each other again, and the cold hard truth is we have to get used to this long-distance thing. It just sucks so fucking much. It took us how long to finally get together and now we're still apart. It'll take time to figure out what actually works for us, I know.

Today went by fast, at least. I ended up staying up until four-thirty in the morning writing after Sam left on Tuesday evening—and made a lot of progress with my book—and then slept in until eleven. I had lunch with Rory, and Dad and Wendy came back here and we ordered pizza and had a late dinner.

Sam didn't get home until close to nine tonight, and he FaceTimed me as soon as he got to his apartment. We texted throughout the day, and we'll talk again tomorrow. I'm in bed now, looking at flight information. I was going to stay here and go right to Chicago since it's not that far, but I miss Spartan and I need a whole different type of wardrobe for a hot weekend with my boyfriend.

I fall back into bed, smiling like crazy.

I book my flight home for tomorrow afternoon. It doesn't give me much time to be in LA, but I don't need much time. I just need to do some laundry, visit my big guy, quickly repack for the weekend, and spend the rest of my time typing away. I didn't finish my book this trip like I hoped, but my inspiration is back and the words are flowing.

I screenshot my flight info and text it to Sam. He told me he turns his phone to silent at night, and he tries to be in bed around ten when he has to get up early for work the next morning. We have very different schedules, and it will be interesting to see how it works—I'm getting ahead of myself.

It's easy to, though, and I can't help but think with absolute certainty things crashed and burned with every single other person I dated because Sam and I were meant to be together all along. I turn off the bedside lamp and plug my phone in, settling down in bed. The nighttime chorus of katydids and crickets fills the room, and I fall asleep with a smile on my face.

"DON'T FREAK OUT," I SAY INTO THE PHONE TO FARISHA. DAD just dropped me off at the airport, and after a bit of a tearful goodbye, I collected myself and got through security and to my terminal in record time.

"When you start a conversation with *don't freak out*, I know you have freak-out-worthy information."

"Oh, I do." I angle my body away from the older lady who sat right next to me, even though there are plenty of open seats. "I slept with Sam."

A few seconds of silence tick by. "You're not joking, are you?"

"No."

"Oh, God, Chloe. I'm so sorry. Are you okay?"

"I've never been better." I wish she could see the smile on my face. "Because he's my boyfriend now. I'm going to his house this weekend. In Chicago," I add.

"I'm going to need a lot more details than this."

I slip my carry-on bag over my shoulder and get up, going to the large windows so I can look at the planes coming and going as I talk. "He kissed me, and I told him I couldn't have a one-night stand with him because I've loved him for years. And then he said he's been in love with me too, he regrets not chasing after me that night at the party, and has wished every day for a way to make things right."

"Fuck."

"I know, right?" I get a goofy smile on my face again.

"You believe him?"

I wasn't expecting her to say that. The smile comes right off my face. "Yeah. Why would he lie?"

"To get in your pants," she says like it's obvious.

"He went through a lot of effort just for that, and why would he invite me to stay with him this weekend if he was just trying to get in my pants."

"To get in your pants again."

Frowning, I shake my head. "No, Sam isn't like that. He doesn't need to con and trick someone for sex. He could easily get anyone he wants. Flying back and forth to each other is the most involved booty call I can think of, and kind of the opposite of what a booty call is supposed to be, isn't it?"

"Yeah, you're right. I have a hard time trusting someone after they've hurt me or someone I love."

"I know, and that's what makes you such a ruthless bitch and a good best friend."

She laughs. "Thanks. I just want to make sure you're not letting your heart overrule your head here."

"It does have a tendency to do that."

"And that's why you make a good best friend."

"I trust him. He's grown up a lot since that stupid party. He goes to bed early and doesn't drink alcohol very often."

"Wow. He has grown up a lot," she laughs. "Now, I have an important question."

"Shoot."

"Does he really have a big dick like everyone said he did in high school?"

Heat creeps over me as I think back to having sex with Sam. "It's huge, like I wasn't sure it would fit inside me without splitting me in two." I turn and realize a couple of teenage boys are within earshot, staring at me incredulously. I pull my hat down, hoping it's a good enough disguise and I don't get recognized today. Without Charles on my arm, I'm easily overlooked.

Farisha laughs. "That's all I'm going to be thinking about the next time I see him."

"I'll try to sneak a dick pic for you when he's sleeping."

"I know I should say no, but if he's as well-hung as you—oh shit, my mother-in-law is here. They're visiting from India and have been staying with Prasad's sister. She's still single and they keep trying to arrange her marriage."

"Ugh. Poor girl."

"Right? I got lucky my parents valued education and didn't push to arrange mine like my grandmother wanted. I got to fall in love the old-fashioned way, and I still ended up with a 'nice Indian boy' who my grandma approves of."

We laugh and she says a rushed goodbye, needing to quickly hide dirty dishes in the sink before her mother-in-law criticizes her housekeeping skills. I end the call, go back to my seat, and get out my computer. I told myself I'd try to write five thousand words from the time I got to my terminal to the time I landed in LA. I have an hour and a half left before we even board the plane, and at least an hour and a half hour plane ride back home. That's plenty of time to write that much. I can write it in just about three hours if I concentrate, but my mind is preoccupied.

I don't want to put any merit into what Farisha said. She wasn't there, she didn't hear our conversations or see the way Sam looked at me. But I'd be lying if I didn't say I was a little scared. Not because of Sam, but simply because I've wanted this so long I'm terrified something is going to come in and take it all away from me...that the universe will punish me simply for being me.

I squeeze my eyes closed, trying to center myself, and reread the last chapter I wrote. It's good and gets me amped up to continue. I stick my headphones in and crank up my music, not looking up until I finish this chapter. We board soon, so I quickly load up my stuff and use the bathroom. Sam calls just minutes before I'm called to get on the plane.

"Hey," he says, and hearing his voice quells all the nerves I have inside me. "I only have like a minute before I have to go back inside, but I wanted to call and just say hi."

"I'm glad you did. I'm just about to get on the plane."

"We just have to make it through tomorrow," he says. "And then we can say we'll see each other tonight."

"I cannot wait."

"What do you want for dinner? I'll pick something up on the way home from the hospital."

"Chicago pizza," I say without having to even think about it.

"Sounds good. I'll get—fuck, I'm being paged. I'll call you tonight. Love you," he rushes out before ending the call. I'm all fluttering inside, and hearing a call for *Dr. Harris* is so fucking hot. I'll text him Friday and remind him to bring home some scrubs so we can role play sexy doctors on TV.

Friday is going to take forever to get here.

"Hey, big guy," I whisper, sliding Spartan's stall door open.

It's late, and most of the horses are settling down for the night. Only Olivia is here, one of the trainers, and she was getting the barn ready to be closed up for the night when I pulled in the parking lot. "Did you miss me? I missed you."

My big gray horse comes over, nosing my jacket pockets for treats.

"Really?" I laugh and reach inside, pulling out a peppermint. His nostrils flare and he impatiently waits for me to undo the plastic wrapper. I give him the treat and then move to his side, wrapping my arms around his neck. I landed in LA not long ago, and sat outside on my patio talking to Sam. He sounded tired and said he had a very long second half of his day at work. There was a bad car accident and several victims were brought to his center, needing to be rushed into surgery.

I fell asleep on the plane, and now I'm not tired. Instead of doing what I should do and focus all my energy into my book or take some melatonin, going to sleep and then getting up early, I drove out to the barn to visit my horse. Makes sense, I know. It's late and the horses have a decent routine here, so I only stay for about fifteen minutes, running a brush over Spartan's soft fur. His tail has been braided, and Olivia told me the barn girls even added flowers. Spartan had to have just eaten up all their attention...and the tons of treats I'm sure they gave him.

I leave the barn feeling refreshed, as I always do, and end up staying up late again writing. At some point, I should get myself on a sleep schedule, but this works for me now and I don't have to get up early tomorrow.

I sent everything new that I've written to my editor and climb into bed. It feels good to be home, but I'm very much looking forward to leaving again. Exhausted from staying up so late, I fall asleep rather quickly, and sleep in until nearly eleven again, only waking up because Lupe sent me a text message. I probably could have slept for another hour or so, but I need to get my ass up, shower, and pack so I can make it to the airport in time.

I smile when I see her text, which is just a bunch of fire emojis. Yeah, I might have really spiced up my sex scenes thanks to all the inspiration Sam has given me. With the smile still on my face, I get up and make myself coffee, mentally calculating my day down to the last minute. I'm going to have to rush to get to the airport, and I haven't done any laundry like I said I would. There's no time to start now.

I repack my suitcase while I drink my coffee, putting in much more clothing than I need. We're staying in tonight and going out tomorrow. Sam is on-call Sunday, so our plans are up in the air, but lounging around with him does sound wonderful. We were so close for so long, and then we went all those years without even talking. We definitely caught up in more ways than one, but we still have a lot of *getting to know each* other to do. What are Sam's annoying habits? What little things will I do that drive him crazy? We both want our relationship to work, and spending time together is the best way to put things to the test.

Which we will pass, I know.

My plane lands at seven-thirty, and Sam wasn't sure if he'd be able to make it here to pick me up. I know he feels bad about it, but it was either land at seven-thirty or not until close to midnight. I assured him it didn't bother me one bit to get my own luggage and take an Uber to his apartment. By that time, he'll probably be home from the hospital and it'll work out perfectly.

And it does.

He's in the lobby waiting when the Uber drops me off, and comes running out the door as soon as he sees me. I'm pulling my suitcase behind me, hurrying to him. We meet halfway, and Sam pulls me into a tight embrace.

"Fuck, I missed you," he breathes before kissing me.

"I missed you, too."

He runs his fingers through my hair and kisses me once more. The city is still very much alive all around us. I'm not familiar enough with Chicago to know exactly where we are, but I know we're somewhat close to the hospital where Sam works.

Sam takes my suitcase and carry-on bag for me and leads me inside the apartment building. I can tell right away it's super nice, and the attendant at the door knows Sam by name. Two other people get into the elevator with us, but it doesn't stop Sam from slipping his arm around me, fingering the hem of the black dress I have on.

The elevator stops at the sixth floor, and Sam pulls my suitcase out, going down a long hall, stopping to unlock his door.

"I put the pizza in the oven to keep it warm," he tells me as he pushes the door open, letting me step in first. The light above the kitchen island is on, and I look around as I take my shoes off. Sam has a one-bedroom apartment in the corner of the building, and the corner walls have floor-to-ceiling windows that give an impressive view of the city.

The entire place is nice and neat, and I can tell it wasn't from him frantically cleaning before I got here. The decor is minimal and modern, mostly done in bold, blue colors. Sam shuts and locks the door behind him.

"Do you want to eat now or...?" he asks, taking his shoes off and pushing them with his foot away from the door.

"I have to pee."

"Bathroom is right there," he tells me, pointing to an open door. I grab my carry-on bag, wanting to freshen up a bit after sitting on a plane for hours on end today. I close the door and flick the light on. Even his bathroom is clean, but I'm comforted a bit by a damp towel discarded on the floor.

I pee and go to the sink, washing my hands and rinsing my face. I quickly run a brush through my hair, adjust my breasts in my bra, pulling them up so they look fuller than they really are, and go out of the bathroom, finding Sam in the living room. The lights are still off and he's looking down at the city below.

"This is an amazing view," I say, and he turns, snaking his arms around my waist. I get the feeling of butterflies and am instantly turned on from being in Sam's embrace again. He's dressed simply right now in a white t-shirt and gray sweatpants, and part of me wonders if he speed-read some of my books to know that gray sweatpants are one of my biggest weaknesses, exhibited by pretty much all of my characters having the same flaw.

"It's why I picked it. Corner units can be hard to come by. I moved in the floor above and the next month, this one opened up. It was not a cost-effective move to come down here, but I like the natural light coming through in the morning."

"That would be nice."

He tightens his hold on me, and I stand on my toes to kiss him. One kiss is all it takes to fan the flames between us, and we quickly end up naked and having sex on the couch. Sam gives me his t-shirt to put on when we're done, saving me "the trouble" of having to go through my suitcase to get something else to wear.

Dressed in only his boxers, he gets the pizza from the oven and brings it over, setting the box on the coffee table. He turns the TV on and gives me the remote so I can pick something for us to watch.

"I like this," I say, sliding a slice of deep-dish pizza onto a plate. "Sex, pizza, and murder documentaries."

"This is my ideal Friday night."

"With anyone?" I tease.

"With you," he says right back, turning to look at me. "I've never done this, you know."

"Eaten in your living room?"

"No, I usually eat in here while watching TV. I mean…this."

I slowly shake my head. "I'm not really following."

"Be with someone…someone I love. It's really fucking nice."

I smile. "It is, and I haven't either."

"You've never been in love before?" he asks, and I can tell he's a little afraid of my answer.

"There were times I thought I was," I confess. "But there was always one problem with every relationship."

"What was it?"

"They weren't you."

"I had the same problem, but with you." Sam grins. "We're here now, together, and that's what matters."

I rest my head on his shoulder for a few seconds, heart so incredibly full. This is the start of something amazing, I can just feel it.

"You know we'll get to have a 'coming out' of our relationship for the tabloids," I say and take a bite of my pizza.

"You mean like leak a sex tape?" Sam asks hopefully.

I laugh. "No, I was thinking more along the lines of eating outside while holding hands or something. But we can totally make a sex tape."

"We should get started on it tonight. I'm thinking the shower will be a good place to say we 'accidentally' recorded ourselves."

"My phone case is waterproof."

"Perfect. I'll make sure to turn on the mood-music too."

"And what will that be?"

"For you," he starts, cocking an eyebrow, "the *Lord of the Rings* soundtrack."

"Hey!" I laugh, playfully swatting him. "But yeah, I could actually see that getting me in the mood."

"See? I was right."

We both laugh, snuggling a little closer together as we finish our pizza. Deciding to put the sex tape off until the morning since we're both tired, we get ready for bed together. There are double sinks in the bathroom, and it's almost silly how something as mundane as brushing our teeth can have such significance, yet it does.

"Did you hear more from the network who wants you to write for them?" Sam asks, taking two decorative pillows off his bed. I'm impressed, really, by how well put together his whole apartment is.

"My agent emailed me today saying she was arranging a meeting for Monday or Tuesday. I don't think I'm going to take it, though."

We get into bed, and Sam takes me right into his arms. "Why not?"

"It would take time away from my usual writing, and it would require me to be in LA more." Maybe I shouldn't have said that out loud, but the one thing that brings us both comfort about being in a long-distance relationship is our ability to travel back and forth. I have more freedom to travel than Sam, and signing the contract to work on a TV show would change that.

"I selfishly want you to myself."

"I selfishly want that too," I say back, feeling sleepy already. There is no place on earth more comfortable than Sam's bed—as long as he's in it with me.

"Good thing I have you all weekend."

Everything is perfect, and I know that right here, snuggled up in Sam's arms, is right where I'm meant to be. All the pain I've held onto, all the fear that's kept me in the dark, melted away the moment Sam kissed me.

We sure took our sweet time coming together, but now that we're here, there's no going back.

I am in love with Sam Harris.

And he is in love with me.

CHAPTER TWENTY-FIVE

SAM

"You're going to miss your flight." I run my fingers up and down Chloe's back.

"Would that be a bad thing?" she mumbles.

"Not for me." I lift my head off the pillow and kiss her forehead. "You can stay as long as you want. It's quiet here during the day so you'd probably get a lot of writing done."

"Well, when you put it that way, it would be irresponsible if I didn't stay."

I sweep my hand down her back to her thigh. We're both naked in bed, and Chloe is supposed to be leaving for the airport to take a red-eye back to LA. The weekend went by so fast, and I can't believe it's fucking Sunday already.

Things couldn't be more perfect. We started Saturday morning by sleeping in and then having sex in the shower. I showed her around the city, and we ended our night with a dinner cruise and walking around Navy Pier. The weather wasn't quite as nice today, and since I was on-call, I couldn't venture too far from the hospital.

We stayed in, ordering Chinese takeout, and played video games most of the day. Chloe is almost irritatingly good at them, though it was more of a turn-on than anything else, and I only got slightly irritated that she beat me three times in Mario Kart.

She's the definition of perfection, and I still can't believe she's mine. She's beautiful and successful, yet still humble and kind. She's quirky but not ashamed to be herself. And she challenges me, not afraid to speak her mind or have a different opinion. All of the research she's done for her different books makes her a well-rounded person, and her knowledge and interest in politics surprised me. She told me she didn't realize until recently how important it is to be involved and to know what's going on around us. If there's a chance your vote could make a difference, you should be sure to use it.

"You did say being with me was inspiring." I run my fingers through her dark auburn hair, having no intention of letting her go.

"You are. Though I run the risk of turning my books from romance to erotica."

I chuckle and pull her into me. We're both naked from having sex not that long ago, and having her lying here like this makes it even harder for her to get up, I know. Is it really that selfish of me to want her to stay when I know she wants it too?

"That wouldn't be a bad thing, would it?"

"As long as I can work in a little plot, not too many people would complain." She hooks her leg over mine. "I'll change my flight to one in the morning."

I groan, wanting her to change it too. "You have a meeting with your agent tomorrow," I remind her. It was finalized last night, hence her taking the late-night flight back today.

"I'll ask her to postpone it."

"I know I should be a good influence on your here, but I really want you to stay." I run my hand up and down her thigh. "But if you do go, have your meeting, visit Spartan, and want to come back…I'll give you a key."

"Really?" She lifts her head off my chest and looks into my eyes, smiling.

"Yeah. This long-distance thing is rough, and I know things are new between us, but I love you, Chloe. We're able to go back and forth to see each other, and I want you to be just as comfortable here as you feel at home."

"I'm more comfortable here." She puts her head back down on my chest. "Right here is my new favorite spot."

"Mine too."

I CLOSE THE APARTMENT DOOR BEHIND ME, FEELING EMPTINESS tugging at my heart. I just got back from dropping Chloe off at the airport. She got emotional when we said our goodbyes, and dammit, it was hard for me to keep it together too. We'll see each in less than a week's time, but it's going to be a long fucking week.

My heart aches for Chloe, and the apartment seems dimmer without her, even though she was only here for a few days. We haven't quite figured out what we're doing next. If she gets her work done early, she'll come back here. If not, I'll fly out and stay with her for three days. It fucking blows that the flight is as long as it is, taking up most of the day. I might have three days off, but really only one is spent with Chloe.

I should go to bed, getting some sleep before having to work tomorrow. I don't have to be there at seven at least since I'm coming off of a night of being on-call even though I didn't end up called in at all. The thought of getting into bed without Chloe depresses me, so I sit down in the living room and play video games instead.

Finally, at nearly five in the morning, I drag my tired ass to bed, collapsing onto the mattress. The pillows smell like Chloe, and I pull one to me, wishing I'll roll over and see her next to me. I drift to sleep pretty quickly and dream of her, only to be rudely interrupted by someone knocking on my door.

I blink my eyes open, not sure if I actually heard knocking

or if it was in my dream. My eyelids are heavy, and I fall back into bed only to hear the knocking again. Maybe if I ignore them, they'll go away.

It doesn't work, and whoever is outside my door knocks more persistently. Annoyed, I throw the blankets off and pad my way through the apartment. The knocker raps against the door again, quick and frantic.

"I'm coming," I mutter, rubbing my eyes. How the hell did someone get up past security? If it's a neighbor again, I'm going to lose it. I'm running on two hours of sleep and have to work later today.

Yawning, I unlock the door, too tired and crabby to bother looking through the peephole to see who it is. It doesn't matter, because I'm going to tell whoever is outside my door to fuck off and don't bother me again unless the building is on fire.

I twist the doorknob and throw open the door, harsh words on the tip of my tongue. "The fuck?" I mutter instead when I see Stacey standing outside my door and not an annoying neighbor.

"Hi, Sam," she says and rests her hand on her stomach. "We need to talk."

Desperate Times, book two in the Silver Ridge Series, comes out this October!

THANK YOU

Thank you so much for taking time out of your busy life to read Backup Plan!

I appreciate so much the time you took to read this book and and would love if you would consider leaving a review. I LOVE connecting with readers and the best place to do so is my fan page. I'd love to have you!

www.facebook.com/groups/emilygoodwinbooks

ABOUT THE AUTHOR

Emily Goodwin is the New York Times and USA Today Bestselling author of over a dozen of romantic titles. Emily writes the kind of books she likes to read, and is a sucker for a swoon-worthy bad boy and happily ever afters.

She lives in the midwest with her husband and two daughters. When she's not writing, you can find her riding her horses, hiking, reading, or drinking wine with friends.

Emily is represented by Julie Gwinn of the Seymour Agency.

STALK ME
www.emilygoodwinbooks.com
www.facebook.com/emilygoodwinbooks
Instagram: authoremilygoodwin
Email: emily@emilygoodwinbooks.com
Sign up for my mailing list here.

ALSO BY EMILY GOODWIN

Contemporary romance:
Stay
All I Need
Never Say Never
Outside the Lines
First Comes Love
Then Come Marriage
One Call Away
Free Fall
Hot Mess (Love is Messy Book 1)
Twice Burned (Love is Messy Book 2)
Bad Things (Love is Messy Book 3)
Battle Scars (Love is Messy Book 4)
Cheat Codes (The Dawson Family Series Book 1)
End Game (The Dawson Family Series Book 2)
Side Hustle (The Dawson Family Series Book 3)
Cheap Trick (The Dawson Family Series Book 4)
Fight Dirty (The Dawson Family Series Book 5)

Paranormal romance:
Dead of Night (Thorne Hill Series Book 1)
Dark of Night (Thorne Hill Series Book 2)
Call of Night (Thorne Hill Series Book 3)
Still of Night (Throne Hill Series Book 4)
Immortal Night (Thorne Hill Companion Novella)

Dystopian Romance:

Contagious (The Contagium Series Book 1)
Deathly Contagious (The Contagium Series Book 2)
Contagious Chaos (The Contagium Series Book 3)
The Truth is Contagious (The Contagium Series Book 4)

Printed in Great Britain
by Amazon